Please return/renew this item by the last date shown. Books may also be renewed by phone or internet.

🖥 www.rbwm.gov.uk/home/leisure-and-culture/libraries

☎ 01628 796969 (library hours)

☎ 0303 123 0035 (24 hours)

Royal Borough
of Windsor &
Maidenhead

www.rbwm.gov.uk

A SEASON
IN EXILE

A SEASON
IN EXILE

OLIVER HARRIS

Little, Brown

LITTLE, BROWN

First published in Great Britain in 2022 by Little, Brown

1 3 5 7 9 10 8 6 4 2

A CIP catalogue record for this book is available from the British Library.

Hardback ISBN 978-1-4087-1292-4
Trade Paperback ISBN 978-1-4087-1291-7

Typeset in Palatino by M Rules
Printed and bound in Great Britain by Clays Ltd, Elcograf S.p.A.

Papers used by Little, Brown are from well-managed forests
and other responsible sources.

Little, Brown
An imprint of
Little, Brown Book Group
Carmelite House
50 Victoria Embankment
London EC4Y 0DZ

An Hachette UK Company
www.hachette.co.uk

www.littlebrown.co.uk

For Pamela Harris

También yo estoy en la región perdida

'La Golondrina'

ONE

No one stopped him as he disembarked. He looked for police waiting on the runway but it was empty. Benito Juarez airport sprawled beneath a petrochemical sunset, and Belsey paused at the top of the mobile stairs to fill his lungs. The stewardess grinned as if she was in on the joke.

'Buenos noches, señor. Bienvenido a Mexico.'

Everyone went to collect their luggage. Belsey had no luggage, which made him feel curiously purposeful, strolling through the corridors alone, empty-handed. A bored-looking immigration official glanced at his passport and nodded him through. So he was first out into the glare of the arrivals hall, greeted like a celebrity by the taxi scammers and luggage handlers. Belsey realised he was smiling at them, amused that they took his existence seriously, the idea he had money and somewhere to go: an Englishman arriving in Mexico City on a Saturday night with nothing but the suit on his back. He was smiling because his life as he knew it was over and he was in Mexico and it felt beautiful.

Shutters started coming down on the airport's facilities. He checked the signs fast: autobús, cambio de moneda, polícia, cerveza. He emptied his pockets onto a ledge by a closed café and tried to figure out what resources he had. Twenty-six pounds in sterling and several cards of dubious credit. A cleaner mopped by his feet. An old man came up to him and opened a carrier bag, as if furtively revealing his shopping. It was filled with cartons of duty-free Marlboro. Belsey gave him a tenner and took a carton, put it under his arm and walked on.

Sixteen pounds, three debit cards, four maxed-out credit cards, two hundred Marlboro. But a few things in his favour: the weekend, time difference, the fact that most businesses processed transactions in batches at the end of the day. All this created a fissure of opportunity between expenditure and consequence that might be wide enough for him to slip through. At least two of the cards would let him go over the limit at the risk of heavy fines attached to billing addresses he no longer remembered. The concept of financial penalties felt weak. He tried a cash withdrawal but that didn't work. Nor did the bureau de change, but he managed to buy a bottle of water from the 7-11 using an old Amex, which meant the card was alive. He had credit.

He skipped the international car-hire companies and went to the last on the row: Optima Auto Rentas. A sleepy kid roused himself and turned his computer on. Belsey asked for the most expensive car they had and was offered a Dodge Charger for forty dollars a day. He requested use of it for six days, gave his address in Mexico City as the Hilton.

'Hilton Reforma?'

'That's the one.'

Belsey watched with a mounting sensation of weightlessness as the boy typed it in, took a carbon paper copy of the Amex, had Belsey sign a couple of forms, then found keys in a drawer beneath his desk. He led Belsey down to the car park, and ten minutes later Belsey was on the road.

This was the real test. The slip road fed into a crowded dual carriageway. Eight lanes of traffic poured into town with an attitude somewhere between a race and a carnival procession: high end SUVs and cars held together with string, all weaving and nudging, everyone driving like they were on the run a thousand miles from home, which was an edgy kind of incognito. Indicators weren't a thing. Sometimes they came on but whatever it meant it wasn't what he'd previously understood. Neither were lanes. If you opened up a gap between you and the car in front someone would cut in so you had to become one with the flow. People threw the hazard lights on before braking. Traffic cops stood on every corner, watching this communal death-wish without judgement. Belsey's adrenalin pumped, everything very vivid now, a plan becoming real even if he wasn't sure what it was.

A carpet of concrete slum homes stretched up the hills either side towards a night sky dulled by light pollution. The silhouette of a volcano came in and out of view. Cars heading east had a coating of ash. He kept an eye on road signs. Mexico City didn't exist. On the signs it was Distrito Federale. 'Federales' was the name painted in white letters on the paramilitary trucks tearing through the traffic: open-backed jeeps with men in black combat fatigues stroking their assault rifles. They were something different from the Policía Municipal, who cruised in convoys of seven or eight vehicles with lights and sirens on. Belsey kept alert, but after a while he realised there was no emergency: that was just how they moved. Or it was all an emergency. He stopped checking the mirrors every time they flashed.

The city grew around him, street-level chaos closing in: little cafés next to glass blocks with armed guards; heavy churches sinking crooked into the ground. No one was ever going to find him here. He reached the centre of town on a big, buzzing avenue called Insurgentes. Everything was fine. He let himself breathe.

What did he look like? Just some *caballero* heading home from work. No one even glanced at him. So this was exile, he thought, like a lucid dream. He could move through it. He could breathe in it, and it felt like being able to breathe underwater. What was the catch? Just keep going, stay out of trouble. He needed to switch vehicles, get some cash, that was all. The plates on the car were still tagged to his name, and while he couldn't imagine a transatlantic manhunt leaping into effect any time soon, it cramped his sense of freedom. There was no such thing as half escaping.

He kept heading south into a lot of cheap construction with wiring feeding into homes from pylons. Isolated pools of yellow streetlight caught curtained doorways. The stop lights in this part of town flashed continuous red as if they had a dark sense of humour.

Belsey stopped when he saw a *cantina* called Salon Casino. Maybe he could win some money, he thought. What games would they have? He parked right outside so he could keep an eye on the Dodge through the doorway.

Salon Casino had no casino, it turned out, but sold a beer called Techate at ten pesos a bottle. The place was small, low-lit, with football memorabilia on the walls. Men stopped drinking to watch Belsey enter. The barman had a deep crease up one side of his bald scalp. Belsey offered a box of Marlboro in return for a couple of drinks. He tried to rustle up some of the Spanish he'd been learning.

'*Uno box, dos cervezas. Sí?*'

The barman reflected, then tossed two beer mats in front of Belsey and set down the bottles, beaded with condensation. He placed the pack of cigarettes in his top pocket. Belsey lifted a bottle in thanks.

The man seated on a stool beside him laughed. He wore

4

overalls, had greasy hair and high Aztec cheekbones. He'd been glancing at the Dodge outside with quiet curiosity. Now he raised his own beer in a respectful *ola*.

'Cheers. I just got here,' Belsey said.

'Doctores?'

It took Belsey a while to understand what he was saying. It turned out he was in an area called Doctores and that wasn't a good idea. Not for tourists anyway.

'I'm not really a tourist,' Belsey explained. He offered the man his second drink. The man accepted. He spoke good English. He said he'd spent several years in California.

'Would you like to buy some cigarettes?' Belsey asked.

'Why not?'

The man paid for the cigarettes out of a roll of grubby, untaxed notes.

'You're a mechanic?' Belsey asked.

'Sure.'

'Perhaps you can help. I've got a car outside that I'd like to trade. Drives beautifully – a Dodge Charger. Not many miles on the clock. Just too big for my needs, and I could do with some money fast.'

'It's a nice car.'

'Any idea where I should go if I wanted to sell it quickly? For cash?'

'How long have you had it?'

'About an hour.'

'How much do you want?'

'Say a hundred dollars and some alternative wheels. Nothing fancy.'

The man laughed, sipped his beer. When the beer was gone, he surprised Belsey by getting up, glancing out through the doorway again. 'Come,' he said.

They went out. The mechanic asked to see inside the Dodge. Belsey gave him the keys. He stuck his head in, checked the mileage, the upholstery, breathed deeply. He came out, circled the vehicle, crouched and dug a thumbnail into the tyre tread. Then he straightened and they crossed the road to a breakers' yard with big metal gates. The road sign next to it said 'Dr Lavista'. The man unlocked the gates and dragged them over the stone pavement, firing sparks. He went inside, hit the lights. A neon-lit cave appeared, filled with jacked-up cars, the sides piled high with rear-view mirrors, windscreens, radios and steering wheels. There were more cars at the back, in a high-walled yard, a lot with US plates, a lot with identifying tags burned off.

'Any of these drive?' Belsey asked.

'Sure. You used that car in a crime?'

'No. I've only been in the country a couple of hours. I just need some cash.'

'It's a hire car.'

'It's a hire car, sure.'

The mechanic's eyes cut to the front. He sucked air through his teeth, then led Belsey to a 1970s Maserati, chocolate brown apart from the front passenger door, which was a black replacement. If you squinted, it had a profile like an old Jag.

'This one drives. I give you this, hundred dollars, we shake hands.'

'Two hundred.'

'One hundred.'

'Okay.'

The man gave Belsey some more sticky notes and the keys for the Maserati. He seemed happy enough. 'Make sure you pump the brakes. Give it plenty of time. And the steering will need a bit of muscle.' He mimed steering vigorously. He looked a little concerned.

'I'll try my best.'

'Any more I can do?'

'Which way's the sea?' Belsey asked.

The man brought up a map on his phone.

'There's a lot of sea. Where do you want to go exactly?'

Belsey touched his finger to the screen and moved the territory around until he saw what he wanted. 'Acapulco,' he said.

TWO

He was out of the city by daybreak and felt safe enough to park for a few hours behind a service station and sleep. When the heat woke him, he got out of the car and stretched, and felt like he was in exactly the right place for the first time. He bought three litres of water, sunglasses and a fold-out road map. It looked like Highway 95 would take him to the coast. He could make Acapulco in a few hours if he floored it, a couple of days if he went more scenic.

The car drove for now. The radio worked. He played rock music as he accelerated out of a national park, keeping the volcano to his left, which meant he was going south. Onto Highway 95, through villages with stone houses, into the state of Guerrero. Get to the sea, he thought. There would be space to think there. Then, once he'd decompressed, he could work his way back into something. But he needed to fully escape first.

He met Esmerelda at a petrol station where Highway 95 met a toll road heading north. She was standing in the shade of the canopy, watching Belsey as he filled the tank and paid. When he walked back to the car he gave her a nod in greeting and she walked over.

'*Buenos días*,' Belsey said.

'*Americano?*'

'*Inglés.* Need a lift?'

'Where are you going?'

'Acapulco.'

She smiled. 'Me too.'

She had long black hair, sandals and shorts, a canvas over-night bag with tassels. She put the seat back so she could stretch out. He wondered what her eyes were like behind the shades.

'What's your name?' she asked, when they were on the road.

'John.'

'Johnny B. Goode.'

'That's the one.'

She said she was Esmerelda, and had been on her way to visit her sick mother when her previous ride broke down. She didn't try to make it convincing. Belsey thought back to when he first saw her and realised she was on the watch for something. Their click was the encounter of a police officer and a criminal. He didn't give a fuck. He had eighty dollars, a Maserati and quite possibly an international arrest warrant on him. She could only enhance the situation.

'Are you on holiday?' she asked. 'On your own?'

'Holiday of sorts. I'm taking a break from things. Needed some space.'

'What is your job?'

'I'm between jobs. I'm an actor. I do bar work. Whatever's going.'

'Are you famous?'

'Not yet. Getting close.'

He gave her a pack of Marlboro and she lit a cigarette for him. They drove, chatting about life, its twists and turns, through Iguala, with its tamarind trees shading the road, then into the mountains, rising above industrial grime and more ramshackle buildings. They passed Zumpango del Río, where she said there were abandoned silver mines but he didn't see any. The hillsides were lush with greenery now. Belsey stopped and they got lunch from a roadside restaurant with a terrace overlooking the valley, which used up a lot of his currency. But it was nice to have company. His passenger took her shades off and her eyes were chestnut brown but deep with a knowledge of things that could happen and were to be avoided. He checked her bag when she went to take a picture of the view and found six cheque books in different names, none of them Esmerelda.

They were still on the road when it got dark.

'Let's get dinner,' Belsey suggested. 'Then we can rest and start again in the morning. Can you do that?'

She took a second to consider this. 'Sure. It's a good idea.'

So they stopped at Chilpancingo, a decent-sized town which promised nightlife. Belsey found a motel. He offered to pay for two rooms. Esmerelda said one would be fine, which made the dinner a lot more relaxed. They went on to a club decorated in the style of old taverns with a mechanical bull in the centre of the dancefloor.

'I've never seen one of these in a club before,' Belsey said. 'It's a great idea.'

The tequila was cheap. Esmerelda had pharmaceuticals: sky blue rocks of crystal meth and something like codeine in white pills. They smoked the meth from a glass pipe and dropped a couple of the tranquillisers and walked around Chilpancingo, checking out other bars, dark ones where they had to lean close to see each other's eyes.

'In the car park, where I picked you up,' Belsey said, 'you were looking for something.'

'Was I? Maybe I was looking for you.' She smiled.

'You looked like you were going to steal a car.'

'Me? Steal a car?'

Crossing the forecourt back to their motel room Belsey felt the earth rising up towards him, lifting his feet. Mexico was just another place, but a new one, and the thousands of miles between him and the UK swaddled him, just like the night air did. And he was heading to a twenty-dollar motel room with a woman whose real name he didn't know, less than forty-eight hours after arriving in the country. What greater sign was there that all was well in the universe?

They hit the road early the next day, stopping for breakfast and then a couple of remedial cocktails. He was starting to hurt – little stabs of pain in specific organs. But he put it down to a hangover. Esmerelda introduced him to something she called a Michelada, which was like a Bloody Mary with beer instead of vodka, and he introduced her to the Easy Flip with stout, bourbon and black coffee. The caffeine was valuable. By the time they reached El Ocotito, a town with two bars, a post office and an industrial park, they were low on money. She told him to stop outside the post office. Belsey watched her go in, and after five minutes she left again, climbed back into the Maserati and Belsey drove fast.

'I'm good at gambling,' he said. 'Poker, slots, whatever. If there's a casino I reckon I can double what we've got.'

There was no casino. They passed villages of pink stone, then larger towns with small demonstrations going on in their central squares. Against corruption, Esmerelda explained. It seemed like something was kicking off in Guerrero state. They did shots of white rum at roadside bars and smoked the rest of the Marlboros. Fifty miles north-east of Acapulco they hit a checkpoint.

Men in ambiguous uniforms with unambiguous weaponry stood across the road, manning a roadblock constructed of concrete sections from the side of the highway. Esmerelda told

11

Belsey to put away any valuables, to approach slowly and not make any sudden movements. She'd do the talking.

'Police got issues?'

'It's not the police.'

She was right. The cars were faded and they wore trainers.

'Who are they?'

'People. Maybe soldiers.'

When it got to Belsey's turn the men stuck their heads in, walked around the car and made Belsey get out and open the boot. He realised he hadn't looked in the boot but all it contained was a flat spare tyre and someone's snakeskin boots. Esmerelda smiled sweetly, talked about visiting her family and her cousin's first communion, and they got through, but it felt lucky. After that they stuck to toll roads. Most of the time it was *mesa* either side, rugged with low peaks. When they passed a church ringing its bells Esmerelda put her fingers in her ears. She said she couldn't stand the sound of church bells.

'Why?'

'Have you heard of the earthquake in Manzanillo?'

'No.'

She told him about her childhood, further up the coast in a small town called Manzanillo. There had been a terrible earthquake when she was eight, she said. Took most of her family. She held back tears as she described waking up in the middle of the night and all the church bells were ringing on their own. She never forgot the sound. 'My life would have been different if it hadn't been for that earthquake. I would have gone to college.' She said she'd never been in a nice hotel, never really been on holiday.

Belsey checked the map and decided on a diversion. Hotel San Luis Lindavista was by an archaeological site on the Río

Papagayo. It was only a couple of kilometres out of their way. 'One night,' he said. 'Let's blow the rest of my money.'

She smiled, and slid a crooked finger behind her sunglasses to wipe each eye in turn. 'Let's do it.'

The hotel greeted them warmly. Belsey did the talking this time, and they signed in as Mr and Mrs Cash. It had a pool and a restaurant. They wore the bathrobes, opened the minibar, ate the chocolate and Pringles and drank the miniature bottles of wine.

Belsey stood in the light of the bathroom mirror wondering if his skin was yellow or if it was the light. He had a dawning sense that he wasn't well, in a profound way; that he hadn't been for some time. The drugs helped temporarily, but he was putting something off. The medication he needed wasn't the kind he was getting. They finished the wine, smoked the rest of the meth. Belsey considered telling her he'd started urinating blood. It felt like a big confession when they'd known each other only a day or so.

When he woke up she was gone. He was in a very bad way then. The sheets were bloody, and there was a sharp reek of bile. He thought at first she'd left because he'd vomited blood over the bed, which would have been understandable. His belongings were strewn everywhere, wallet gone, along with paperwork and car keys.

That stung, but he could look back and see it as the conclusion of a far more elaborate hustle, one he'd wandered into before he could remember. Life was a con. It was worth every penny. He laughed and a white pain cut through him. He sat down on the bed and held his head in his hands.

After a few minutes Belsey had the strength to get to his feet and mop up the last of the drugs from the bureau. This gave him the presence of mind to take the clothes iron out of its little linen bag and empty the rest of the minibar into the bag. He left the hotel, nodding at the receptionist, saw his car missing, made it to the road where he hitched a lift.

The first group that picked him up took offence when they realised the state of him. It was a crew of four men, drunk, driving a van. They tried to rob him but couldn't find anything to rob, so they kicked him out of the vehicle, then got out and started kicking him in the head. When they were done, Belsey remained curled up for a while, letting his new injuries throb.

Next lift was a serious guy in a brown suit, who seemed to understand something about Belsey's situation. He gestured solemnly at the passenger seat without taking his eyes off the windscreen.

The man drove steadily. His car was falling apart. The exhaust system rattled beneath them, and both wing mirrors had departed. He had a handsome, unevenly shaved face, and elegant fingers, which he drummed on the wheel as if to music Belsey couldn't hear. He asked Belsey for help reading signs and Belsey realised he was partially blind. They shared drinks. Belsey gave the man some of his minibar haul. The driver had mezcal in a litre Coke bottle, crazy moonshine that tasted of burning tyres. Belsey felt momentarily fortified and lucky. He imagined the two of them helping each other as they made a slow but important journey across the decimated surface of the earth. The man said he was going to see his son, who worked in a hotel and whom he hadn't visited in twelve years. He hadn't driven for a while also, he said. Belsey persuaded the man to let him drive and they swapped places. The man talked more from the passenger side. He had been driving many days, he said. He was a Jehovah's Witness. He fell into a stupor. Belsey put the seatbelt on him to stop him falling face first into the dashboard. At some point Belsey must have blacked out too because when he next opened his eyes they were parked at the side of the road, the man asleep beside him. It was night. Belsey could smell the sea.

He took the remaining pesos from his pockets and put them into the man's jacket along with a couple of miniature Smirnoffs. Then he stumbled out of the car and walked the remaining distance to the coast, each step a victory against whatever was going on inside him.

After a couple of hours he got to a beach with small boats lined up on the sand. Houses made of corrugated metal and raw concrete faced the sea. Waves glittered in moonlight. It wasn't Acapulco but it would do. He stood right by the water so he couldn't see anything else and had a sense of having arrived at the far shore of his life. His peripheral vision was gone. The sea was in his shoes. He let himself sink down until he was kneeling in the amniotic warmth of the Pacific, salt water lapping his thighs, and everything within him said good night, game over, and he understood now why he had been coming here, what he was here to do.

THREE

For a long time there was darkness. He felt dull pain, but had no sense of who he was or where. Then there were voices: children laughing, a woman speaking Spanish. Sometimes she was joined by a man. They stood over him, muttering, concerned. When the man left, the woman spoke for a while on her own and Belsey realised she was praying.

The next thing he was aware of was the voice of a TV presenter followed by applause. Belsey opened his eyes. A picture of the Virgin Mary hung on a roughly plastered wall. It looked like a chapel, but a chapel wouldn't have a TV, he reasoned. He was in someone's home.

He turned onto his side. His clothes were folded on a crate beside the bed. Belsey reached under the blanket and felt someone else's T-shirt and pants on him. He lifted himself up and saw he was in a small home with a low roof and uneven walls carefully decorated with prints of saints and flowers. A middle-aged woman stood in the doorway watching him. She called over her shoulder and the man joined her. The woman was small, with a kind, attractive face and hair tied in a long plait, the man wiry and deeply tanned. He wore a baseball cap and a frayed blue polo shirt with the Ferrari logo on the breast. They looked concerned and apologetic, which seemed wrong in the circumstances.

'I don't know what happened,' Belsey said. 'But thank you. I'm fine now. I'll get out of your way.' He swung his legs out of the bed and stood up.

Everything moved sideways. He felt a splinter of pain straight through him and went down heavily, reaching for the bedside table and spilling it onto himself.

'Sorry,' he said.

They moved the table off him, helped him onto the bed again.

He slept. Occasionally the woman gave him water. Then she brought some bread, and when she saw he could eat this, she brought him beans and eggs on a tin plate.

'*No sabíamos a quién ...*' The man and woman both had attempts at saying something. Eventually they fetched a teen-age girl who spoke some English.

'They don't know who to tell,' she said.

'No one,' he said. 'Please. *No persona. Por favor. Gracias.* I'll be gone soon. I can give you some money. I'll get some money.'

There were other kids: a young boy and a girl, possibly more boys – though they might have been from other families. Belsey would open his eyes and they'd be there. They helped him as he staggered between the bed and the bathroom. Eventually, the kids began to speak to him.

'*Americano?*'

'*Inglés.*'

'*Cuál es su nombre?*'

'*John.*'

'*Juan.*'

'Juan sounds good. Don Juan.'

He lay in the house, recovering. The woman fed him spicy broth with corn, sometimes chicken and plain tortillas. He drank cold, minty tea. She placed an egg in a glass of water

17

beside the bed, which she said he shouldn't drink. There was a towel she'd lay across his forehead with rubbing alcohol or something on it, from a bottle with flowers floating inside.

He could walk a bit further now. A TV took up half the front room, which had a bare bulb, an electric fan. There was one room in the back where they all slept. He realised, horrified, that the parents had moved there because of him.

'Really, have your bed back,' he said.

'Soon.'

At night, the lights all flickered when the wind blew, and there was a sense of the world entering and flowing through their home. Sometimes there was no electricity and they lit candles.

When he was strong enough Belsey went to the front and looked at the sea. The front door opened straight onto the beach. The kitchen was outside, with a thatched roof and a clay oven. On the other side of the house an open-fronted workshop was filled with boat parts. The path to the front of the house was marked by piles of swept-up palm leaves, fragments of coconut shell and plants in soil-filled tyres. He got into the habit of sitting on the tyres as it became dark.

The kids wanted to play with him. He learned their names. The thin, intelligent-looking one was Francisco. Then there was cherubic, golden-skinned José, silent Arturo, the twins Rosa and María Isabel, and the older María Luisa, who showed him English textbooks and got help with her homework. They called him Juan and he liked it. In his own mind, Nick Belsey became someone he'd heard of but couldn't place, and sometimes he struggled to recall the name altogether. He liked the idea of being on a continent where no one knew him. He saw the concept of Nick Belsey float away over the ocean, like a helium balloon.

He didn't want to be nursed, didn't understand who these people were or why they were helping him, but knew, with a deeper instinct, that he wasn't fixed, so he didn't have a choice. This was survival: waiting, suffering their generosity. He would find a way to repay them. That was what he had lost, he realised, the means of repaying debts. That was what a life was. He needed nothing himself, but sometimes life sprang debts upon you and you had to be prepared. That gave him something to think about.

Eventually he could walk for ten minutes at a time. The place he'd arrived in was thirty or so homes of varying degrees of solidity, arranged along a sandy cove with rocks piled at either end. The fishing boats that went out each morning ranged from new motorised ones to old wooden crafts with peeling paint on the hull, but none big enough for more than three or four men. There was no hotel, no bar. A real place, for living and fishing.

He explored more as his strength returned. A dirt track ran up the hill to the main road, where a bus passed every hour carrying workers and tourists between the bigger resorts. A faded sign advertised 'Sport fishing'. Behind it was a small cemetery, the graves all horizontal slabs painted in pastel colours. There was a statue of the Virgin Mary, eyes covered with children's stickers. Concrete fragments of abandoned building projects choked the palm trees either side. Fields of rock and cacti led towards mountains.

The men went out to sea at 4 a.m., came back at six or seven, running the boats up over sticks laid out on the sand. Belsey was usually awake so he'd go out and help pull the boats up, untangling the nets, unloading the ice boxes of fish. The father's boat was called *Tigresa del Mar*. Birds circled above them: long-beaked herons, small grey seagulls. Men gutted the fish on tables at the back of the beach. People carted off the day's haul in plastic beer crates, balanced on mopeds, blood dripping. A van went out each day to the local towns, piled high.

Sometimes a few tourists came down in the afternoon from hotels further up the coast. They dived or sunbathed – German students, elderly American couples, travellers with the optimism of the happily lost. A couple of times a week a battered bus pulled up with backpackers hanging on, tattooed and tanned. The father would take out divers and anyone who wanted to fish but there weren't many. They enjoyed the picturesque poverty, then got out of there before night fell.

Games of football began once the sun was safely behind the hills. The sea retreated, leaving an expanse of glistening wet sand so it looked like the boys were playing on water. After a week Belsey was able to join in with the kick-about. They were good. He'd get a heat up and go for a swim. That became his thing: swimming under the stars. They seemed brighter than the lights of a city. He liked floating on his back, watching them, listening to the electric hum of cicadas.

One time he was sitting on the sand, drying off, when María Luisa came over and asked him why he swam at night.

'Why not? We don't have this where I come from. I think it's good for me.'

She sat beside him, hugged her knees to her chest.

'What is England like?'

'Cold. *Frío*. A lot of rain.'

'It rains here.'

'The rain here is warm.'

'You have the Queen.'

'That's true.'

Other kids gathered – his football crew. They asked him about London. María Luisa translated for the younger ones.

'When do you go back?'

'Not sure I can.'

'You live here now?'

'Maybe.'

'You will fish,' José said.

'I could learn.'

He was hit for the first time by a sudden wave of emotion: a response to the beauty of the place or grief for his old life, or the two entangled. It caught him by surprise.

The daughter showed him a magazine with pictures of people in London on a red carpet.

'You have been here?'

'Yes. That's Leicester Square.'

'It is very beautiful.'

'Very beautiful. Right in the centre of town.'

'Everyone is rich.'

'A lot of them. Not everyone.'

At the children's prompting, the younger María sang him a song called 'La Golondrina'. The children explained that it was about a bird that had migrated across the ocean, but was missing its homeland. Belsey asked her to sing it again the next night, until he knew a few words. She seemed shy when she saw how carefully he listened.

Sound took over when it was dark: dogs barking, men laughing. The breaking of the waves gained a deeper tone, of something ominous but too far away to touch you. The night air was oppressive, like being chloroformed. A crescent moon appeared on its back, flattened by the heat.

Belsey started hanging out more with the other men. At night, they sat at the edge of the boat shed playing cards. They drank bottles of Pacifico beer, ate little dried fish, smoked a brand called Delicados, which had sour tobacco and sweetened paper. They gave Belsey a beer and raised a toast.

'*El hígado no existe.*'

'What does it mean?'

'The liver does not exist.'

'That's brilliant. More a diagnosis in my case.'

They clapped him on the back, raised their bottles again.

'*Dios esta borracho.*'

'God is drunk?'

'*Sí, sí.*'

'*Es verdad.* For sure.'

They called him John Wayne. He watched the men play cards by the light of a bulb buzzing with insects. They played poker with a Spanish deck. The kings wore big floppy hats, the jacks were women. The poker itself was a variant of five-card stud, with no eights, nines or tens and a single joker. People played it like lottery poker, loose and passive, chucking the cards impatiently.

One day he helped carry an extra big load up to the main road and was surprised by a couple of notes being pressed into his hand. It bought him into the card game. The trick, he soon saw, was to stick to playing pairs: pound aces and pairs and fold everything else. Only bluff if you knew no one had the joker. He won a few dollars, tried to refuse the money, but this was bad etiquette. They slapped him on the back again, toasted, laughing.

El inglés afortunado. Johnny de la suerte. Un hombre muy dichoso.

That night he lay with the money in his pocket feeling different, not sure what it meant.

The next day Belsey hitched a ride into town. He sat in the back of the fish van clutching ice boxes. They passed through urban sprawl, shanty towns, houses built with waste from other construction projects. Cattle and goats grazed the steep rocky slopes. There were shrines set back from the road, pine trees a pale chalky colour from the dust.

He got out at the junction where the highway met the road for the nearest town, La Cada. Barefoot squeegee merchants plied their trade, kids hawking packets of Clorets, people selling indistinct items off trays strapped to their bodies, faces scarved against the carbon monoxide. The driver said he needed to make a delivery to San Marcos a few miles inland but would be passing back through in a couple of hours and would wait for Belsey here. He sped off once Belsey was out of the vehicle, as if finding the place distasteful.

Belsey headed into town. The air filled with the cloying sugar and smoke smell of distilleries. He passed several *fabrica de mezcal*, then anonymous factories, into the town itself. La Cada was ten or so long, straight roads forming a grid, each road leading to a view of brown and yellow hills. The day was bright and silent. Clouds hung in the sky, stranded there as if something had broken.

A lot of the shops appeared to have closed down. Others had simply drawn their shutters against the heat. Signs were hand-painted onto plaster above dark, uninviting entrance ways: *Dentisto, Funerales*. The police station was a block of peeling pink stucco with white bars over the windows. *Cantinas* hid behind beaded curtains, interiors unlit, histrionic football commentary echoing off the tiles. But the most unnerving two places were the luxury car dealership and the designer fashion boutique, conspicuous as blood at a crime scene. Someone in this district was making money.

An army truck passed through, sending up dust, men in fatigues and helmets on the back staring out. It was closely followed by Policía Municipal, Policía Estatal and Prividad

23

Securidad. Finally armoured vehicles with no windows, like squat tanks, trundled down the narrow road as if somewhere just out of sight was a war zone. A moment after the tanks, Belsey heard music approaching, and a convoy of flashy cars sped past, driven by chubby men with shark eyes. They almost ran him down, and one passenger gave him an evil stare as he jumped back onto the pavement. He watched them park outside a pool hall with black windows covered in mesh. On the roof there was a giant rack with billiard balls. Outside were shiny pick-ups, a gleaming black Cadillac Escalade, a white Mercedes Grand Marquis. A man in sandals guarded the entrance, with a long-barrelled rifle slung across his body. Belsey decided not to make it part of his itinerary.

He walked past. The man with the rifle called something. Belsey kept going. He called again and Belsey turned.

'*Ola.*'

The man stepped closer, studied his face. Maybe he didn't like new people around. He lifted his phone and took a photo of Belsey.

'You want my photo?' Belsey said.

'*¿Quién eres tú? ¿De donde eres?*'

'*Inglés. No hablo español. Adiós.*'

Belsey backed away and the man watched him go. He didn't turn his head, didn't raise the rifle either. Belsey crossed the road to an arid square of park, and when he was sure the man wasn't following, he sat down on a bench. There was a bandstand, a few sickly looking trees with their trunks painted white, ornamental rocks lining the path. Someone approached, carrying what looked like a tool box. Belsey tensed, then saw it was a young boy.

'*Señor. Buenos días.*'

'*Buenos días.*'

'¿*Limpiabotas?*'

'¿*Qui es limpiabotas?*'

'Shoe shining.'

'*No, gracias.*'

'Where are you from?' the boy said, setting his box down and starting to unpack his kit. The box was full of crap: old rags, rusted tins. The kid's own shoes were in a bad way.

'England.'

'You need this, *señor.*' He showed Belsey a torn cardboard box.

'Yeah?'

'Very special liquid. For rain. *Para lluvia. Sí?*' He wiggled his fingers, whistling softly. '*En inglaterra hay mucha lluvia.*'

'Sure. I'm wearing trainers, though.'

'No problem.'

He set about his work protecting Belsey's shoes from a London downpour he was never going to feel again. After he was done, Belsey gave him some pesos.

'Where's good for booze around here? Alcohol? ¿*Comprar alcohol?*'

'*No ahí.*' The boy waved in the direction of the billiards hall. '*No ahí. Ve allí. Muy barato.* Over this way.'

'What's going on in that place?'

'*Mala gente.*' He shook his head. 'Bad people. Bad things.'

Belsey followed the boy's directions into the sanctuary of the back streets. Grandmothers sat in front of their homes on fold-out chairs selling homebrew: tequila, *pulque*, corn beer. He got a lot for his money. Then he went to the supermarket and bought fruit juice, bottles of lemonade, some coloured syrups, limes, plastic cups, candles.

When he picked Belsey up, the delivery driver appeared impressed by the bags. He looked glad to be getting out of there. He kept checking the mirrors and Belsey saw a black

Cadillac Escalade behind them, keeping its distance. It was the car from the billiards hall.

'¿*Problemos?*' the delivery man asked nervously.

'I hope not. I think maybe they don't like visitors.'

The car stayed behind them for a mile or so. Then they turned off towards the beach and it didn't follow. Both Belsey and the driver swore quietly in their own languages, shook their heads and laughed.

Back at the beach, Belsey set up two sticks and strung old netting between them, a card table beneath it, punctured holes in some old tins, lit the candles and put them inside. He unfolded a cardboard box and wrote up a cocktail menu. As it got dark he stepped away to admire his work from a distance and was impressed. He waited for tourists.

Eventually a Dutch couple wandered by. They'd been out fishing, asked if he had water and took a couple of beers instead.

'This is great,' the man said.

'Thanks.'

'You sound English.'

'I am.'

'How long have you been working here?'

'This is my first day. This is the bar's first day.'

'Well, good luck with it. You've got a great spot.'

They paid for the drinks, then had to go for the bus. Belsey packed up, feeling the eyes of the locals on him. He wondered if he was going to try again. It was a lot of stock to drink by himself.

The next day the Dutch couple came back with seven friends. Belsey watched the crowd arrive and whistled softly.

'What drinks do you do?' a woman in her twenties asked.

'What do you want?'

He got inventive with tequila-based cocktails. Tequila

Sunset, he called one – tequila, triple sec and orange juice, with some pomegranate syrup for the sunset effect. Margaritas with fresh lime juice were popular, and he could bang them out in seconds. He garnished the rim of the glass with salt, which impressed people. Tequila and ginger beer worked, tequila and pineapple juice for the sweet of tooth.

'You've got *pulque*?' one guy said, looking across the bottles. 'What do you do with *pulque*?'

'Let's see.'

What he did was mix it with lime juice, cane syrup, mezcal and ice. Finally, like he knew what he was doing, he tossed in some roasted habanero chilli.

'This is wild,' the man said. 'It works.'

'I just invented it.'

'What are you going to call it?'

'I don't know. What's your name?'

'Rudi.'

'Let's call it Rudi's Dream. Enjoy it while it lasts.'

Locals watched in wonder. They brought out snacks: the dried fish, bowls of nuts. They brought a tape player and then someone with a small guitar began playing along to the music. There was dancing. The tourists hung around for three hours, drank him dry, left Belsey with a wad of over three thousand pesos.

Belsey tried to give it to the mother. She refused. The kids took a few notes each, with smiles.

'Buy something for your parents, okay? Persuade them to take this.'

He went back into town the following day with the rest and topped up supplies. Maybe this was it, he thought. Maybe he was here for a while.

That evening the kids helped him arrange the place. Some of

the women grilled fish for tacos. Belsey had twelve customers in total – two different parties. They were up for it, had heard about the *pulque* cocktail and the live music. The kids helped Belsey serve, running to get ice from the cool boxes. By 9 p.m. he had exceeded the previous day's takings. Then the men turned up.

Someone had made a joke about a flambé cocktail and Belsey said he could do it. He'd seen someone using a blowtorch to fix their boat, so he went to borrow it, and when he was halfway back to the bar carrying the torch he saw the black Cadillac Escalade driving down onto the beach.

It stopped and two men got out. One was fat, in a red Adidas vest and red shorts, one taller, darker, in polo shirt and jeans. They went straight to work, trashing the bar, pulling down the netting, smashing bottles. Women screamed. The tourists fled to the main road. Belsey ran towards his bar. As he got closer, he saw the fat one grab María Luisa. The mother took hold of his sleeve and he pushed her off with a hand in her face.

'Hey,' Belsey said. They turned towards him. Both wore a look of dumb cruelty. Both moved languidly, their pupils dilated. They were drunk and drugged. In his experience that meant anything could happen apart from fast responses.

'What's the problem?' he said.

The fat one tossed María Luisa aside and walked towards Belsey.

Belsey read his swagger and decided this wasn't time for a negotiation. Which meant he needed at least one of them out of action fast. Belsey took a step towards the man, which made him stop. Made his knees lock. Belsey stomped on his kneecap and the man collapsed, howling. Belsey took advantage of his friend's shock to fire up the blowtorch. By the time the second man had tugged a gun from his waistband, Belsey was aiming the flame at his gun hand. He yelped and the gun fell to the sand. Belsey aimed the blue flame in his face and he staggered backwards, tripping over remnants of the bar.

Belsey threw aside the torch and dropped on the man with all his weight, turned him while he was winded and got a knee into the small of his back, reaching instinctively for handcuffs that weren't there. What was he doing? He was conscious of people watching. He got to his feet, kicked the gun away.

'Get the fuck out of here,' he said.

The taller man pulled his friend up, staring at Belsey. There was a moment of calculation, but they'd lost their flow. And, Belsey suspected, they knew this wasn't their last chance. The two men moved towards the car.

'¡Puto! Estas muerto.'

A few seconds later the engine started, wheels spinning momentarily on the sand. The Escalade reversed away.

'Hasta luego,' one of them shouted.

Then they were gone. Everyone went to check the daughter was okay. The father had a bleeding lip. The mother cried. Others watched Belsey with a degree of awe but also as if a mask had slipped. Belsey looked around: upturned tables, broken glass, candles guttering.

'What the fuck was that about?'

People shook their heads.

'What did they want? A cut? Mafiosi? They want pesos?'

'No lo sé,' the father said.

'What did they say?'

'Nick.'

'Nick?'

'Un nombre. Señor Nick Belsey.'

'Nick Belsey? Really?'

'Sí. Nick Belsey.'

He glanced down at the ground where a sheet of paper lay among the broken glass. Belsey picked it up. It contained an enlarged copy of his own passport picture.

The father stared flatly at Belsey now. *'¿Quíen es Nick Belsey?'*

FOUR

She hadn't heard the name for a long time. So it was hard to believe she'd really heard it at all.

'Who am I speaking to?' Detective Inspector Kirsty Craik lifted herself up in bed. The clock said 5.15 a.m. She took the phone out to the hallway so as not to disturb the man sleeping beside her. If it hadn't been so odd she might not have answered at that hour. But not many people had her personal number, and the caller ID said: *Funeral Care.*

The person at the other end spoke carefully in lightly accented English.

'I am looking for Nick Belsey,' he said. 'Do you know where he is?'

'Nick Belsey?'

'He will know what this is about. Do you have a number for him?'

Belsey. The last name she expected to hear. They had worked together over eight years ago, and been close in less professional ways longer ago than that. It belonged to a different part of her life. But if anyone was going to randomly resurface in troubling ways it was Nick Belsey. And with the stab of concern was the undertow of old cares, of having wondered where he was more times than she'd admit.

'Who is this?' Craik asked.

'Someone who would like to speak to him. Perhaps you could let me know if you hear anything. It would be in his own interest.'

'How did you get this number?'

'I know you live alone, Miss Craik. I am worried for your safety. You must consider what it means – a woman living alone. Tell Nick Belsey that you got this call. Tell him you will be dead by Christmas if I have not heard from him.'

The caller hung up. Craik stood in the hallway, staring at the phone, trying to gauge the appropriate level of concern. Could it be dismissed as a prank? There was a bit too much personal information for that. The voice sounded cooler, as if performing a function.

She went to the kitchen window and checked the street outside. They were probably guessing about her living arrangements. A woman answers the phone at five in the morning, it's a strong possibility she lives alone. And if they were really watching the house they'd know she wasn't alone tonight. An ill-advised lover occupied half of her precious bed.

Craik could see her boss, Chief Inspector Robert Price, propped up on one bare arm, watching her from the darkness when she returned.

'What was that?' he said.

'Nothing.'

'Really?'

'Someone offering to help me claim accident compensation.'

'In the middle of the night?'

'Maybe it's not night where they are.'

The chief inspector closed his eyes. 'You know that's technically illegal now,' he said.

'I'll tell them next time.'

'Unless you've opted in,' he said. 'Who opts in?'

'Lonely people. It's not five thirty. We can get another hour's sleep.'

He rolled towards her, throwing a thick arm over her body, lips to her shoulder.

'Imagine,' he said. 'How lonely you'd have to be.'

Craik didn't have time to think about it again until she was in the office. Price rushed off to a meeting with the Crown Prosecution Service. She made her way through the darkness of a London winter morning into Organised Crime Command.

The OCC shared a new office block in Vauxhall with Narcotics, Kidnap, Armed Robbery and the National Criminal Intelligence Service. It was a hub of elite units, a reminder of how far her career had come since the days of being mentored by Belsey in Borough CID. Stakes in the Organised Crime unit were high, camaraderie tight. As Craik passed through the layers of security into the office she was greeted by the sound of laughter.

Three of her team stood around a mobile phone, watching a video. Craik heard a police raid, the smashing of a door, and then her own voice yelling orders amid the ensuing chaos. Detective Constable Ciaran Gibson, the unit's junior member, held the phone. The rest of Craik's team stood humouring him: Nelson Obiri, their towering tech specialist, and Craik's own mentee, DC Jocelyn Summer.

'Not bad, ma'am,' Summer said. 'He wants to put it on YouTube.' She grinned.

'Not before the trial,' Craik said.

She joined them and watched herself storm into a multi-million-pound apartment as several men were forced nose-down into the shagpile. It was hard not to feel a glow of satisfaction. The bust had been the conclusion of a twelve-month operation into a sprawling criminal empire responsible for 80 per cent of London's recent drug and gun crime. It had been set up in response to governmental pressure to get a grip on UK narcotics. The water in the Thames was testing positive, the Yard was under fire. Price had been given the green light to develop his pet project, Operation Goldmine: turn off the taps, hit the dealers hard, as high up the chain as possible. Thirty-seven associates of various gangs had already pleaded guilty or been convicted. So this was rewarding, a career high. But it made the call about Belsey feel like the puncturing of an illusion: that there was a reason it had come now, just when she was winning.

'Put it on a screen at the Christmas lunch tomorrow, maybe,' Gibson said.

'Or maybe not.'

Craik sat at her desk and considered the mountain of paperwork she had to get through before the world closed down for the rest of the year. Did she have time to pursue that random call? It had begun to feel unreal, a phenomenon of the night.

First duties involved dealing with several messages and emails from her long-term boyfriend, Lawrence, a property lawyer who had already gone to his parents' place in the country for Christmas, and was expecting Craik to complete the cosy set-up as soon as possible. He was passing on several requests for cooking ingredients and last-minute presents. Craik had seven more Old Bailey trials to prepare for and no idea when she was meant to go Christmas shopping. Then she had the emails from Forensics and Firearms analysis to deal with, plus a press conference to arrange. But she wasn't focusing, she realised.

She booted up the national police database and typed in

Belsey's name. He came up as WoW – Wanted on Warrant. He had absconded midway through an investigation into him that had begun three months ago, concerning theft, corruption and assault. It had been bumped from the local Professional Standards Department to the IOPC, which meant it was serious. The Independent Office of Police Conduct investigated the most sensitive allegations involving abuse of power. She scanned down the list of advisers and saw Price himself offering the support of Organised Crime Command should Belsey's corruption prove more significant than a few minor misdemeanours. So he knew of the man. There was nothing Craik could find that told her what he was currently up to or where he might be. She set up an alert on Belsey's name to ensure she was notified if any new information was uploaded.

Someone had connected Belsey to her personal number. That was the most puzzling bit. She remembered him taking her number, many years ago. He had written it down on a piece of paper that he kept in his wallet. When she asked why, he said he didn't have a mobile. In truth, he had several. Still, more often than not, the best way to contact him was via the telephone in the Wishing Well pub, and it was this number that frequently showed when he attempted to contact you.

Tell Nick Belsey that you got this call. Tell him you will be dead by Christmas if I have not heard from him.

Craik took out her mobile. The Funeral Care ID had been spoofed, she was pretty sure. It was a technique used by nuisance callers and identity thieves, and easy enough these days. When she tried to ring the number back, the line was dead.

She knocked at Obiri's office. Nelson Obiri was an all-round genius, in Craik's opinion: a former Bank of England software engineer who had got bored of economic forecasts and turned his skills in data analytics to tracing criminal networks, modelling patterns of violence, weaponry, drugs distribution. Few in the police hierarchy knew exactly what he did, but there was a general understanding that it was effective and cutting edge, so he was left alone. He was very beautiful, with a quiet intensity and a bachelor lifestyle about which he never spoke and which made Craik curious.

She showed him the ID on her phone.

'Reckon Technical Support could see behind this? Find out who was really calling?'

'Sure. What's it from?'

'I can't go into details right now. But it's a call to my personal number.'

'The source number is only blocked for the recipient of the call. It will be on phone company records. Might need a warrant, though.'

'Would you send it through, see what they can do?'

'Of course.'

Craik wrote down the time received and her mobile number and network. 'Use the Goldmine code,' she said. 'That should clear a warrant.'

Obiri hesitated for a second. 'Okay, boss.'

She didn't have a chance to think about it again for a couple of hours. She was in a meeting with Gibson, Summer and the officer in charge of trial prep: DS Jackie Weller. Weller was the smallest and loudest in the office: a chain-smoker on her fourth husband, dogged when it came to evidence. For an hour she guided them through the legal challenges of using social-media posts in court. Gibson, who'd recently transferred out of the undercover unit and worked tirelessly to prove himself, wrote everything down, between glancing at Summer, who seemed to absorb technique more effortlessly. Craik had once caught Gibson proudly showing her photographs of all the doors he'd destroyed during raids, possibly missing what seemed apparent to herself: that neither broken doors nor testosterone-fuelled male officers were Summer's thing. But they all worked well as a team, and she trusted them, and having a secret concern, no matter how small, felt strange. The meeting finished at 11 a.m. Craik was about to call Belsey's old number when Price arrived.

'Kirsty, quick word,' he said, marching through to his corner office.

They were both good at keeping a straight face. Craik knew this was half of the appeal of their affair. Gibson had once told her how addictive undercover work could be, the life of deception, and she understood that now. It seemed to provide what real life was missing. She followed Price into his office, and the fact that their bodies had been entwined twelve hours ago hung silently in the air.

'CPS okay, sir?'

'Fine, just cautious. Some of the Belarusians have filed a complaint saying you used excess force in their arrest.'

'They filed or their lawyers filed?'

'I know. But still . . .'

'They had three Kalashnikovs in the place. How much force would have been reasonable?'

'Apparently there's a skull fracture.'

Price spread his hands and grimaced. He self-identified as a 'results person', which meant a disproportionate amount of time thinking about defence lawyers. He had papered the walls of the open office with the faces of those criminals they'd put away, lines through them. He liked the Hollywood touches, and he liked promotions. Without the secrecy involved in their relationship, Craik knew there wouldn't be much depth to it, or much mystery to the man. Price was ambitious, career-oriented, an East End boy whose grip on a managerial position depended on the skills of those he headhunted. One of those charming men who appear to be moving at speed, but whose wheels, upon closer inspection, are frequently spinning on ice. Over-promoted divorcees. Why were they the ones she found herself attracted to?

'It's all on bodycam,' Craik said.

'Can you make sure I get any relevant footage?'

'Of course.'

'Aside from that, the CPS are delighted. As is the chief constable.'

'Good.'

Price studied her face. 'Something's up.'

Craik wanted to tell him about the call but held back, partly because his involvement with the IOPC investigation meant he would have formed his own opinions about Belsey, partly because she had already lied once. Not for the first time, she wondered what it was about Belsey that made you cover for him, as if his own misdemeanours were contagious.

'Nothing,' she said. 'A lot on.'

'Is it about us?' he said.

'No.'

'Okay.'

Then she realised what in particular was troubling her at this moment. In the centre of his office, Price had hung a large, framed photograph of a former colleague collecting a commendation after being shot in the course of an investigation. The officer concerned, DI Scott Montgomery, was wheelchair-bound, his face a mess of transplanted tissue. It was only thanks to seventy-five hours of surgery that he'd survived, and the picture didn't flinch from what looked like a work in progress. A few months after the collapse of the investigation into the attempted assassination Price had set up Organised Crime

Command, vowing a new, more effective approach to prosecuting those gangsters who considered themselves beyond the law. The photo was the first thing he put up, a reminder of their cause. But right now it was also a reminder of the stakes. *Threats become real*, it said.

Price glanced at the photograph then back at Craik, curiously. 'Scott would be delighted at how we're doing.'

'I know,' she said.

Craik went to the bathroom, locked the door and stared into the mirror. Her face looked very intact. No one had shot it yet. But it didn't seem untouched by her role. When she'd got the OCC promotion she'd taken the opportunity to let her hair grow and buy some new clothes. She wasn't going to be attending pub brawls any more so she could afford a little femininity. But the constant exposure to organised crime had its own hardening effect; the act of facing violent men in interview rooms, and needing a countenance for that. It felt like there was a dust of criminality in the air that wasn't going to wash off.

Her phone rang. It was Lawrence. 'Sweetheart,' he said.

'Hey. How's the country?'

'The country is idyllic. The eccentric old couple I'm stuck with are increasingly irascible. But they haven't driven me crazy yet. Have you packed?'

'Almost. Halfway.'

'I've got some specifics on my mother's wish list that might help. Gardening gloves.'

'Right.'

'Have to be leather, apparently. With elasticated wrists.'

'I don't think I'm going to have much of a chance to shop around.'

He went silent for a moment. 'Well, do what you can. But

don't leave it too long. My father's hitting the port. I'd like him to have some recollection of seeing you.'

'I'll be extra memorable when I get there.'

'You sound stressed.'

'It's the last-minute rush to get things done. You know what it's like.'

'Don't let them push you around. Even detectives deserve Christmas.'

'That's true. I've got to run.'

He'd sent her links to various stores. Last week he was sending her links to estate agents. Soon they would move in together. Then he would propose. Craik's own parents were already delighted, wondering if his presence in her life meant she'd move on from the police, which they'd always seen as a phase she was going through. They, like Lawrence, couldn't understand why it had to consume so much of her. That was why police ended up with fellow police: the rhythm. Crime doesn't rise and fall with the sun, doesn't take holidays. Fucking your colleagues was awful, but they understood. You didn't have to try to be someone else. At the same time, you didn't want to go home to all that either. Welcome to Hotel California, Belsey had said, on her first week at Borough. You can check out any time you like ...

Belsey, she thought. What was it about that past mess of emotions that seemed so simple now? Just the fact that it was past? That stakes were lower then, and memory relinquished all the conflict and left you with snapshots? Craik studied herself in the mirror and realised that the 5 a.m. call had opened up more than she'd initially been aware of.

On her lunchbreak, she tried the last number she had for Belsey, then sent a speculative email to his old Hotmail account, which he rarely checked at the best of times. *Hope you're okay. A weird thing happened last night . . .* Finally, she called a mutual contact who had worked at Hampstead police station with them.

'Any word on Nick recently?' she asked.

'Nick Belsey?'

'Yes. Got a strange call about him last night. Do you know where he is?'

'Off radar. That's all I know.'

'Since when?'

'Since Hampstead police station shut down. Nick vanished. No one's spoken to him for months, as far as I'm aware.'

Vanished could mean several things. Craik probed as to the exact nature of this vanishing but that was all they had. Belsey had 'gone on his toes', in police parlance.

Craik called a contact in Border Force, just in case he'd fled the country, but without knowing Belsey's passport number or exact date of birth it wasn't going to get an immediate result. They said they'd have a trawl and get back to her. That was all she could do for now, it seemed.

She prepared for the afternoon. Then one final avenue of investigation occurred to her. Craik went back to the database and searched for recent reports of threatening phone calls. Five had been logged in the last twenty-four hours. Two people had mentioned 'Funeral Care'. One of those had just been shot.

Craik stared at the report. Male, fifty-eight years old, in Camberwell, south-east London, shot outside his home at approximately ten o'clock this morning. Currently in intensive care at King's College Hospital. Further details had just been sent through to her own unit, on the understandable suspicion that this might connect to organised crime.

Josie Summer already had the notes and was working her way through them, searching for connections to their own investigations.

'How does it look?' Craik asked.

'It's an odd one, ma'am. Possibly a mistaken identity. Victim is called Trevor Hart. A retired postman. It seems he saw someone outside his flat and went out. There was a confrontation with two men in a parked car and a shot was fired. He's in intensive care, so we don't have anything more yet. Hart's on the system: a charge back in the nineties for handling stolen goods, and one a couple of years later for unlicensed bookmaking. Almost twenty years ago, though.'

'Suspects?'

'Nothing yet.'

'Something made him go out and confront them.'

'Hart's wife says he saw men watching the house, and that he was agitated because he received a call in the night.'

'Did she say anything more about that?'

'Not much. Something threatening. The caller used an ID that said "Funeral Care". Beyond that, it's not very clear.'

Craik took her own look at the details available so far. Nothing that told her very much except that she was in danger.

'Tell them to keep us in the loop.'

'You want updates?'

'Direct to me. Yes.'

The other person who'd reported a similar call from Funeral Care last night was a forty-seven-year-old woman. According to her police report, it had included the threat that she'd be 'killed in the next week'. She lived just a mile away, in the heart of Belsey's old territory: Borough. Her name was Samantha Topping.

Craik tried to sound relaxed when the woman answered.

'Samantha Topping?'

'Yes.'

'Detective Inspector Kirsty Craik here. You reported a nuisance call. I just wanted to check in with you, follow it up.'

'I didn't think you'd take it that seriously.'

'We try. Has anything else unusual happened in the meanwhile?'

'There's been another call.'

'When?'

'About an hour ago.'

'What did they say?'

'Similar things. I'm getting genuinely worried.'

'Where are you now?'

'Home.'

'I'm going to come round, if that's okay. I'd like to have a word. Stay there.'

Borough, the area where she'd cut her teeth as a police officer, was only a ten-minute walk from the Organised Crime HQ, down into south London proper, although she rarely went in that direction these days. Now she did. Craik crossed the border represented by Kennington Park Road, into the borough of Southwark, past people with rolls of wrapping paper sticking out of shopping bags, past gritted roads and memories. Walworth Road had changed, as if mirroring her own retreat back into professionalism. It looked smarter, more aspirational, but more soulless too. The woman who'd reported the threatening call lived in a new block of beige cladding and dull glass that resembled an architect's digital image. Craik scanned the street around it for men in parked cars, then pressed the bell. Topping buzzed her in and directed her to the first floor. The doormat in front of her flat said: 'Come in if you have Prosecco.'

Topping opened the door, smiling anxiously, make-up creasing around attractive green eyes. 'Thanks so much for visiting.'

The flat involved a lot of pastel colours, with bright furniture

43

and Christmas cards. Photographs of Samantha Topping among her friends and relatives had been preserved in sparkling frames. A print on the wall said: 'The most wasted of days is one without laughter.' Craik sat on the sofa as the woman described receiving the call.

'It was horrible. I don't know why I answered it. I saw the caller name – Funeral Care – and it was three in the morning, and for some reason I thought it must mean something. Then I assumed it was a horrible prank – some guy saying I was going to be killed. But I don't know who'd do that. Now the second call, going on about drugs . . . I've got nothing to do with drugs. Never have done.'

This caught Craik's attention. A more concrete detail.

'What was it the caller said about drugs?' she asked.

'Something about cocaine – that I knew where it was. I told them they had the wrong person.'

Craik felt the first, vague sense of a rationale emerging. 'Can you remember the exact words they used?'

'Not really.'

'Any suggestion why you'd know anything about these drugs?'

'No.'

'Any idea who the caller was?'

'None at all.'

'Did the caller seem to know anything about you? Your living situation? Your life?'

'There was one odd thing.' The woman hesitated. 'They referred to me as Samantha Vagabond.'

'Samantha Vagabond.'

'Yes. On the first call, when I answered. It took me a second to understand what they were saying. It sounded like: "Is this Samantha Vagabond we're speaking to?"'

Craik had a strange feeling she knew what that meant. 'How long have you been in the area?' she asked.

'All my life.'

'There's a bar, Vagabonds.'

'Yes.' Topping looked surprised that Craik should share this knowledge. 'That's what I thought. It's closed down now. How do you know it?'

How could she forget it? Vagabonds, a few minutes from Borough police station: a basement of spilled drinks and shamelessness; sticky red booths, curtained walls, nocturnal solidarity. Dodgiest dive in the area and a lot of fun. 'Used to go there myself,' she said. 'Back in the day.'

'Yeah?' Topping's face lit up.

'Thursday nights.'

'Two-for-one cocktails.'

'Lethal.'

'You lived around here?'

'I used to police here as a local bobby. Used to go to Vagabonds to unwind.'

Used to go there with Nick when it was the only place still serving, following the flow of the area's late-night drinkers as licensing laws washed them towards the gutter. One pound a shot, Stella for one fifty a pint. More flashbacks: someone's birthday, Belsey putting a shot from every bottle in one pint glass. Music playing: *I fought the law and the law won* . . .

Craik took the plunge. 'Odd question: have you ever come across a man called Nick Belsey?'

Topping flinched, then the look of puzzlement returned. 'Yes. Why? Is this to do with him?'

'Do you know him well?'

'No. I've really only seen him a couple of times.'

'When was that?'

'About ten years ago.'

'Are you in touch at all?'

'Not for ages.'

'But he had your number at one point.'

Topping nodded very slowly as pieces of the puzzle started to connect.

'I probably met him there.'

Samantha Vagabond. How you write someone's name when you're taking their number in a rush, near a loud dancefloor, and there's other Samanthas, and you have trouble keeping track of the women you meet at 3 a.m. in south London bars. Craik thought about the morning's shooting – Trevor Hart and his illegal gambling sounded very Belsey. Now she thought about it, hadn't there been a Trevor who used to drink with Belsey back in the day? Samantha Topping, Trevor Hart and then Craik. Three people potentially connected by one man. Belsey would have met Craik around the same time he met Samantha Topping. No doubt their mobile numbers shared the same smudged scrap of paper somewhere. The caller was working down a list.

'Someone else who got a similar call mentioned hearing Belsey's name,' Craik said.

Topping frowned. 'I didn't want to say because I didn't think it would mean anything – it sounded weird. I thought maybe I didn't hear it right. But, yes, the caller said his name, said they wanted me to pass on the message.'

'Any idea where he might be?'

'Not now. I barely knew him then. No idea where he's been the last ten years or so.' She watched Craik carefully. Craik had the vague sense of looking into a distorting mirror. She imagined Belsey taking fleeting sanctuary in Samantha Topping's arms. 'Is he in trouble?'

'I hope not.'

'What do you mean?'

Craik considered how much to tell her. She didn't want to terrify the woman without knowing what on earth this was about. But it was becoming clear that something was going on, and whatever it was, it wasn't a prank.

'The situation's unclear at the moment, but there's a chance that someone has accidentally put you at risk, so I want to connect you with officers who'll be able to help further. They'll want to know about the call, and they'll be in a position to decide what precautionary measures you should take.'

'So this is serious?'

'It might be. And I want us to treat it like that until we're sure there's nothing to worry about.'

Topping paled. 'It could still just be someone having a laugh, right?'

'Sure.'

'Did *you* know him?'

Craik hesitated. 'We crossed paths.'

The woman nodded, alert to something unspoken.

'It could be nothing,' Craik said. 'But if you do see anyone acting suspiciously, don't approach them, okay? Just call us.'

Topping began to cry. Craik made a few calls, located the senior investigating officer on the Trevor Hart shooting and was put through to the incident room directly. She explained the situation and possible connections and he said he'd send detectives to Topping.

'She may need Protected Persons Services,' Craik said.

'Okay. We'll evaluate.'

Craik hung up. She gave Topping her direct line and promised she'd be doing everything to pursue this.

'There are officers coming over now,' she said. 'Tell them

what you know. Then think if there's somewhere you can go for a couple of nights while we try to find out what's going on.'

FIVE

Craik returned to the high street, calling a friend in Narcotics as she walked.

'Anything odd going on in the world of cocaine right now?' she asked.

'Odd thing is it's light, reports are down. Doesn't seem to be much on the streets.'

'What are the streets saying about that?'

'Nothing as far as I'm aware.'

'Really?'

'Maybe our hard work's paying off.'

Craik forced a laugh. 'Maybe.'

Investigators weren't plugged in like they used to be. There was only so much you could discover trawling databases. What would Belsey do? She heard his voice: *If anyone knows anything about what London puts into its bloodstream it's old Tiger Teeth. Devious and ingenious.*

'While you're on the line,' Craik said, 'is there any recent intel on Eric Jackson? He's a dealer, works Borough area.'

'Not recently. Still up to his old tricks, I'm sure.'

'Have you got a current address?'

'Hang on.' She heard him typing. 'The system just says no fixed abode.'

Craik knew where that was. She crossed through Elephant

and Castle, past the Brazilian and Nigerian clubs, into the back streets. The Wishing Well remained in the shadows of the railway. Where there'd been an arcade of shops – launderette, newsagent, chippy – three glossy blocks of flats stood emptily. But the pub was still there: paint peeling, windows dusty, open. Craik gathered herself and walked in.

The place had aged. Its red velvet banquette seating was missing in places, tarnished to blackness in others. A corner of the front bar had been taped off, like a crime scene, where a leak had made it unusable. Across this decay, the Sky Sports bunting was a dazzling touch. A single horizontal line of tinsel curled above the bar. But the unique perfume of the Well remained: decades-old tobacco smoke, yeasty layers of spilled beer, surface cleaner and urinals.

Eric Jackson was on the public phone around the corner of the main bar. Craik heard him as soon as she entered. She took a glimpse. He had his head down, two mobiles stacked on top of the payphone, deep in a stressful conversation by the look of it. Eric was a coke dealer and south London landmark. He wore a suit too large for his skinny frame over a floral shirt. He was the only person in SE1 Craik knew who'd been arrested for trading in illegal wildlife – the tiger teeth from which he took his nickname – which he said he'd been paid with in Chinatown by some restaurant workers desperate for their fix. Belsey used to call him the Oracle, the fly on the wall, a compendium of information. Used to call him slippery as fuck. *Eric knows everything. Plays the sides against the middle. Don't buy the persona, he's a devious rat.* This was the kind of street-level contact you needed.

The pub's landlord, Rod Thompson, appeared behind the bar, a little more cadaverous than last time Craik had seen him, in a stained T-shirt and jeans. He put his hands up.

'I've paid my taxes, Officer. No one smokes in here. The karaoke's bad but I keep it the right side of the law.' He winked. 'What can you do me for, Copper?'

'How've you been, Rod?'

'Alive. Heard you're a big cheese now. What are you after?'

She nodded towards Eric. Rod rolled his eyes.

'I'm not getting rich running some kind of probation office, Kirsty. I can tell you that much. Hard times for a pub like this. You should bring your top-brass buddies. Have a birthday. Get me some feet through the door.'

'Give me a lime and soda, then. What's Eric drinking?'

'He'll be happy with a Southern Comfort and lemonade.'

'I'm glad someone will.'

The landlord fixed the drinks. Craik could hear Eric on the public phone: *Nothing*, he kept saying. *I wouldn't lie, would I?*

The phone was mounted on the wall between the jukebox and the cigarette machine, framed by minicab stickers. It was an iconic phone. The office phone, Belsey called it. His office phone, at least, where you were most likely to get through to him – at a time before mobiles, when people were identified with a geographical routine out of necessity, no matter how sordid. And it served no shortage of purposes to be both in and out. Craik had thought he was joking when he called the place his office but there was truth to it: his theatre of operations, for sure. Belsey liked the Well because other police avoided it. Not because of the low-level criminality but because it was shit. Rod had inherited the place from his father and wore the pub with a weary affection, like a house you were never going to afford to do up. Owned outright, though, no brewery knocking. God knows how many developers circling hungrily, smelling death. So, its charmlessness was a sneer of sorts.

She paid for the drinks, gave it a moment, soaking up the lack of atmosphere, waiting for Eric's call to finish. The first time she'd come here there was still an hour of shift to go. 'It's okay, this is training.' Belsey winked, lining up the drinks. 'You're at the bottom of the Well, collect the coins.' People nodded at him, shouted greetings, shook Craik's hand. Enough of a crowd for them slowly to become less noticeable. When Belsey decided the ambience was suitably blurry, he started pointing out people and types and how to use them: your grass, out for himself; your entrepreneur, looking for leverage; your show-off, the bragger, the one who can't hold his drink; the needy, the attention-seeking, the psycho, who will get picked up in a street brawl and be willing to make an emotional turn against his former associates. Learn to tell their addictions: drugs, money, women, adrenalin. 'Sink in,' he'd said. 'Have fun. But never forget that they're more desperate than you are. Play them.'

Eric saw Craik when she got closer. Instinctively he checked the windows for the silhouettes of an arrest team.

'Going to have to go, mate.' He hung up. 'Ma'am. What are you doing here?'

'Wanted a chat.' She gave him the drink.

He looked uneasy. 'Not here,' he said.

'The back still open?'

They went to the old pool room, with its shuttered bar, cue rack and dartboard. This used to be where the deals went down. Now it was a graveyard of unsalvageable furniture. Craik leaned back against the pool table and watched Eric sip his drink. He looked sharper and more serious now. This was the other Eric, a successful businessman, for whom the jokes and chaos were a cloak. He'd progressed from dealing crack to supplying raves with ecstasy to providing south London's expanding middle class with their cocaine. Simply surviving for so long had gained him respect among the various currents of criminality. People didn't know how far his connections spread, just that he'd been around for twenty years, which must mean something. He kept in with the bigger gangs, avoided unnecessary noise. And he was charming, which counted for as much in the criminal underworld as anywhere else.

'Trevor Hart,' Craik said. 'I've been trying to think where I know the name. He used to drink in here, didn't he?'

'Once or twice.'

'Have you heard what happened?'

'He was shot.'

'That's right.'

'How's he doing?' Eric asked.

'Reckon he's been better.'

'It's nothing to do with me, Kirsty.'

'I know. But something to do with coke, maybe. Someone looking for something that's gone missing. Thought you might have heard about that.'

'Yeah?' Now he looked distinctly perturbed.

'I couldn't help overhearing your phone conversation. Got the impression of a drought, things running dry. Is that right?'

'Maybe.'

'And has that got anything to do with people getting threatened?'

'What makes you think I know anything about it?'

'You know everything.'

Eric glanced towards the main room of the pub, then fixed Craik with a stare. 'What are you after, Kirsty? Not your beat any more, I thought.'

'Everything's my beat now.'

He took a breath. 'Really wouldn't trouble yourself with this one. You know what I mean?' His eyes strained with something desperate.

'I can decide what to trouble myself with.'

'You were smart, I thought. There's no joy for you here.'

'What's going on?'

'Supply-chain issue. That's all I can say. Trust me.'

'Tell me about that.'

'It was all Belarusians running it the last year or so. They've been put away. So have the Albanians and the Turks. The show's wrapped up. Left a bit of a gap.'

It was nice to feel the impact of her last twelve months' exertion. But Craik had never kidded herself that London would pack up its vices.

'Is that right? You were tight with some of them, weren't you?'

'I've got nothing to do with any of it. Glad they're being locked up. I give you my blessing on that one.'

One of his phones rang. He took out both mobiles, identified the correct one and answered. 'I'll speak to you later,' he said. 'What?' He glanced at the doorway. 'Wait there.'

A couple of kids stuck their heads into the back room as he was hanging up and he sucked his teeth in anger, shooing them out. 'Give me a moment, Kirsty.'

She heard him outside, berating them: 'I'm with someone, aren't I? Do you know who they are? No. Then you don't just walk in, do you?' Then silence while something less pedagogical went on. He returned a few moments later. 'Sorry about that.'

'What's the supply-chain issue?'

'No comment.'

'Eric, I'm not going to ask you to say anything you don't want to say. But you know how it goes once people start shooting each other. Everyone gets hauled in. We can't control who wants to talk to you. Favours don't mean anything. You're usually good at avoiding that kind of situation. You don't want this sticking to you.'

'It's not going to stick to me.'

'What do you want? Some cash?'

'I want you to not worry yourself about this.'

'You're scared.'

'Yeah.'

'It's someone big.'

'Yeah.'

'Do I know them?'

'That's all I'm saying.'

Craik was heading back to the main bar when he began speaking again. 'Let's say some gang's been supplying for a while,' he said. 'Then they go away. London still wants its sweeties. Rumour starts: there's someone who can sort it. Mysterious, but the word is they're effective. And people sign up. This man's come along and said, "I can sort you big-time. But I need money up front." A lot of people are owed a delivery right now and it's all fucked up. And that's all I'm saying. You're right, it's going to go nasty.'

'What happened?'

'What I just said. Someone had a very big thing coming and it didn't show. It was going to be enough snow to cover the streets.'

'Okay.'

'Christmas-morning pure. Made everyone pay over the odds. Mexican connections and all that. Direct lines.'

'Mexican?

'Big boys. Cartel boys.'

'How much exactly?'

'One hundred.'

'One hundred grand?'

'One hundred kilos, Kirsty. That's what I'm saying. One hundred keys of the bloody stuff.'

Craik made a rough calculation. The going rate for a kilo of cocaine was thirty grand on the street. One hundred kilos was more than three million pounds' worth of narcotics. 'So where is this mountain of Mexican snow?' she asked.

'Vanished.' He paused for effect. 'Like when you run outside, all dressed up, ready to play, but it's gone. The fucker's melted into thin air. Someone somewhere along the line has played it naughty, is my guess. Maybe someone in Mexico. They might be laughing but there's a hell of a lot of people who aren't.'

Now it was Craik's turn to glance at the front before pursuing her next line of questioning.

'Any contact with Nick Belsey recently?' she asked.

'Nicky? Haven't heard from him in a long time. Why?' Eric looked puzzled. 'Thought he'd been fired or something.'

'Yeah, he has. Thanks, Eric. I'd appreciate hearing if any news about this snow turns up.'

'You won't be hearing from me, Kirsty. Mind yourself. I'm serious.'

She walked out and stopped. Beyond the superficial new gloss, Borough remained: grey and secret, old and deep. 20 December: the city was slowly building to hedonism, its will to oblivion given permission. A city of work and grind releasing itself into festivity.

How had she arrived back here again?

She had messages. Her contact in Border Force had tried to reach her. She gave them a call.

'Nick Belsey gets a result,' the officer said. 'If it's the Nick Belsey born March the twelfth 1977, his passport was used to leave the UK on November the eighteenth. Believed to have boarded a Virgin Atlantic flight from Heathrow to Mexico City.'

'He's in Mexico?' Craik said.

'That's how it looks.'

'Any suggestion what he's doing there?'

'Not on here. But he's just been input as of interest to the FBI. So, something big.'

Craik walked to the bus stop across the road and sat down, head spinning. 'Really?'

'From what I can tell, they don't know much about Nick Belsey either. But a lot of people suddenly want to talk to the guy.'

SIX

The mother pleaded with him. *'No vayas,'* she said. Don't go. Not La Cada. Not to those men. She said it in various ways, all of which he understood clearly enough.

'I have to,' Belsey said. 'What's going to happen otherwise? They'll just come back here. I've got to find out what's going on.'

There was an attempt to explain that these were not good people. *Hombres peligrosos.*

'That's pretty evident. But they've got something mixed up and I need to straighten it out.'

He'd been awake all night, deciding on a course of action. There was little choice. He needed to find out what he'd brought to this idyll by the sea. Why were men looking for Nick Belsey? When dawn broke he'd got up and tidied as much of the previous night's damage as possible. There were fishermen on guard duty, armed with sticks and baseball bats. Belsey got dressed, took a knife from the kitchen, one of the small, mean-looking ones used for filleting fish, checked the delivery man was driving into town and said he'd like a lift. The driver looked wary.

'El hombres . . .'

'Hombres peligrosos, sí. Know them?'

'Very bad. Mafiosos.'

'I need to speak to them. I need to do something about this. Because I figure police might not be so helpful.'

The driver winced. '*Sin policía. Ellos no son nuestros amigos.*'

'Right. So I don't see what other options we have. They're going to come back, maybe hurt someone badly. I know the bar where the Mafiosi drink. I can speak to them, clear the air.'

The mother held onto his clothes when he set off and he had to twist them out of her bony hands. Kids lined up, staring.

'Look,' Belsey said, 'it's coming back to me one way or another. They're not going to forget last night. I don't want it here. It's nothing to do with you.'

The van driver looked despondent when Belsey got in. María Luisa ran up to Belsey's window. She handed him a necklace. The pendant had a picture of the Virgin. 'From our mother,' María said. 'To keep you safe.'

'I don't need a necklace,' Belsey said, but she insisted, so he put it on. 'How does it look?'

'It protects you.'

'Let's hope.'

They drove into town. The necklace was cool against his chest, knocking against his breastbone. The delivery driver dropped him at the same junction, shook his head, drove on.

The town was still dead. Belsey walked past the dentists and undertakers to the billiards hall. The Escalade sat outside, sand from the beach on its wheels.

He walked past, got a coffee from a café on the corner, went to the park and sat down, trying to focus his mind. Taking a last minute before whatever was about to happen. Street kids watched him. The shoeshine boy came up, smiling.

'Mr English.'

'Señor Shoeshine.'

'How are you? Shine today?' The kid was already unpacking his kit.

'Got anything that keeps blood off?'

'Blood?'

'I'm joking.'

'Are you okay?'

'Not really.'

The boy wiped his shoes with an old T-shirt and Belsey gave him all the money he had. Then he crossed the road to the billiards hall. It was a different guard, younger, but with the same long rifle.

'I'm Nick Belsey,' he said. The man studied him, then turned his head away with a sniff.

'People want to speak to me.'

The man glared at him. '*Vamos.*'

'They came last night.'

The man called out, over his shoulder. An older, pot-bellied man in a black shirt appeared from inside. He walked over to Belsey. '*¿Inglés?*'

'*Sí.*'

'What do you want?'

'I was going to ask you the same question. People came last night. Wanted Nick Belsey.'

The man looked up and down the street, pushed Belsey into the bar.

Inside it was weird: UV strip lights, pink baize, pinball machines. A mirror behind the bar had an engraving of the Last Supper. The place was empty. Then a door at the back opened and the men from last night appeared, one of them limping.

Belsey felt the adrenalin kick in.

'I came to apologise,' Belsey said. '*Lo siento. Soy Nick Belsey.* I think there's been a misunderstanding. What do you want? Where did you get my name?'

He braced himself. They stared, hungover, caught on the

back foot. His turning up voluntarily had spooked them. The barman reached down, found a pistol and passed it over the bar to the fat man. He trained the gun on Belsey while his friend made a qall. There was a chain of command somewhere.

'Nick Belsey?' the guy on the phone said, after a while. 'You?'

'Yes. Where did you get that name?'

He turned back to the phone.

'*Él está aquí. Sí. Bueno. Sí.*' He put the phone back in his pocket. '*Ven con nostros.*' He beckoned for Belsey to accompany them. When Belsey drew closer, the man stuck a hand out and grabbed Belsey's throat. Belsey knocked his hand away. The man drove a punch into his stomach and Belsey doubled over.

'Okay,' he said. 'You win.'

He was led out through a service door to a Toyota Land Cruiser and ordered into the back seat.

SEVEN

They drove out of La Cada, but not far. Half-built developments began to line the sides of the road, half hidden behind advertising hoardings showing swimming pools and golf courses. The grey foundations of these luxury blocks had been laid into the dry soil, skeletons in various stages of coming to life. No construction work currently going on that Belsey could see. Ragged tarpaulin hung limp in the windless air.

If this kept someone from the beach being killed, it was worth it, he told himself. He had nothing to lose. And if he could establish the source of the misunderstanding maybe there was a way forward that didn't involve too much pain, but he wasn't counting on that.

They stopped at the furthest building site. One car was already there, gleaming under the midday sun. Belsey was bundled out, marched to the half-constructed apartment block, down bare concrete stairs to a room with stainless-steel sinks, a pair of refrigerators wrapped in plastic and a single chair on a sheet of tarpaulin. It was baking hot. Two men in suits stood by the chair, lit by narrow gaps of daylight waiting for windows. One of the men searched Belsey, pulled out the filleting knife and laughed, stabbed it into his upper arm just deep enough to draw blood, then tossed it across the room. He was pushed into the chair, hands tied behind him with a cord. The fat one spat in his face. The suits stared at him, conversed. Then nothing happened.

'What do you want? I'm here to talk. Let's talk.'

It turned out they were waiting for more to arrive.

Over the next half-hour a succession of figures came and looked at him. One wore a shirt unbuttoned so you could see the tattoo of a man's face on his chest. One stank of cigars and held a folding knife with an ornate ivory handle. He was accompanied by a couple of heavies, who stood to the side, watching. At one point, police turned up: two uniformed, two with the swagger of plain-clothes officers. They looked at Belsey, consulted with the criminals, smoked a cigarette and departed.

Belsey was slapped hard. One of the heavies approached with a bucket and poured filthy water over him. The other waved a lighter in his face and under his right ear until Belsey spat curses. They showed him rusty tools, then surgical equipment, and he tried to find a place behind the fear, thought of swimming at night, kept his breathing steady. He was compared to photos he couldn't see. The men in suits hitched their trousers to crouch down, eye level with him.

'*¿Dónde está?*' they asked. 'Where is it?'

'Where's what?'

After an hour the first real punch came, hard to the side of his head. He tumbled over in the chair, hitting the other side of his head on the concrete floor. Here we go, he thought. They lifted him back up.

The man with the knife did most of the talking, but instructed the others to hit him when he'd had enough. One of his security – a huge guy with a ponytail – stood quietly at the back, as if disinterested in mere violence. Belsey felt he might be the one they called in to finish the job. He began to wonder about his exit plan.

Men took calls, walked out. One put his phone to Belsey's ear.

'We know what you did,' a man said in English. 'You won't get away with this. Your family are already dying.'

'What did I do?'

The man yelled '¡No me chingues!' and the phone was taken away. Occasionally they'd go as far as pointing guns at his head but no one killed him. He had a sense that something was protecting him: an importance or incongruity, or just the information he was meant to have.

Belsey started piecing together what was going on. Some of his ID connected to a theft. He thought back to that morning waking up in the hotel and finding Esmerelda gone. He wondered how she was doing. From what Belsey could tell, his missing passport and possibly cards had been used by people up to no good: people who'd pissed off the crew here. It was the passport that Esmerelda had taken. These men thought Belsey had been involved. There'd been an alert out for him and then he'd been spotted in La Cada, eventually traced to the beach.

So this was his end, over a case of mistaken identity. Of course it would be. As if he hadn't done enough to earn his own execution.

'You are a thief.'

'You've got me mixed up with someone. I haven't taken anything.'

'Nick Belsey.'

'Yes. What is it you think I have?'

A punch hit him in the centre of the face. Blood began to stream into his mouth, thick and warm. He wondered how he might survive this. Being entirely random didn't necessarily seem a good idea. Random could be killed and written off as a mistake. Nobodies disappeared. He started considering an alternative tactic.

'I'm a police officer from London,' he tried to say, through the blood. 'I have connections. I think I can help you. I need someone who speaks English.'

'*Policía?*'

'*Sí*. Senior detective.'

The guy with the ornate knife made a call. There was a brief hiatus. Belsey spat blood, felt his skull throb. His request for water went unanswered.

Half an hour later, a young guy with US-accented English arrived. He was tall, preppy-looking, in a blue shirt and glasses, clean-shaven, expressionless. He placed a leather wallet satchel on the floor, crouched beside it, close to Belsey. He smelt of deodorant, which was a relief after the raw sweat and *cerveza* stench of Belsey's companions so far.

'Who are you?' he said.

'Nick Belsey. I want to talk about options.'

'Talk.'

'Can I get some water?'

The man instructed them to fetch some. Eventually a bottle was found and poured into Belsey's mouth. Belsey swilled out his blood. He didn't want to spit at the guy so he just let it dribble down his chin to his neck.

'I don't know what you're looking for,' he said, 'but I reckon I can be helpful in other ways. I was a senior police detective. I know the system inside out.'

'Where is the consignment?'

'What was it? Drugs?'

'You know what it was.'

'I really don't.'

'Where were you on December the fifteenth?'

'I don't know. What date is it now?'

'December the nineteenth.'

'I've been living in a place by the sea, a mile or so south of La Cada. That's where your guys found me last night. It's just a few fishermen. I've been there maybe five weeks. Maybe six. I don't know. I've been ill. I was recovering.'

'Is Nick Belsey your real name?'

Yes. Detective Constable Nick Belsey. Metropolitan Police.'

The young man left the basement. When he came back he held his phone and Belsey could see there was information on his screen.

'You're currently wanted for questioning by the Independent Office of Police Conduct.'

'Exactly.'

'What did you do?'

'Plenty. I can tell you all about it. Maybe you'll see how helpful I can be.'

The man considered this. 'How long have you been police?'

'As long as I can remember.'

'In London?'

'Yes. Scotland Yard, Customs, Drugs Squad. In and out of them all. This may actually be quite a lucky meeting for both of us. Let me at least talk to you somewhere a little more civilised.' The man considered Belsey, like he was an unwanted and unwieldy gift. Eventually he touched Belsey's upper lip with a knuckle, wiped away a drop of blood before it reached his lips, then took a handkerchief from his pocket and wiped his finger clean.

He left the room again, scrolling through his contacts. When he came back he turned to the men, nodded to the door and they untied Belsey.

Belsey was blindfolded with a sweat-stained bandanna. He assumed he was going to be killed. Ended up in Paradise.

EIGHT

They drove deeper into the territory on quiet, winding roads with sudden gradients. After fifteen minutes Belsey began to taste mountain air. After an hour they passed what must have been a roadblock. The car slowed to a stop and Belsey heard jokes pass between the men outside and the men inside. Someone reached in and ruffled his hair. He smelt gun metal and cigarette smoke.

Ten minutes later they stopped for another check, without laughter this time. The car made a sharp turn to the right and gates whirred open. Then they were on smoother tarmac. Private tarmac. It went on for a mile or so and there was a scent of flowers. He heard sprinklers ticking.

Finally they stopped and he was led, still blindfolded, into an air-conned interior, up carpeted stairs. When the bandanna was removed he was in a bare office with the preppy blue shirt and a guard he didn't recognise. The room was windowless. The blue shirt told Belsey to sit at the bare desk. He gave Belsey a box of tissues and left the guard watching over him, then returned with a pile of papers, a laptop and an ashtray, and told the guard to leave. He lit a cigarette, pushed the pack towards Belsey, opened a fresh yellow legal pad. In the surroundings of the office, he looked like an ambitious corporate analyst. In some ways, it seemed that was what he was.

The pile of papers he'd set on the table included statements for several debit and credit cards. They covered the last few weeks. Some of the transactions were circled. Several of these, Belsey saw, had been declined. They were his: he recognised a few card numbers.

'Which police unit do you work in?'

'CID. Most recently Hampstead. North London.'

'What are you doing in Mexico?'

'Just travelling around. Looking for opportunities.'

'Have you ever met this woman?'

He slid across a mugshot of a woman. It took Belsey a second to recognise her as Esmerelda. In the picture she had short blonde hair. The name under the photo was Ana Martinez. Belsey felt a pang of nostalgia for a simpler, more optimistic time. What had she got him into?

'Maybe. I'm not sure.'

'You were with her from November the twentieth to November the twenty-second.'

'Was I?' It felt a bit late to try to protect her with lies. 'Oh, right. She said her name was Esmerelda. I was giving her a lift, that's all. You think she connects to a robbery?'

'What do you know about this robbery?'

'Just that people keep saying: *Where is it?* You mentioned a consignment of some kind. I don't know anything about that, but I know about UK policing. Anyway, I'm sure Ana Martinez isn't involved. She seemed a nice girl.'

'The people responsible had your bank cards.'

'Well, I lost them.'

'You say you weren't involved?'

'Of course not. Why would I hang around near La Cada if I'd robbed you? I'm a visitor here. I haven't been anywhere. Someone's using my ID.'

'We need your bank details,' the analyst said. 'For all the cards that were in your wallet. And passwords, PINs, security answers – anything you can remember. Do you internet bank?'

'I don't think so.'

'Set up voice recognition?'

'No.'

Belsey wrote down what he could. The analyst's phone rang. He took the call outside. Belsey sifted through the paperwork. Beneath the transactions was a creased sheet from a lined A4 pad, with his own writing across it. It was his phone numbers. Christ. It had been in his wallet. Why had someone annotated it with red crosses? A cab company, a number to do with horse tips, several one-night stands, bankruptcy advice.

Kirsty Craik.

That was why he'd kept it. Kirsty. It had sentimental value.

'Where did you get this?' he asked, when the man returned.

'We found it.'

'Why have you written on it? You called those numbers?'

'Why?'

'Those people are really nothing to do with me. I'm not in touch with them any more.'

'This is unfortunate. For you and them.'

'You have people over in the UK?' Belsey asked.

'We have people everywhere.'

'Have they done anything yet? To hurt my contacts?'

'They have done enough that people are concerned. Your friends and family are concerned. They would want to know you are cooperating. Think about how you can help us.'

'I'm trying.'

'If it is too difficult, I have a suggestion. We drive you back to the beach and swap you for the teenage girl, María. Is that her name?'

Belsey felt his muscles tense. He knew the analyst felt satisfaction at this. One on one, there wouldn't be any contest. But where would that leave him? Back in a basement, tied to another chair. In the end he just stared at the man. They were silent for a moment. Then the analyst said, 'Think about it,' and left the room again.

Alone, Belsey firmed up a plan. Play them for everything they're worth. He could do this: use them to get back to the UK. First step was to sell them a dream. He needed to channel the anger like he channelled the fear. Keep breathing, keep imaginative. Revenge would be sweet.

When the analyst returned, Belsey asked to use his pen. He flipped a bank statement to its blank side and began drawing a web.

'I'm going to give you a glimpse of how UK policing really works,' Belsey said. 'What are you trying to do? Trafficking, right?'

'Go on.'

'Moving drugs into the country is going to make you of interest to three major departments, none of which are uncrackable.' He drew a diagram of the national policing structure. 'The thing you have to understand about UK police is there's factions: NCA, Customs, Drugs Squad. You know the word fiefdoms? *Territorio*? There's a lot of tension, which you can exploit.'

The analyst nodded.

'Shipping narcotics into Europe, the access comes under Customs, trafficking under the NCA, but moving it around once in the UK, it's going to be Drugs Squad or Organised Crime Command. They answer directly to the commissioner and then the home secretary.' Belsey drew a triangle. 'You own them, you're eighty per cent covered.'

'It's possible?'

'Everything's possible. The trick to Customs is knowing which loads get searched. They use algorithms, but the logic is obvious enough. Say you're entering the UK at Tilbury Docks, the Customs officers at Tilbury will check twenty per cent of traffic originating in Mexico, but if you can get it to Spain first, clear the paper trail, that's a soft route. Madrid into Tilbury, only four per cent of those consignments are going to come under scrutiny. Then you need just one person on the inside keeping a lookout for the container, and they can tell your people when the delivery's arrived, let them in the back door, clear out what they want before it's even unloaded. This is all straightforward enough. What's going to trip you up is surveillance, especially on any communications. The police and security services need a warrant before they can initiate a phone tap. Surveillance warrants go through a judge, but judges are like a gang in themselves. Most warrants for high-level crime operations are issued by one of three judges and at least two of them are open to conversation.'

'You have their names?'

'Sure.' Belsey wrote some down. 'The big picture I'm trying to show you, and which I can tell you a lot more about, is that policing resources are thin and you need to know which specific projects are flavour of the month. Operation Geronimo, for example, that's been up and running for a couple of years and focuses on class-A trafficking. And it has solid inside sources, with gangs penetrated, especially Dutch and Russian. Then there's Operation Kingfisher, which pursues the bosses, and gets a lot of offshore access. Where do you bank? They have insiders at the foreign exchange shops, at HSBC, Barclays, Coutts. There's no such thing as private banking any more.'

The man nodded. Belsey sensed him becoming pliable.

'Tell me what you need. I think the UK coke market can go higher. I think it's the place to target. There's not much sunshine, you know, not much native *joie de vivre*, but people like to let off steam.'

'I understand.'

'I think you do.'

The analyst opened another file, took out copies of official Metropolitan Police documents and passed them over. He watched Belsey's expression. There was sensitive stuff: command structures, staff lists, home addresses of personnel. They either had good hackers or deep sources.

'So you've already got access,' Belsey said. The analyst smiled. Belsey looked closer at the documents. 'This is all about Organised Crime Command,' he said.

'Yes.'

Belsey checked the staff list. There was a dot by 'Detective Inspector Kirsty Craik'. He hadn't realised where she was working now. The man came around the desk and touched a finger to her name.

'This name is on your list too.' He found the list of phone numbers and showed Belsey.

'Oh.'

'You know her?'

'Not well.'

'You think she is a threat to us?'

'No,' Belsey said. The man waited for elaboration. 'She's fine.'

'Persuadable? Open to conversation?'

'She's no one, is what I'm saying. I wouldn't waste time on her.'

'Why's she on your list?'

'I met her once, that's all.'

'You said Organised Crime Command was one of the departments we needed to be careful of.'

'They'll only target you if you stumble onto their radar. They do very little proactive work, and each job takes years. It's a cushy posting. Office-based.'

The analyst watched Belsey as if trying to decide whether to believe him. Belsey pointed to the sheets, tried to move the focus of their discussion away from Craik.

'You're only scratching the surface of the computer systems here. Anyone shown you how to use them properly?'

'Properly?'

'I mean get deep. Use them like a detective would.'

The man stood up. 'Come with me.'

Belsey followed him out of the room and got his first glimpse of what kind of place he'd arrived in. They were in a grand home, up on a mezzanine level overlooking a ground floor with a firepit and a lot of expensive rugs. The analyst led Belsey along the corridor. Beneath them, a woman in a cleaner's uniform carried a baby.

They went into a large control room with a heavy-duty security door and cameras on both sides. The room contained radio equipment, a satellite phone and three PCs. He had the UK Police National Computer System up on one of the monitors. It felt bizarre seeing it there. Belsey took a seat, had a play around. 'You've got third-party access.'

'What does that mean?'

'The police allow some third-party organisations to have limited access, if they need it for security reasons. This is the data something like the Post Office would have, or the border agency, or anyone involved in cash transportations. It will give you checks against vehicles and people, you can view convictions and cautions, but not much else. With enhanced access you can search vehicles by description rather than plate, get a history of previous checks, all that sort of thing. It can be useful. You can see which other officers are interested in someone. You probably want ongoing investigations, right?'

'Yes.'

'To access that area you need an ID number and a password that changes every week. That gives you real-time updates.'

'Okay.' The man was interested in this. He wrote something down in a pocketbook. While he wasn't looking, Belsey typed his own name into the search field. His IOPC investigation appeared. *Wanted on Warrant.* Theft, corruption and assault. That made him laugh. He had known they were investigating him but not why or what exactly they were looking at. No access to the file itself, which was external, but he could see a recommendation from the regional director that his case be passed on to the CPS for criminal charges to be brought. The accusations were phrased vaguely enough to be catch-all. The Police Federation didn't seem too exercised about defending him. The whole thing was a crock of shit. Still, there was something grimly amusing about being able to see it thanks to the wiliness of a Mexican drugs cartel.

He was closing the screen down when he saw the tag placed on his name. Yesterday, an officer had requested an alert on any updates relating to himself. That officer was DI Kirsty Craik.

The analyst shut his notebook and came to sit beside Belsey. Belsey swiftly clicked back to the search page, wondering urgently what had made Craik interested, and whether it might connect to the cartel's own interest in Craik.

'Talk me through this system,' the analyst said.

Belsey showed him around the areas of the database he could get to, demonstrated its strengths, limitations, some shortcuts with inputs and search fields. When the guy seemed content, Belsey said: 'Let's work together. I can get you someone inside the port, and someone inside the police. But I need to go back over there.'

'Who can you get?'

'There are a number of options we can talk about. But you need to listen to me: leave the people on the beach alone.'

'You care about those people.'

'Yeah. And I've got my own codes of conduct. You don't like that, shoot me or whatever.'

'For now, I'd like you to stick around.'

'I'm not going to be much help here. We need to move fast. I need start-up capital – new papers and ten grand to play with. Get me over there and I'll secure you the port.'

'First things first. We need to find who is using your old paperwork.'

They went back to the bare room. A doctor came in, checked Belsey's injuries. He was elderly, with a dour expression, and moved about Belsey as if inspecting an object.

'*¿El dolor?*' he said. Belsey wondered how much to tell him. Something about this unreal figure inspired faith.

'*Dolor*, yes. I had some kind of episode a while back, sharp pains inside. Maybe my kidneys or liver. I was drinking a lot. I could get something for that, maybe.'

He gave Belsey good painkillers, like a form of compensation for whatever was about to befall him. Then someone brought water and coffee and he was left alone to consume them. Eventually the analyst returned with a man holding a digital camera.

'We've made progress. Your bank details were very helpful.'

'What kind of progress?'

'You'll see. There's still a lot to do. In a minute, an important person wants to meet you.'

He asked Belsey to stand in front of the blank wall as the

photographer took headshots. Belsey thought back through what he'd said and wondered which part could have inspired progress, and what that meant for himself. He wondered what meeting important people might mean.

'You are ready?'

'Who is it?'

'The boss. He's very interested in what you have to offer.'

Belsey expected to be led to a big office. He pictured Al Pacino behind a mountain of coke. But they headed to the garden.

'You might not see me until tomorrow,' the analyst said.

'Could I have my phone numbers back?'

The man shook his head. 'They are our insurance.'

'Those are personal.'

'That's why it works. I will introduce you to the boss. Be respectful.'

'I'm respectful to everyone.'

'Be extra respectful.'

The building was a mansion, hacienda-style, set in grounds that extended as far as the eye could see. They followed covered walkways into a garden with palm trees, fountains, terracotta urns and brash pink bougainvillaea. It was evening and the sky was indigo, with expensive people having fun beneath it.

A party was going on, a couple of drum-shaped barbecues spitting flames as men in chef whites flipped steaks and lobsters, claws clattering on the grill. Uniformed catering staff hurried to and fro, some with bottles, some servicing tables with tacos, pizzas, grilled meat and seafood. There was a chain of turquoise pools at varying heights, around which women with a lot of silicone in their bodies sipped cocktails. A mariachi band in red trousers and cummerbunds set up their instruments. Belsey heard a screech and turned to see a peacock opening its tail while a woman in a bikini tried to take a picture of it.

The security pretended not to watch the women. These men were everywhere, once you began to look: suited, ear-pieced, strolling and alert. Belsey tried to get a sense of exits, in case he got a chance to run. He glimpsed high fences, and imagined there wasn't much life-sustaining on the other side. He couldn't hear a road nearby.

They reached the boss. He stood between two huge bodyguards, which made him seem smaller than he was. But he was still a head shorter than Belsey, wearing a black polo shirt tucked into pale chinos. Muscular, though, with a healthy tan, a strong jaw and close-cropped brown hair, all of which gave him a military vibe. He was drinking a Sprite.

'This is the man,' the analyst said, gesturing at Belsey. The boss studied Belsey with dark eyes. Was he meant to bow, Belsey wondered. They weren't doing names, it seemed. He certainly wasn't going to initiate a handshake.

'You are the Englishman.'

'I try to be.'

'Fallen into our laps.' His English was good.

'That's right.'

'You must be thirsty.' He gestured at an ice bucket of Coronas. Belsey took one. 'Thanks.'

The boss looked Belsey up and down again, nodded. 'Miguel will show you around.' A blond man in a double-breasted suit stepped forward, hair slicked back from a widow's peak, reeking of cologne.

He smiled, and looked cruel. 'Mr Belsey. I am glad to meet you. Please, let's walk.'

Miguel clapped Belsey hard on the shoulder and steered him onto the tour. Two armed security walked behind them.

'Where are we?' Belsey asked.

'A very nice place to be,' Miguel said. 'Have some food. Help yourself.' He gestured at the buffet. Belsey hadn't eaten for a long time. He took a slice of pizza and a burger. There was a strum of guitar, then the live music began and everyone cheered.

Belsey ate while they played. It was rhythmic, waltz-like music, the singer balladeering over the top with dramatic flourishes. People cheered the story he was telling. There were mock gasps, and sometimes they sang along. When the song finished, Belsey took another beer. Then Miguel continued the tour, away from the pool, past tennis courts to what looked like a stage set, with façades of buildings. The security guards followed them a few metres away.

'They tell me you work with police,' Miguel said.

'I am police. I try to work with as few of them as possible.'

Miguel laughed. They passed the set of a bar. 'Have you seen *La Mercancía*?'

'No.'

'You must know Alejandro Capilla, the actor.'

'The name rings a bell.'

'This is where they shot it. It is online. *Estoy en una misión de dios – una misión de venganza.*'

'Is that a line from the movie?'

'Yes.'

'I'll check it out. If I'm ever able to.'

They walked on. Further out there were huge empty cages with sand and straw on the floor, and a smell of large animals, although Belsey couldn't see any. For a terrifying moment he wondered if he was going to be caged.

'How long have you been in Mexico?' Miguel asked.

'Only a few weeks. Feels longer.'

'You have been a busy man.'

'Not half as busy as some people think.'

'But you are ready to do business now.'

'Absolutely.'

They left the abandoned zoo, out of the lights, towards the perimeter. Belsey could see a guard up on the ramparts, silhouetted against a floodlight. The path turned right and they passed through an arch into a landscaped garden. Security lights came on. The structures lining the sides were tombs.

There were twenty or so mausoleums, the size of small huts. Narco tombs, baroque, carved from varying shades of marble, with air-con units and wreaths of bright orange marigolds at the front.

'These are our people,' Miguel said. 'These are my brothers.'

'I respect that. I can see what it must mean to you.'

They walked in silence.

'The tombs have air con,' Belsey said eventually.

'Families go inside, drink with them. It is a tradition. I will show you.'

He stopped at a particularly elaborate mausoleum in orange marble, with a mural of the deceased on the side and lamps by the entrance. It wasn't clear if this individual had a personal connection to Miguel, but he had a small key with which he opened the front.

Inside, there were benches along the walls carved from the same stone as the rest of the tomb, a shrine in the centre that doubled as a table, with framed photographs, candle stubs, dead flowers, an empty beer bottle filled with cigarette butts. Miguel lit a candle, sat down at the back, gestured for Belsey to sit beside him. He removed a gun from his jacket and placed it between them. It was a silver Glock with mother-of-pearl grips. He reached into the other side of his jacket and produced a freezer bag of cocaine. Inside it was a silver spade and silver straw. He offered the bag to Belsey. 'Please.'

'You first, I insist.'

'I am okay.'

Was it a test? Belsey took a dab. The coke was crystalline. No chemical aftertaste, just instant numbness. It was astonishingly pure. Miguel gestured for Belsey to take more. Belsey snorted a spadeful. 'It's good.'

'You want to work with us?' Miguel said.

'One hundred per cent.'

The man reached to Belsey's shirt front and undid the top three buttons. He slipped his hand in, cool over Belsey's heart. Then he picked up the gun, released the safety and pressed the barrel into the side of Belsey's head.

'If this fucks up we kill everyone. You understand that.' His eyes looked yellow in the tomb light.

'If what fucks up?'

'What we're doing. What's about to happen.'

'Kill me if you want. This isn't about other people. Why bring them into it?'

'A life is the people in it.'

'You don't know who's in my life.'

'We kill everyone.'

'Okay. Well, let's try not to fuck it up.'

The man removed his hand and slipped the gun back into his jacket. When Belsey tried to return the bag of coke he waved it away. Perks, Belsey thought, pocketing it. He could feel great when he was killed. 'The other guy suggested you were making progress,' he said. 'This will be over soon.'

'I'm sure he is taking care of it. When something like that happens, order has to be restored.'

Belsey wasn't sure if this was good or bad. He thought of

Esmerelda crying at the sound of church bells and hoped, whatever she had to do with a load of stolen cocaine, she was currently a long way away from Guerrero state.

They went back to the party. The women watched Belsey with curiosity. Miguel ordered him into the house, up the main stairs, through to a different corridor. One of their accompanying guards unlocked a door. Inside was a suite with pale new furnishings, a rug like a dead animal. A fan turned in the ceiling. There was a basket of fruit on a cabinet.

'This will be your room for the night. Anything you need, this man will be just outside.'

'Got it.'

'Want a woman?'

'I should get some rest.'

Miguel nodded. Belsey went in and the door was locked behind him. He walked to the window, opened it. A man beneath it looked up and waved. Belsey waved back and shut the window. He couldn't see any cameras in the room. He checked the bathroom. It was brightly lit, same colour as the mausoleum, with gold taps. He went back to the door and knocked once. The guard on the other side opened it.

'Could I get another beer?' Belsey said. The guard spoke on his radio handset, closing the door again. It arrived a few minutes later: another ice bucket with three bottles of beer nestled in the slush. Belsey ran a bath. He had a beer in the bath, which took the edge off the coke. He thought of Kirsty Craik, their nights together, then her predicament now. If she was in danger, what could he do?

Belsey closed his eyes. They'd had good times. He hadn't fully realised the depth of their connection until he'd ruined things. He drank his beer and thought about that. Then he brought his attention back to the present. The cartel seemed to have plans for him. Was he heading back to the UK? He wanted very badly to let Kirsty know something was going on and she needed to watch her back. Wanted to ask her what had put her on to him, why she'd set up an alert.

He imagined seeing her again. Then he just stared at the necklace pointing towards his bruises, wondering what they wanted him for, why he wasn't dead; thought through how you'd set up a cocaine-smuggling operation, how you'd get yourself into a position to enjoy the rewards.

NINE

Craik was in the office at 5.45 a.m. checking the reports for any more attacks, but it looked like things had quietened. The Camberwell shooting victim, Trevor Hart, was still in intensive care, too injured to be interviewed. One witness had come forward, reporting a black Jeep, two men inside it, both white, one possibly wearing a suit. They didn't see the incident but had noticed it parked up a few minutes earlier. A 9mm cartridge had been retrieved from the brickwork of a house next door, and investigators were seeing if it matched any other hits.

At 8 a.m. Craik called Samantha Topping.

'I'm still alive,' Topping said. 'I'm at my sister's.'

'No more calls?'

'No.'

'Let me know if you notice anything that makes you uneasy,' Craik said.

Belsey had left the country on 18 November, six weeks ago. Interpol's list of fugitives now included his name and the designation: *wanted for obstruction of justice*. No one had chased extradition yet. The FBI had requested information on Belsey without including any information of their own as to the cause of their interest. Craik had tried to call yesterday but there was no answer.

Of course, it was possible he had nothing to do with any

drugs. It was possible he was on a Mexican beach, dozing on a sun-lounger. But then you'd have to explain the rest of it.

And something would have to explain what was going on in the UK.

Overnight, two call-centre workers in Reading had been rushed from Silktown Snooker Club to the Royal Berkshire Hospital with detergent in their lungs. Same happened to a banker in Clapham. Another finance-industry employee was reportedly in cardiac arrest and two remained in a critical condition after taking cocaine that turned out to be eighty per cent phenacetin, a banned painkiller linked to kidney failure.

Similar incidents in the East Midlands, North Wales and Hartlepool. Tests were throwing up all sorts: protein powder, fentanyl, lidocaine, MSG, laxatives. It was quite a roulette. Several people had reported to hospital with purple blotches over their faces; all of them turned out to have been snorting levamisole, a de-worming medication taken off the market due to its effect on white blood cell counts.

You'd expect 30 or 40 per cent adulteration, but 90 per cent – and then you snort a gram of the stuff ... Regional squads were all saying the same: the real deal didn't seem to be about. Prices were skyrocketing. At least two violent incidents – in Salford and Sunderland – connected to gangs who'd paid for drugs that never showed.

Eric was right. A lot of cocaine was missing.

DC Josie Summer was in early, sifting the reports alongside Craik. She was that rare breed, the officer who joins the police post-doctorate. Not even your usual criminology background, but something to do with medieval manuscripts, which Craik assumed had contributed to her eye for detail. With her jet-black hair and silver jewellery, she made no attempt to blend in or conform to the various stereotypes. She was twenty-nine, headstrong and champing at the bit to lead her own investigation. You didn't join Organised Crime Command for a sedate life.

Their first task for the day was building a profile of the man they were looking for: the importer. If Eric was right, and one figure had promised a large load direct from Mexico, with people actually believing them, the question was why they were trusted. UK gangs had been trying to transport cocaine directly from South America for a long time. None had succeeded so far: the bulk trafficking was too difficult, routes too conspicuous. People fell back on established techniques: mules from the Caribbean; lorries from Holland or Germany; occasionally a small boat over from the Continent. It meant you had to pay a lot of mark-up, but when you were handling the most profitable commodity in the world, expenses could be written off.

Trafficking direct was different. Italian Mafias did that – the Calabrians and Neapolitans – not many others. You needed capital, infrastructure, security, reputation. You needed connections in the producer country. Most of the people who could tick those boxes had been put away.

The office filled as they searched. They were still knee-deep in European networks when Obiri came over.

'That spoofed phone call you gave me, we've got the real phone used. It's a pre-pay, dead since just after ten a.m. yesterday, but I've got a list of usage.'

He showed her the records. It wasn't much. Sim card activated at 9 p.m. the night she'd been called. The location tracking was off but usage could be roughly pinned to various parts of central London: Euston, Camden, Victoria. No messages sent or data used. Four calls made in total. 'To Trevor Hart, a woman called Samantha Topping, then a mobile registered to yourself.' He glanced at her.

'That's correct. What's the fourth?'

'The fourth one's odd. At nine thirty a.m. there's a call to a beauty clinic in Hampstead.'

'A beauty clinic?'

'It's called U+. The call lasts almost three minutes. I don't know what you'd make of that.'

Craik looked up U+. The clinic was on Heath Street. The website had a lot of very close-up images of people's eyes. *Welcome to U+ Aesthetics, where the art of beauty meets the centre of excellence! Here at U+ we want to help you look and feel the best version of you.*

Craik ran the clinic's name through the police database to see if they'd reported any harassment but there was nothing.

'Maybe a mistake?' Obiri said.

'Not for a three-minute call. I think the mistake was to use that phone. They got their lines mixed up.'

This made it even more intriguing: a slip. Mistakes were what you pounced upon in investigations.

But a beauty clinic?

Craik wondered if it was mad – or overly desperate – to pay them a visit. She'd never been to a beauty clinic. Obiri was right: it was an odd lead. But sometimes you follow the odd ones because they're the only ones you have.

Heath Street wound up from Hampstead station to the Heath, past bijou restaurants, galleries, antiques shops, and various forms of medical treatment. The front window of U+ was frosted. Inside, it looked like a spaceship decorated by someone with bad taste. The reception was entirely white: white sofa, white floor and walls, white Christmas tree. The receptionist, in a black top with ruff, looked like a spillage of ink. She stood in front of a mirrored shrine of U+ products, all very small and expensive.

One customer was paying at the desk, another waiting on the

sofa, so Craik took a seat. She watched a flatscreen displaying a menu of treatments ranging from chemical skin peels to tattoo removal. As the woman beside her got up, she turned to Craik with a smile.

'Don't worry. They're miracle workers.'

The woman gave her name to the receptionist and was invited through a magic doorway to a land of spiralling wooden stairs. Then the receptionist beamed at Craik. Craik showed her badge.

'We're looking into a series of threatening calls in this area, and I wondered if you'd experienced anything like that, anyone causing you concern.'

'I don't think so.' She looked puzzled.

'More specifically, there was a call made to this clinic yesterday morning which I'm interested in.'

'Hang on.'

The woman lifted a phone. A moment later a short woman in a white coat appeared. Her name badge said 'Dr Choudra'. She led Craik anxiously away from the public area, up the wooden stairs to a treatment room with its own chandelier.

'Threatening calls?' she said, when Craik explained again what she was there for. 'Not that I'm aware of.'

Craik showed her the phone records from the pay-as-you-go. 'Specifically this call, from this number.'

The doctor studied it. 'I don't remember anything unusual at that time.'

'Would you be able to tell if the call related to a booking? If someone made an appointment at that time?'

'I wouldn't know what time the appointments were actually made. And the girl who probably took the call is off today.'

'Okay. This a long shot, but does the name Nick Belsey mean anything to you?'

It meant nothing and, somewhat unsurprisingly, he didn't turn up on their database. Nor did the phone number in question. Then the woman's face lit with an idea.

'Is this about New You?'

'New You?'

'The clinic in Belsize Park that opened last year. They claimed we used an inferior type of filler. A customer made a complaint, but we think it was someone they'd put up to it. It was in the local papers.'

'Right.'

'But that's all dealt with. They backed down when we threatened legal action.'

'It's unlikely to be about that.'

'So who was this caller?'

'I don't know.'

'Did they call New You as well?'

'I don't think so. I don't think it's about dermal fillers.'

The woman spread her hands, as if to say: what do you expect from me, then? Craik could see her point. She said she'd be in touch if she had any more questions, took an embossed business card and left the world of beauty. Once she was heading back down the hill her phone rang. It was Price.

'You requested an alert on an officer called Nick Belsey,' he said. He sounded breathless.

'Yes.'

'Why?'

Craik thought quickly, deciding how much to share. 'His name was mentioned in some threatening calls to people, possibly to do with missing cocaine. Turns out he's on the run, wanted for questioning, so I was curious. Has something come up?'

'I'm heading to a meeting at the US Embassy in just over an

hour. There are senior people asking about Nick Belsey, and I'm expected to report on him. If you know the man, I'd appreciate you coming along to share whatever you can.'

'Sure. I can try. What's going on?'

'I've got to smarten up, Kirsty. Let's talk on the way.'

TEN

The new American embassy was five minutes from their HQ, west along the river to Battersea. They walked fast, beneath dove-grey clouds, both striders by nature. The occasion had made Price excited but uncertain, a status-conscious man heading to a make-or-break performance.

'There's a couple of pretty senior people over here,' he said. 'It looks like something's happened. I don't know what exactly, but Belsey's name has come up. How well do you know him?'

'We worked together. Briefly.'

'Really? Did you get any sense of where he's gone?'

'Yes,' she said. 'It looks like he flew to Mexico six weeks ago.'

Price stopped. 'He's in Mexico now?'

'Possibly.'

The chief inspector nodded as he processed the news, then set off again. 'This is good. This is going to be helpful. I'd like to position our unit as a potential lead on any investigation they're considering. What else do we know? Tell me about this missing cocaine.'

'I don't have any more to tell. All I know is that it wasn't heading to any of the usual suspects. I think there's a new supply chain.'

'Involving Belsey?'

'That doesn't sound plausible to me. He's not the type for this level of criminality.' This got another glance from Price.

'Okay. We're going to need something a lot juicier than that.'

The embassy building was a futuristic, thinly disguised fortress set back from the road behind a hundred defensive feet of landscaped gardens. The main building was a cube of thick glass inside a plastic membrane, surrounded by an ornamental lake that served as a moat. Its concrete bulwarks were hidden beneath earthworks, anti-truck bollards buried within hedges. Next door to it were the barracks assigned to the marines who guarded the complex, looking like a mid-budget hotel.

Plenty of marines about. One pair directed them through the metal detectors into the embassy grounds. Another escorted them into the building, where they were issued with security passes. Craik had liaised with agents here but had never been inside before. The interior was stylishly bland, like a Starbucks with ambitions. The FBI's overseas legal attaché met them in the foyer, a broad, fleshy man who introduced himself as Doug Brown, pumped their hands and led them to the FBI section on the second floor. They walked into a conference room with the blinds drawn, the FBI seal on the wall partially obscured by a projector screen showing a map of Mexico. In the shadows, two men and one woman watched them enter.

One of them Craik knew: Chief Superintendent Philip Horne, chief of the Yard's Drugs Squad, in full dress uniform. The others Brown introduced as Michael DeLuca from the FBI's Criminal Investigative Division and Alicia Perez from Mexico's Policía Federal Ministerial. DeLuca was clean-shaven, with black hair neatly parted, Perez a petite woman with intense dark eyes, wearing a crisp white suit. Both looked like they'd stared into a lot of abysses.

Craik and Price gave nods as they took the seats opposite.

'Thanks for joining us at short notice,' Brown said. 'I'll let Agents DeLuca and Perez talk you through where we're at, but I understand you have some familiarity with Detective Constable Nicholas Belsey.'

'That's right,' Price said.

'Any update on his whereabouts?'

'We've just received word that Nick Belsey flew to Mexico last month,' Price said.

This didn't appear to surprise the assembled investigators.

'His passport was used to fly from Heathrow to Mexico City on November the eighteenth,' Craik said. 'We don't have visuals yet.'

'Is there existing intelligence that he's been operating in Mexico?' DeLuca asked.

'No.'

'Not as far as we're aware,' Price added.

'Any idea how many times he's been over there?'

'Possibly never before,' Craik said.

'And he's suspended from police duties, right?' DeLuca said, rolling an expensive-looking pen between finger and thumb.

'He was suspended four months ago, pending an investigation into some serious misconduct charges,' Price said. 'The theft of police funds, amongst other things. Now he's absconded.'

Craik told them about the threatening calls and the Trevor Hart shooting. There was an exchange of glances between the FBI officers. Horne looked interested. He said he'd arrange for the Hart file to be sent through to them.

'There may be more we can get you,' Craik said, 'but it would be useful to know as much background as possible.'

'Okay,' DeLuca said. 'We've got a mystery and we need help. Fast. Are you familiar with the ATO?'

Price looked blank.

'It's a drug cartel,' Craik said.

'That's right. The Ayón-Tallón Organisation, or ATO, is a major drug cartel run by Joaquin Ayón and Salvador Tallón, based in Guerrero state.' He pointed at the map. 'Originally a branch of the Sinaloa Cartel, it split off around 2017 before fighting a long and very unpleasant war for control of the transportation and wholesaling of cocaine, heroin and marijuana. Both ATO's leaders are former paramilitary commanders who retain significant influence in the military and police. They're sophisticated, use advanced technology in pursuing intelligence on investigators and rivals. And, as of a couple of years ago, they have their own labs. They bring in the paste raw from Colombia and produce cocaine of unprecedented purity. That's helped them win friends abroad. Right now ATO control most of the major drug-trafficking corridors within the country and beyond. Last year they began a series of targeted assassinations with the intention of sealing control of the remaining trade from Mexico to Europe. That's when we set up Operation Flyway, a joint US-Mexico operation dedicated to ATO's foreign ambitions.'

'One of their primary goals of the last year has been to monopolise supply to the UK,' Perez said. 'This is where you might be able to help. Ayón acquired what we believe to be a new ally over here. He seems to believe that this individual has connections that can ensure a safe route into the country. That was all we could get for a long time, but last week something happened that might give us a lead.'

She clicked to a shot of a room in a nice house covered with blood and broken glass.

'We know that several kilograms of cocaine belonging to the ATO were due to be flown to the UK earlier this month.

On December fourteenth, the drugs were moved from one of the labs to a safe house en route to Cancún airport, where presumably it would have been hidden in a legitimate cargo. The safe house was on a private, gated, residential estate just off the Cancún-Tulum Federal Highway.

'In the early hours of December fifteenth ten individuals stormed the place using smoke grenades and tear gas, and proceeded to rob the ATO of several million dollars' worth of cocaine. It was a well-coordinated heist lasting about seven minutes. They clearly had inside intelligence. Three ATO members died, two still critical. We believe the stolen drugs may have already travelled to Europe in the last twenty-four hours. The gang will be trying to offload them as fast as possible. So we know what happened, but not exactly how, or where it is now. That brings us to your area of knowledge.'

Perez clicked the PowerPoint again. The next image gave Craik a jolt. It was the photo page of Belsey's passport.

'We believe there are connections between Detective Constable Belsey and the group suspected of carrying out the robbery. So far, this is what we know: Belsey arrived at Benito Juarez airport on November nineteenth, hired a car, swapped it a couple of hours later for a stolen vehicle. It seems pretty clear he went over with a plan, and with considerable preparation in place. Early the following day, Belsey rendezvoused with a woman attached to the gang suspected of carrying out the Cancún heist.'

A woman's face appeared on the screen: high cheekbones, dark eyes, hair scraped back. A mugshot stamped *Detenida*.

'Ana Martinez first came to our attention as a possible player in a string of frauds around Cancún and across the border in Los Angeles and San Diego,' Perez said. 'Her parents were killed in a mass shooting in Temascalapa village in 1993, by men connected to Ayón. She has long-term affiliations with Ayón's rivals, in particular a breakaway group of criminals and con men, former members of Los Zetas who've struck out on their own and now mostly concentrate on extortion and robbery. Martinez connected with Nicholas Belsey somewhere between Mexico City and Chilpancingo on the morning of November twentieth. She was seen with him in Chilpancingo later that day and stayed with him at the Hotel San Luis Lindavista a few miles south the following night. They parted ways soon after that. Ana Martinez joined the robbery team in Taxco. Belsey disappeared off the radar entirely. Or almost entirely. His ID was used to book the hotel that the gang stayed in before carrying out the operation.'

'He's the piece we can't figure out,' DeLuca said. 'But he's potentially involved with both sides, and playing a somewhat audacious game. From what I've gathered this wouldn't be out of character.'

'No,' Price said. 'It very much fits what we know.'

'He'd be unlikely to use his own ID,' Craik said. 'For the hotel booking.' Something in her tone got a curious look from the others. She regretted speaking too fast.

'True, but then there's a lot of things about his activity that seem unlikely,' Perez said, measuring her words. 'Did you work with him?'

'Yes.'

'That was one of the things that drew DI Craik's interest,' Price said. 'She knows him personally.'

'Before we put resources in,' Craik said, 'I want to say that I worked with the man for several years and I wouldn't say he fitted the profile for organised crime on this level. He was a somewhat maverick detective, but with a sense of principles. That's my personal opinion.'

'But his disciplinary record,' Perez said. 'He has extensive criminal connections. Is that correct?'

'In our line of work ...' Craik began, then stopped herself. 'He has a large pool of contacts, formal and informal. That's true. But they are mostly low-level: eyes and ears on the street.'

The room considered this. Craik felt like she'd stolen a bone from a dog.

'But you say these recent threats connect to him,' Horne prompted.

'There have been threats connected to a missing load, yes,' Craik conceded, 'to people who may be associated with Belsey.'

She gave them more details. It was clear that the shooting of Trevor Hart lent the whole thing a new urgency.

'It reinforces our suspicion that they have active members over here,' Perez said. 'From what you've described, it sounds like the suspects were surveying the victim's home in preparation for further action. Which suggests the ATO think Belsey is in some way responsible and are ready to elevate this. If they believe someone is a friend or associate of Nick Belsey, that person will be used to apply pressure. The next step will be abduction and torture. Belsey will be sent recordings of this. That's how it goes, in our experience.'

Craik's stomach turned.

'This is how they operate,' DeLuca said. 'Psychological intimidation using loved ones, friends and family, anyone they can get their hands on. They use the same technique to intimidate police and journalists. It is brutally effective. And they cast the net wide. If there has already been an attack, then it is likely there are cartel members here attempting to exact revenge or locate the drugs. We would like to help you identify them. Officer Belsey may be key to that.'

'Is there anything else to suggest who they might be working with in the UK?' Craik asked.

'There is one other piece of the puzzle. In July this year there was a meeting in London, possibly about refining transportation processes. Ayón sent his trusted lieutenant, Efraín Xavier, one of the cartel's top logistics specialists. A *sistemista*, as they call them, commissioned with establishing a secure route and method.'

They brought up a blurry image of a man crossing the pavement in the Strand, between a glossy black hire car and the entrance to the Savoy. Craik wondered how much surveillance the FBI was conducting on British soil, and what kind of sign-off they got for that. She couldn't imagine the Home Office putting up a fight.

'From what we managed to intercept it seems he is dealing with a group that have managed to remain off the radar – *un sindicato sin nombre*, he calls it. Approximately seven men. Central to it is an individual Xavier calls *el jefe*. *El jefe* is slang for "the boss", the chief. This person will only meet him once, away from the rest. We believe this meeting occurred around lunchtime on Sunday, July twelfth. It was after this encounter that Xavier confirmed an arrangement to advance the relationship.'

'Any details of this meeting?' Craik asked.

'The cell-phone data suggests it was in an area called Harlesden.' Perez checked her notes. 'Is that how you pronounce it?'

'Harlesden. Yes.'

'Does that area carry any significance?'

Not one of the most salubrious areas, Craik thought. A busy, gritty district on the outer reaches of north-west London. No longer a crime hotspot, but even London's ravenous gentrification chipped its teeth trying to chew into NW10. It carried no particular significance, and Craik wondered if that was the point.

'Nothing specific,' Craik said.

'We know Xavier stayed at the Savoy.. But we have reason to believe that on July twelfth he travelled to Harlesden for a meeting with this man he calls *el jefe*. We have no idea what exactly this meeting involved, but it is the only occasion we can find when this leader has shown his face, so to speak. In his calls to Mexico, Efraín Xavier emphasises his faith in this individual. He is described as someone "who will make this work", by which we believe he means an increase in shipments using new smuggling techniques.'

A gang with no name, Craik thought. No more people involved than necessary. Careful operators, individuals who knew not to flash the new-found wealth of cocaine importation – who paid taxes and maintained day jobs and never talked business on phones or in cars or homes.

'We're going to put resources into establishing what Nick Belsey has been up to over the last year or so,' Horne said. 'Obviously, we will share the fruits of that investigation with you as they come in. At the same time, we will be tracking events that might reflect trouble among those who had anticipated the delivery of cocaine. In my experience, this is when people show their hand.'

Perez nodded but she was still watching Craik. Then her phone rang. The Mexican investigator turned it face up, like a card in poker, leaned to her colleague and spoke to him. He, in turn, spoke to Brown who announced a break for lunch. Someone wheeled in a trolley of food and coffee.

Brown and DeLuca went to get refreshments. Price leaped to his feet and hurried over to Chief Superintendent Horne. Craik turned to Perez. The investigator had finely manicured nails, and Craik imagined this was part of the poise needed, operating with a price on your head: that you'd want to look sharp in the face of death.

'You said they manufactured their own cocaine,' she said.

'Yes. They have labs hidden in the forests north of La Cada. Last year, Colombian police seized several hundred kilos of coca paste from a Mexico-bound plane. Intelligence indicated it was destined for the ATO, so we know they can process it.'

'Do you have chemical analysis of the cocaine they produce?'

'Yes.'

'We're in the process of compiling a database. I'd be interested to see the fingerprint, see if any's turned up in UK seizures. That might be a step towards establishing who's running this operation.'

'Sure.'

Craik caught a flicker of respect. She sensed the investigator warming.

'Is there anything else you know about this UK connection?' Craik said.

'The intercepted phone calls are quite revealing, in an opaque way. According to Efraín, this *jefe* is the individual who assures him the syndicate is still powerful. He is *muy secreto* – the most secret of all those concerned – but provides *la solución*. As far as I can tell, Nicholas Belsey connects London and Mexico and the police. He seems to tick all the boxes.'

'Perhaps.'

'When did you last see him?' Perez asked coolly.

'A while back,' Craik said.

'In what context?'

'Professional.'

There was a moment of consideration, then Perez said, 'Take a look at this.' She lifted the screen of her laptop. 'It has just come through. It is puzzling.' It was seven black-and-white images of what looked like a party in the grounds of a mansion. Craik recognised the odd lo-res angles of a camera hidden on someone's person. It caught a lot of female flesh, bikinis, a peacock, a band of paunchy men in jaunty costumes. There were also a lot of shady-looking men, rich-looking men, and security guards.

'This is Joaquin Ayón's ranch, in the mountains of Guerrero. The images are from last night.' She clicked through, pointing across them. 'The man with the cigar is Sergio Lizano, who was governor of Tamaulipas until 2010 when he was accused of laundering money for the ATO. Next to him is a thug, Miguel Sanchos. He killed one of our undercover operatives in Texas in 2013.' Perez enlarged the final image. 'Over here, in the background, is Ayón himself, and with him is a man we have not seen before, but who our source believes to be British. Could it be Nicholas Belsey?'

Craik stared. There he was, unshaven, looking like he'd been in a fight, clutching a bottle of beer. Chatting away on a cartel ranch in Guerrero. Oh, Nick, she thought. What the fuck are you up to?

'It may be,' Craik said. 'It certainly looks like him.'

ELEVEN

Craik called Summer from the embassy corridor when she briefly managed to escape the meeting.

'There was a shipment arranged from Cancún in Mexico to the UK, December the fifteenth. The cocaine that was meant to be flown was stolen before it could get on the plane. See if you can find out which freight companies use the airport, then which were delivering to the UK on this date. There's a small chance it gives us something.'

'I'll take a look.'

'And I'm also interested in a meeting that happened in Harlesden around lunchtime on July the twelfth this year. That's all we've got, but worth checking any reports from the area at that time, just in case.'

'That's all we've got?'

'Yes.'

'You want me to search for reports of a cartel meeting?'

'Of anything: suspicious individuals, bad parking, anything that could give us a lead. I know it's a long shot, but the FBI think a major UK importer was there, and I don't think we're going to get much else to work off.'

'Okay. You're still at the embassy?'

'For now.'

'How is it?'

'Long-winded, weak coffee. I'll see if I can get anything else useful.'

It was another hour before the meeting ended. Craik had never been a meetings person and this didn't win her over. Price spoke at length about their successes to date: strategies and existing transnational collaborations. The only concrete thing he had to give them was Belsey.

'We'll put all the resources we have into establishing what he's been up to. If there's any truth to this whatsoever, we'll hunt it down.'

When the meeting was over, Price went to clear the Belsey investigation with the director general of the National Crime Agency. Craik returned to the office. She messaged the Transnational Crime Department to see if they had independent intelligence on the ATO's European connections, and whether these might, somehow, involve a UK officer called Nick Belsey. It felt ridiculous even asking. As of now, it seemed, no one knew anything about any of it.

Craik thought of that photo of the pool party and tried to find other explanations. Belsey would be doing some kind of investigation of his own, she thought. Informal. He was the kind of guy who fell in with crowds to see where it led. She tried to imagine being on a cartel boss's ranch, slipping into that life, finding yourself there, then rolling with it. If anyone could, it would be Nick. But he knew the evil they represented. Belsey was happy mixing with anyone who operated on what he called ground level, but reserved disdain for those who considered themselves above it, and who sustained that illusion at the cost of other people's lives.

Josie Summer came over, a gleam in her eye. Craik knew she had a result.

'These are the export companies using that airport on the

date in question.' She placed a list on Craik's desk: seventeen separate shipments booked in for flights to Europe, three flying direct to the UK. One of these had been circled.

'A haulage company called Eurofreight has two refrigerated units booked onto American Airlines flight AA135 from Cancún to Heathrow on the day following this heist. Among the loads are twenty boxes for a pharmaceutical company called Farmaco Mundiales: injectable botulinum, anti-ageing injections.'

'Fillers.'

'Right. It's the generic ingredient in Botox.'

'The clinic.'

'That's what I thought. Twenty boxes, each with four twenty-five-millilitre bottles. Weight is twenty kilograms in total.'

'A lot of filler.'

'I don't know what would be considered normal. Farmaco have a thirty-acre manufacturing plant producing eight hundred million units of dermal filler per year.'

'Who's importing it to the UK?'

'A company called Infinite Beauty Supplies.' Summer passed over more sheets. 'The address on the import documents is a virtual office in Hainault, just a mailing address. When you try to establish ownership of Infinite Beauty you end up at a company called Orchid Securities.'

'Offshore.'

'You guessed it. Registered in the British Virgin Islands, bank account at our old friends Global Pacific in Puerto Rico.'

'Someone knows what they're doing,' Craik said. Even if, by some miracle, they got access to company records, these would contain nothing but nominee directors: random men and women paid a few dollars to file the paperwork.

'Aside from that, everything seems above board. They have a

warehouse, delivery drivers, all the right licences. They've got a website and a phoneline. It looks like they order this amount of filler every month, plus face creams, toner and a bunch of other Farmaco products. They supply seven or eight clinics directly. Customs have previously had an eye on them. I got the file. There've been eight shipments between Farmaco Mundiales and Infinite Beauty in the last six months, and they've all been checked. Nothing's been found, apart from the declared cargo. One time they'd even overpaid the import duty.'

The fact that Customs had taken a look was no surprise. If you were a first-time importer from Central or South America you expected a thorough search. But that was the problem: importers were forewarned, and could play it clever. The Customs documents recorded X-ray, gamma-ray and physical inspections. A Contraband Enforcement Team had even taken the boxes apart. No drugs.

'Decoys?' Summer said.

'Maybe. Or they're playing a long game, establishing credibility. But they clearly expected to get something through this time.'

'What did the FBI say?'

'A Mexican cartel called the Ayón-Tallón Organisation have a connection here, someone they regard highly. They met them six months ago in Harlesden, which coincides with the start of the Farmaco shipments. I'd place pretty good money on that being more than coincidence. I think serious quantities have already been getting over. We need to figure out why Customs aren't finding anything.'

Craik called the FBI overseas office and got a number for Perez. The Mexican investigator answered promptly. Craik told her about Farmaco and Infinite Beauty, and the mysterious Orchid Securities being used to hide ownership. Perez was keen to have the details sent through. In return, Craik got the fingerprint.

Every batch of cocaine has a unique chemical profile telling the story of whichever jungle clearing grew the coca leaves, of the petrol and ammonia used to extract the base, the metal drums it was mashed in and the brick moulds the resulting mixture was poured into. Craik forwarded the analyses to Obiri, with a request for him to search for any local matches. It had been Obiri who had argued for the UK narcotics database. It was time for him to demonstrate its worth.

For much of the rest of the day Craik's time was taken up with the work she had originally meant to be doing. Price had lined up a press conference early tomorrow morning for the sake of publicising their Operation Goldmine success. A budget review was coming up and he wanted the positive PR before the complexities of trials could tarnish it. So Craik had to devote a considerable amount of time to the logistics of transferring bags of marijuana and customised weaponry to their media suite downstairs. She almost forgot about *el jefe* for a moment. It was 6 p.m. when Summer approached her desk, looking anxious.

'There's something you should see, ma'am.'

'Go on.'

Summer laid down a fresh pile of paper. 'I looked through some records. The name Orchid Securities comes up as owner of a clothing company, High Class Fashion and Accessories, from 2016 to 2018. They made three imports from Mexico in that period, from a company called Mexico VIP Shirts, which has a factory outside Tijuana.'

She spread the paperwork.

'I brought up Customs documents on this company. The file came with a previous police reference.'

'Okay,' Craik said cautiously. The reference notified you that someone else had previously requested it, to avoid overlaps or repetition. 'Who was on it?'

'The contact name is Detective Inspector Scott Montgomery.'

The two officers stared at each other, then glanced instinctively through the window of Price's office at the photograph of the disfigured man in the wheelchair.

'That Scott Montgomery?'

'Must be. Serious and Organised Crime Unit, 2018.'

Craik read the paperwork again. Montgomery had requested the Customs records on 1 February 2018. She brought up an online news report of his attack. 'That was a week before he was shot.'

They turned back to the framed photograph: Montgomery receiving his commendation. But not looking like it eased the pain. Sensing their gazes, Price looked up from his keyboard and peered at them through the glass.

'We're going to have to think very carefully about how we proceed,' Craik said.

TWELVE

Price read the Customs paperwork, horrified. 'Scott asked for this?'

'He was looking into this clothes importer, High Class Fashion. They're owned by an offshore holdings company called Orchid Securities, which also owns a distributor of clinical beauty products. They import these from Mexico. I think that was the cargo that was going to contain the stolen drugs.'

Price checked each sheet in turn.

'I don't know exactly how this syndicate is playing it,' Craik said. 'Customs can't seem to get anything.'

'Customs aren't going to get everything,' Price muttered. 'What led you to Infinite Beauty?'

'A call to a beauty clinic that connects to the individuals making threats.' Craik shut the door. 'Rob, there's something I didn't mention. They called me too.'

'Who?

'Whoever's making threats. It was when you were with me, the five a.m. call.'

'Why didn't you tell me?'

'I didn't think it was anything serious.'

'Why did they call you?'

'Because I'm connected to Nick Belsey, I imagine.'

'I thought you didn't know him that well.'

'That's not entirely true either.'

The chief inspector thrust himself back in his chair as if assailed by all this information. 'How close exactly were you?'

'Not that close. But friends.'

'For Christ's sake, Kirsty. Why didn't you say?'

'It seemed too bizarre.'

'You were in a relationship?'

'No. He's not really a relationship type of person.'

Price got to his feet but had nowhere to go. 'What did they say when they called?'

'They wanted me to pass a message to Belsey. I think they thought he had the missing cocaine.'

'Did they threaten you?'

'They said I'd be dead by Christmas if they didn't find him.'

'Oh, Christ.' He ran a hand down his jaw.

'What was Scott Montgomery working on?' Craik asked. 'What do you remember about that last investigation?'

'All I knew was that he felt he was getting close to something. I think he'd been put on the scent by some Financial Crime reports, and it led him to a drugs ring. But I wasn't working with him. I went with him that day to try to put eyes on a meeting between gang members, an unofficial surveillance. But I was there as back-up only. And even he didn't know who was going to turn up. I can try to contact him, but you have to understand, he's not in a good way, Kirsty. He's not the old Scott. And, first, we need to get protection for you.'

'Like what?'

'I can make a referral to the PPS.'

'I'm not going into protection.'

'They can keep an eye on things.'

'I'd rather not have that.'

'Great. And what about Josie? Have you thought about her?'

'I'll give her the choice to move away from this investigation if she's not comfortable.'

'Do you think they know where you live?'

'They said they knew I lived alone.'

Price closed his eyes. When he opened them again he appeared gentler but no less anxious. 'Do me a favour, stay at mine tonight.'

The offer took her by surprise. He had never invited her to his home before.

'I'm meant to be packing. I'm going to Lawrence's parents' place tomorrow.'

Price broke eye contact. He had always been respectful of this area of her life, but references to it provoked the only moments of reflection that she noticed in the man.

'I can find time to pack tomorrow,' she said.

'It's up to you.'

'Are you sure?'

'Of course.'

She took his hand. He ran a thumb across her knuckles, studying them as if they were the precious part of her. Through the office window she saw Josie Summer staring.

'Shit,' Craik muttered, extracting her hand.

Summer was by the printer when Craik emerged, reading sheets as they appeared. Just the two of them left in the main office.

'That's a lot of something,' Craik said.

'Not much necessarily useful. What did the boss say?' Summer asked. Craik thought she heard a sardonic emphasis on 'the boss'.

'We're going to try to approach Scott Montgomery, see what he can tell us about Orchid.'

'I see.'

'Josie, you know we're on uncharted territory here. I think it could be sensible, while we assess risk, if you go back to working on Goldmine. We've rushed into this.'

Summer's expression was a mixture of disdain and disbelief. Craik realised she shouldn't have done this now, after being caught with Price. The look was wrong.

'Are you asking me to step away?'

'I'm just making it clear that the option is there. It wouldn't be counted against you.'

'I'd like to keep going.'

'That's fine too. Let's go through what you've got tomorrow. Get some sleep.'

Summer nodded. Craik packed up in the silence that hung between them.

'See you tomorrow.'

'See you,' Summer said, without looking up.

Price's flat was small and clean, in a superficially glossy building by the river. Through the windows, the river view appeared clichéd, like some off-the-shelf IKEA art. It was the flat a professional man moves into when his wife kicks him out, Craik thought. It didn't feel like he'd fully established himself there. He was someone in transition, which made Craik wonder about her own role.

'Bit poky,' he said.

'Big enough to potentially save my life,' she said. 'I like it.'

Price poured wine, left the lights off, not so much in a romantic way but as if to enhance the sense that they were hiding. He stood by the window. Craik downed her first glass and felt she was communing with Belsey in some way. Although he always avoided wine because, in his words, it went too quickly. 'I can't sip,' he'd complain, which was a general truth about him. Well, he had drunk deeply the past few weeks, whatever was going on. What kind of trouble had he brought himself and those who knew him?

'I never knew what Scott had been working on exactly,' Price said. And Craik realised why he'd left the lights off: he wanted memory, not the present. 'I wasn't on the investigation. But it was the same situation as now, from what I understood. Scott had a hint of something major. He just needed names. How much do you know about it?'

'Not much. I know they never got the person who shot him. I know it happened out west somewhere, near the M4.'

'Middle of nowhere. This supposed lead he'd been given was that when the men involved needed to meet they'd go to a parking area near Heston service station on the M4. The source told Scott there was a meeting coming up the following day, the top names would be there. And I don't know what made Scott believe them. I tried to tell him that you needed to approach this kind of thing with caution, that intelligence like that doesn't just land in your lap. But obviously any kind of official surveillance would have taken weeks to clear. The whole thing's so obvious now.'

'He thought he'd see who it was.'

'Just take a look, he said. He'd become fixated. I've told you how driven he was. No one else was up for backing him, but I was, because it was Monty. I thought he was the best detective I'd met and if he said, "Let's do this, let's take a look" – a detective who had previously always done things by the book – then I thought . . . Obviously, it was a set-up.'

'What happened?'

'The place was just a bit of tarmac behind the lorry wash. No lights, no cameras, nothing. Pissing down, and total darkness by the time we got there. We parked away from where they were going to be, obviously, with some cover from a lorry, and a clear exit back to the motorway, but we had a view. Scott had binoculars and everything, but we didn't want to keep the wipers on, so he had to get out. Soon as he's set foot out of the car someone came from the side and that was that. Bang. By the time I was out, they'd legged it. I saw Scott on the ground and assumed he was going to die. It was the worst thing I'd ever seen. I just sat with him and waited for the ambulance.'

'And the source of this tip-off?'

'Scott never said. There was something shady about it. I don't know. I don't know how the gang got wind he was on to them, either, but he'd been asking around and word spreads.' Price drank, watching the river as if it was a mystery in itself. 'It's incredible what the surgeons did,' he said. 'You know, the guy whose face they used, he'd topped himself the night before. He was a painter, an artist. Decided he'd had enough and swallowed a load of prescription meds. Donated everything, though, head to toe. Sometimes I try to imagine that, having a new face, knowing what happened to its previous owner. Scott has to take these drugs to stop his body rejecting it.' Price turned towards Craik for the first time since he had begun his reminiscence. 'Imagine rejecting your own face,' he said.

'Intense.'

'The point, Kirsty, is that whoever this importer is, he's deadly. If what you're telling me about these companies is true, then I'm pretty sure he was the one who shot Scott.'

'I'm not doubting he's deadly.'

'People didn't get Scott. He had this military background and he was seen as humourless, stubborn, but you have to be stubborn. Management have their fashions, and you have to stick to your guns, especially if you want to take the top men down. He was like you.'

'I don't think I deserve that comparison.'

'He was patient. Never swerved. I let him walk into an execution. I don't want more of that.'

'You saved his life. If you hadn't been there to get the ambulance . . .'

'I saved something. Whatever's he's got now isn't his life.'

They finished the wine, tried to talk about Christmas, but neither had the stomach for it. Finally Price said, 'Do you love him?'

'Lawrence?'

'Nick Belsey.'

The question momentarily startled her. 'I don't know,' she said, eventually. 'It's easy to love someone who never seems entirely real.'

Price nodded. The answer seemed to suffice, or at least gave him enough to chew on. Sufficed for him, if not for her.

'I can take the sofa,' he said, a few moments later. Again, she was caught off guard, even if it had become clear that this wasn't going to be a night of passion. It wasn't necessary, Craik said, though when they were in bed beside each other she wondered if it would have been a good idea. She wasn't going to sleep well. The bedroom felt like a hotel room, with dark wood and midnight blue walls. She tried to imagine a future beside this man. A future in exile. Did every relationship feel like that? She couldn't shake the feeling that something was missing, and it wasn't her.

THIRTEEN

It snowed overnight. Then, just as it was thawing, the temperature plummeted, preserving an icy grey crust of slush. They crunched through it together to HQ, then staggered their arrival, Craik grabbing coffee while Price went in. By the time Craik got inside, Summer had all Montgomery's old paperwork out.

'Spend the night here?' Craik joked.

'Just in early,' Summer said.

At 9 a.m. Craik had to go down to the media suite for the press conference. Arranged on tables at the front were diamond rings, twenty bags of cannabis, a converted Slovakian blank-firing pistol and an Uzi with a gold handle. Everything was bagged in clear plastic, like prizes at a funfair.

Price beamed. Reporters filed in and he shook their hands, like a father of the bride. For him, the job was about moments like this: a fleeting appearance of good triumphing over evil. Craik imagined it connected to the aggressive reek of aftershave that trailed him today. Price took a call just before events were due to kick off and when he came back his expression was less confident.

'That was the chief constable. Someone at the US Embassy has had words about this ATO situation and he's taking it seriously. I need to speak to Customs and Border Force ASAP. Are you okay handling this?'

'Sure.'

'The commissioner can field most of the questions.'

The Met commissioner, Paula Walsh, had taken up position behind the cannabis: a vigorous, silver-haired woman in medals. When the press were seated she read a statement praising Organised Crime Command, listing the criminals they had prosecuted.

'... Shutting down London's criminal infrastructure gang by gang, turning off the taps of hard drugs and illegal weaponry ...'

'Who are you targeting next?' a journalist asked.

Walsh looked to Craik.

'Obviously that's sensitive,' Craik said.

Then one of the journalists at the back raised a hand. 'People are saying other gangs are sniffing opportunity now.' Craik recognised Fraser Dunlop from the *Sun*. He used to hang around Borough, cultivating cop contacts.

'We're here to celebrate success,' Walsh said. 'Thirty-seven dangerous foreign criminals taken off the streets, lives saved.'

'Can you pick it up?' Dunlop asked.

Craik didn't understand what he meant at first. 'Pick up what?'

'Can we get a photograph of Detective Inspector Craik holding the Uzi?'

'No,' she said.

By the time she got back upstairs, Summer was gone. No coat on the back of her chair. Craik felt the mug of half-drunk tea on her desk and it was still warm. Gibson and Obiri emerged from the break-out room, Obiri balancing a MacBook and a sheaf of papers.

'Any idea where Josie went?' Craik asked.

'She rushed off. Not sure. We think we've made some progress at our end, though.'

'Go on.'

'The fingerprint of the cocaine connects to street-level seizures across the UK.'

'Where?'

'Widespread. As far afield as Cumbria, Glasgow, all over the north-west. That's in the last four months. Whoever's importing this seems to have gained a monopoly on supply in these areas. I've never seen such consistent results.'

Craik looked through the paperwork. 'That means they have distribution as well,' she said.

'We've got something on that too,' Gibson said. 'They're offloading it fast and anonymously to trusted gangs, it seems, no more than three or four.'

He passed her documents from a joint East-West Midlands Regional Organised Crime Unit investigation. 'This is Operation Tide, looking into Gerald Rafferty, a forty-nine-year-old sometime taxi driver running a county-lines operation out of Aston. Midlands Regional have bugged two of Rafferty's cars. He was recorded on a device in one of them saying the echo line's gone dry. That's what they call it. Mr Rafferty's second-in-command, Len Bolt, is also not answering calls or taking any orders on the line. You can hear Rafferty on the recordings, furious that a deal's fallen through.'

'What about the other areas?'

Gibson passed another report. 'North West have a source in Strangeways who's been saying the Copeland twins are back in business and have a new supplier but, again, something's messed up.'

Stephen and Ryan Copeland were notorious twins who had run a gangland empire from their base in Salford. They'd controlled much of the cocaine and heroin coming into Manchester before shooting a rival at an Express car wash. Stephen was locked up and Ryan had fled to Thailand.

'Stephen's controlling things from within prison, according to this source. Ryan's back in the country and coordinated a series of robberies to raise capital to buy into this shipment. Now they're somewhat up the creek.'

'We're not getting this intel?'

'Not directly. The Copelands aren't named as current objects of OCC interest.'

'Can we change that?'

'Yes. But the real concern is that, according to this source, the Copelands seem to be in contact with Danny Spiers.'

'You're joking.'

'When the load failed to turn up there was a series of calls between Spiers and the Copelands, trying to establish what had happened.'

The Spiers family had once included some of the most feared individuals in south London, with a sprawling portfolio of organised crime to their name. Back in the nineties Danny Spiers had begun stealing from lorries near his home in Essex, turned armed robber and drug dealer soon after. The last thing he'd been successfully prosecuted for was the kidnap and torture of a rival's family that left three people missing their thumbs. That was in 2006. He'd served five years of a ten-year sentence, left prison, retired from crime and moved into property development. Or so the story went. There was no doubt he was using criminal assets as start-up capital but there wasn't much anyone could do about it, apparently. Often, driving around London, Craik would pass one of Spiers's blocks of flats or identikit bars and sense a lurking violence beneath the banality. He'd been one of their first targets in Organised Crime but the hard evidence slipped through their hands. Craik regularly floated the idea of an investigation into his business empire but these things were a nightmare – a year filling your office with box files only to hit expensive lawyers and confused juries at the end of it. No one wanted white collar, and Price had been burned one too many times on Spiers.

'Spiers is an opportunist,' Craik said. 'If he and his associates are back in the game, someone's tempted them with an offer.'

'All old-school players,' Gibson said. 'All off the radar. All working with a mystery supplier. It's like they've been biding their time.'

'Get everything we can,' Craik said. 'Anyone who might have been buying wholesale off this cartel. Ensure the regional squads are looping us in.'

'What about this guy, Nick Belsey?'

'What about him?'

'Price has tasked us with getting information on him. Is it something you know about?'

'What kind of information did Price ask for?'

'Anything that might tell us what he's up to now. The chief wants a list of his contacts, up-to-date photos, recent addresses. The lot.'

Craik sighed. 'I used to work with Nick Belsey. Let me tell you one story about him. He crossed paths with Danny Spiers back in the day. Danny used to hang around a couple of the pupil-referral units, recruiting kids who'd been excluded from school to deal for him. Belsey couldn't get action from Drugs Squad, so he went to Child Protection and reported Danny Spiers as a paedophile. He wanted to send a message, so he hauled Danny in, got his home searched, pretended they'd found pictures. That was all we could do, but it told Spiers he wasn't untouchable, that we could play dirty too. It didn't stop Danny for good, but he never returned to the school gates. There's no way Belsey would work with these people.'

She didn't mention the rest. As revenge, Spiers had had three officers beaten up in a surprise attack, including a woman police officer who was throttled with a dog leash. It was another two years before police managed to send him down. He was surveillance savvy, forensics savvy, good at terrifying potential witnesses. One of the real untouchables.

'I can see your point,' Gibson said uncertainly.

'Do what you need to do. But chasing Belsey's a waste of time. What was Josie on before she went out?'

'I don't know. Seemed like she had some kind of break-through. Wanted to take a look at something.'

'Alone.'

'Yes.'

'Did she give any idea where she was going?

'No.'

'Was she going to tell me?'

'I'm sure.'

'Fuck's sake.'

Craik emailed Price, outlining the possible network of old-school criminals the importer was working with. She knew Price wasn't going to be happy when he saw these names, having spent a good decade of his life already chasing Spiers and his associates without much success. And even if he was up for reopening all this, there wasn't going to be much they could do before Christmas.

Summer's phone was now off. That gave Craik a bad feeling.

She went to Summer's desk and searched through the files she'd been studying that morning. Most came from Montgomery's investigation into High Class Fashion: photo-copies of endless shipping documents. On a bill of lading from April 2018 Summer had underlined the name given as UK contact: Mr Kenneth Bright, then circled the mobile number supplied. Craik dialled the number but it was disconnected.

She ran a search on the name, but nothing stood out online. So what was this breakthrough Summer had achieved?

As she was stacking the files back up, Craik knocked Summer's keyboard and the screen of her PC came on. It was the sign-in page of the police incident log. Craik typed in her own password then ran a search on Kenneth Bright.

Still nothing.

She sat back, aggravated, watching colleagues with boxes of Christmas crackers preparing for the office party. Then she looked again through Summer's notes. She hadn't circled the name, Craik thought, she'd circled the mobile number.

Craik went back into the incident log and ran a search on Bright's disconnected mobile number. This time she got a result. It was from last night.

Brent police had received a report of an attempted break-in at 3.15 a.m. Men had been seen trying to enter a property, masked-up, carrying bags and cases. It was called in by neighbours who owned the shop next door. By the time officers attended the address, it seemed the men had dispersed. Police then established the registered owner of the property, a company called London Commercial Property Solutions, who rented it out. The property company passed on their tenant's name and contact number: Mr K. Rain. Mr K. Rain shared the same mobile number as Kenneth Bright.

The property in question was on Harlesden High Street.

Flat A, 60 High Street. The Harlesden meeting, Craik thought. On Street View it looked like the flat was above a pub. Her guess: someone had used the mobile number for a limited period of time, a period in which they had set up the import shipment and begun renting this place. On 12 July they had used the address for a meeting. Maybe there was something there they wanted to show the ATO's *sistemista*.

It was 11.30 a.m. The Christmas lunch wasn't until one. Summer had been gone for two hours now. Two hours without contact. Craik went to the lockers and dug out her protection kit: handcuffs, retractable baton, Taser X26 and incapacitant spray. She was putting on her coat just as Ciaran Gibson appeared with a bottle of vodka and plastic shot glasses.

'Save me one,' she said.

FOURTEEN

Harlesden was busy, winter-grey, identical to a thousand other London high streets: pallid people going about their business with their heads down, moving between the pubs and fast food takeaways, past the mobile-unlocking shacks and currency exchanges.

Craik could see why it would be the perfect place to hide.

60 High Street was on the main junction, with a hardware store to its left and a TSB bank across the road to the right. The pub that had once occupied the ground floor had died, windows boarded up, paint scraped off. Its previous identity as the Royal Oak was preserved in ghost letters where the golden ones had been. Multiple layers of posters had been pasted over the boards: club nights; travelling circuses. The pub's own door was secured with a metal sheet and a notice: *No Entry. Dangerous Building.* But a worn black door between the pub and the hardware store had bells for flats A and B. Junk mail carpeted the front step along with takeaway boxes and empty cans but the entrance hadn't been sealed.

Craik pressed the bells just in case. No sound from inside. She walked around to the side of the building. Locked gates blocked access to some parking space and an external metal staircase. The first floor had brown cardboard stuck over every window. She couldn't see the windows on the floor above. The gates were liberally ornamented with coils of barbed wire. She returned to the front and checked the dates showing through the torn scraps of bill posters to determine how long the place had been closed down. It looked like years.

Best Deal Hardware, next door, spilled its contents onto the pavement: ladders, toilet brushes, mops and stacks of detergent. It was hard to see the doorway among the bargains. The abundance continued inside: kitchenware hanging from the ceiling, a single aisle to the checkout narrowed by Tupperware and tools. The woman behind the till looked like she was trapped within her own cornucopia of Chinese plastic. A child sat on her lap playing with an iPhone. Craik showed her badge.

'Did you report an attempted break-in last night at the property next door?'

The woman seemed unsurprised by Craik's arrival. She looked tired. 'That's right.'

'You live here?'

'Above the shop, yes.'

'Can you tell me what exactly happened?'

'We were woken at around three a.m. by some sounds at the back of the property. When I looked there were men with their faces covered. Scarves, masks. So I called the police.'

'How many men?'

'Three or four.'

'And what happened?'

'My husband shouted at them from the window. They went away then, I think. The police came very quickly.'

'Was there anything at all identifiable about these men?'

'I didn't see them very well.'

'Did your husband?'

'No.'

'Can you tell me exactly where they were?'

'Around the back stairs.'

'Did the police say anything?'

'No. Just that we'd scared them off. And if they came back we should call again.'

The child made complaining noises and she set him down on the floor.

'What do you know about the people who live in the flats above the pub?' Craik asked.

'I don't know anything.'

'Have you ever seen them?'

'No.'

'But your home has a view of the back.'

'Yes. I've never seen anything. Sometimes I hear people, late at night. I thought it was to do with converting the place.'

'Do you have any idea when they moved into the property?'

'No. I wasn't sure anyone had done.'

'How long has the pub been closed?'

The woman thought about this.

'At least since early last year. Maybe longer.'

'Has anything else struck you as odd or suspicious in that time?'

'Nothing. Like I say, they were hardly there.'

Craik was about to leave when she stopped.

'I don't suppose you've seen anyone else taking an interest in it this morning? A young woman?'

'I don't think so,' the shopkeeper said. 'I've been in here since six.'

Craik tried Summer's phone one last time, then walked back to number 60 and tried to imagine a meeting there. The building seemed to know something, to contain something, and she wanted to prise open its boarded mouths. Josie Summer would probably be at the Christmas party by now, she thought. They could talk about it. Craik wouldn't reprimand her for going alone, it was a brilliant connection made. Some praise could help rebuild a bridge. They could discuss how to get a warrant to see inside.

The lunch was at an ugly Sheraton hotel around the corner from HQ, in a ballroom with no dimmer switches, so half the room was dark and half under bright neon. Glittery letters across the back wall spelled 'Merry Xmas Organised Crime'. People were drinking hard.

'Here she is.'

There was a tipsy cheer when Craik arrived. She looked for Summer. Her mentee wasn't there. Sixty or so revellers occupied the long rows of tables, numbers boosted by civilian staff, plus guests of the unit, from lawyers and forensics to financial analysts. It was later than she'd realised and the meal was in the dying stages, so Craik had been spared that at least. They were at the end of most of the wine as well.

She asked around as someone poured her the dregs of a bottle. 'No sign of Josie?'

'Not seen her.'

'Maybe not her thing,' someone suggested. Gibson looked disappointed. The speeches began. Price spoke about the foundation of the unit, as he always did on occasions such as these: its mission, its challenges, as ever with reference to Scott Montgomery.

'We vowed to never again have vicious, highly organised criminals getting away with it like that. And this year we showed them what that means.' He was drunk. A mobile rang. Price made a joke about confiscating it, then someone else's went off.

'Fuck's sake.'

A few seconds later someone got up on stage, walked over to Price and whispered to him. Price looked initially annoyed, then, as the man continued to speak, the blood drained from his face. He stepped away from the microphone, looked across the room, met Craik's stare. She felt a wave of dread. Everyone had gone silent. Price approached the microphone, then seemed to think better of it and got down from the stage.

The room filled with murmurs. Craik heard Josie's name.

'What's going on?'

'Something's happened to Josie Summer.'

'What?'

Price walked towards her, tie askew. 'Have you heard?' he said.

'Something about Josie.'

'Apparently she's been shot.'

Craik felt faint. She wanted to sit down but fought the impulse. 'Where?'

'Leyton.'

'Leyton? What happened?'

'Are you sober enough to drive?' he said.

FIFTEEN

Price told Craik all he knew as they marched to her car. There'd been an attack next to a trading estate in Leyton. Summer was involved. It was serious, but he didn't have more than that. 'Do you know why she might have been there?' he asked.

'I have no idea whatsoever. She was looking at an address in Harlesden this morning.'

'Harlesden? That's miles away.'

'How bad is it? Is she alive?'

'I don't know.'

Price made calls as Craik drove, trying to glean more information as she sped through Islington into Hackney, out to London's north-east edge, where the city fragmented and the marshland showed through. Scrappy industry spread itself across a flat grey landscape, the sky suddenly vast and cold with distended clouds and Essex on the horizon.

Argall Avenue Trading Estate was a square kilometre of industrial units presenting windowless sides to the low terraces that surrounded it. Electricity wires sagged from pylons, and weeds grew wild around the rusted fence. They stopped at the outer cordon and were met by a keen young detective sergeant with a blond beard.

'You're from her unit?'

'That's right.'

'An ambulance has just taken her off. Didn't realise it was one of ours at first. Happened around two p.m. Does the silver Fiat belong to her?'

'Yes,' Craik said.

'It's on the other side of the trading estate, just outside the gates, but we'll be quicker if we cut through.'

He led them into a maze of varying structures, some brick, some built out of what looked like corrugated plastic. There were different zones: hangar-sized warehouses of builders' supplies, then smaller units incorporating everything from dry cleaners to recruitment companies. Workers stood outside their doorways, talking to police officers, breath steaming.

As they got to the far corner Craik could see scene-of-crime officers, just beyond the gate, erecting a white tent over a patch of road littered with paramedics' detritus: bandage packs and a scrap of shirt that had been cut away. Summer's blood bronzed the tarmac. She'd been shot less than ten metres from her car, which had both its doors open. On the far side of the road a high fence backed onto the railway.

The blond officer stopped at the inner cordon. Trains rattled past, shaking the razor wire and its rags of greying carrier bags. To the north were the jagged peaks of a metal-recycling centre, presided over by the arm of an excavator.

'Left her car, was shot almost immediately, it seems,' the officer said. 'No suggestion of an altercation. Haven't been able to find anyone who heard it yet. There's a lot of noise from the estate, as you can imagine – music, machinery. Any idea what the victim was doing here?'

'That's not clear at the moment,' Price said.

'Where did the ambulance take her?' Craik asked.

'Whipps Cross.'

'Is she alive?

The officer glanced at Craik's face, and she knew.

'I don't think so,' he said carefully. 'She was shot twice, once to the body, once to the head. No, she's not alive.'

When Price and Craik both fell silent, staring at the tent, the officer cleared his throat.

'You knew her well?'

'She was a close colleague,' Craik said.

'I'm sorry.'

'Any witnesses?' Price asked.

'None we've found yet. It's a pretty secluded corner.'

Craik looked around for security cameras but there were none. The sergeant, reading her thoughts, said, 'It's outside the range of the cameras, unfortunately. This side is only used for heavy goods vehicles. One of the men from the skip hire came through at midday to unlock the gates and saw her.'

He was respectful enough to leave them while his radio crackled and he walked away to speak into it. The day was darkening, sun setting prematurely behind the metal carcasses of the recycling centre.

'What was she doing here?' Price said.

'I don't know.'

'But that's the point. Why not? Why was she operating under the radar?' Then a look of comprehension dawned on Price's face. 'Because it's Belsey,' he said. 'She knew you and Nick Belsey ...'

'No.' Craik turned to the chief inspector. 'Because she was pissed off.'

'About what?'

'Us.'

'What do you mean?'

'She saw us touching hands.'

'When?'

'In the office last night.'

Price looked bemused. 'So she didn't keep you informed of her investigation? Because she was jealous?'

'Not jealous. Disappointed.'

Price shook his head. 'What was this visit you said she made to Harlesden?'

'She'd been at an address in Harlesden that connects to the import paperwork. Flat A, sixty High Street, above a derelict pub. It was rented under an alias. I took a look before the party, but there's nothing useful I could see from the outside. The place is abandoned. The flats as well, I think.'

'That's why you were late.'

'Yes.'

'What time was Josie there?'

'Around midday. We need to get the FBI informed, see if there might be anyone operating over here from abroad. I'm going to the hospital.'

But she didn't move. A second tent went up over Summer's car.

'Are you going to be okay?' Price said.

'I don't imagine I'm going to be *okay*. No.'

'We'll get them, Kirsty.'

'I know.'

'It's not your fault.'

'It's quite clearly my fault.'

SIXTEEN

Whipps Cross was ten minutes further east, its Victorian bricks overlooking Epping Forest and Hollow Ponds.

Craik rushed through the ground floor of the hospital, following signs for the mortuary to a basement level where the lighting was less urgent and original tiles remained on the walls. Double doors led into the realm of the dead.

Homicide officers already crowded the waiting area. Craik was told that the body was currently being examined by a forensic pathologist. When she explained her connection to the deceased, they radioed up the chain of command, got authorisation and let her through to the post-mortem examination room.

It was much like every other she'd been in: bright, chemically scented. But stepping inside had never felt personal before. Summer's corpse was covered, her necklace and earrings in a dish beside her. The pathologist was a middle-aged man with silver-framed glasses and a hairless, antiseptic air. He had taken an initial look and was preparing his tools for the next round, content for Craik to watch from the sidelines.

'Seen things like this before?' he asked, handing Craik protective coverings.

'That depends what it is.'

'I don't know how much you've been told. She was shot

twice, once to the chest, once to the centre of the forehead. The bullet from the head shot is lodged in her skull. I was about to remove it.'

'Could you let me see her first?'

He removed the sheet. Craik forced herself not to recoil. The sight was awful, but not as grotesque as she'd been braced for. Summer's hair had been shaved off, which was somehow more shocking than the wounds, which were disarmingly neat, one to the right of the breastbone, one to the centre of the forehead. They were still vivid red, with a darkened aureole of burned powder meaning the killer had been close when they fired. Craik fought a sense of unreality. She wasn't used to corpses that hadn't been washed, hadn't had time to grey.

'They were close to her,' Craik said.

'Less than a foot away,' the pathologist said.

'You think the chest was first?'

'I'm sure.'

'Any signs of a struggle?'

'Hands and nails are clean, from what I've seen. No scratches.'

'They took her by surprise.'

'Perhaps.'

'Anything you can say about the shot to the head?'

'Again, very close range. I'd assume the killer was standing over her when they fired. There's an exit wound at the back of the skull, but ricochet off the ground drove the bullet back in.'

'They really wanted to make sure,' Craik said.

'That's one interpretation.' He drew his mask up and selected a handsaw. 'You're welcome to stay if you want, but I wouldn't recommend it.'

Price was with the Homicide officers when she emerged. He broke away to speak to her. 'Anything I need to see right now?'

'Not right now.'

'Two shots, is that correct?'

'Chest and head. No struggle.'

'An execution.'

'Looks like it.'

'There's a canteen on the ground floor. I'll be there in five.'

The canteen was filled with those who wouldn't be going home for Christmas. Several who might not be going home after that, it appeared. Garish festive decorations spun on threads Blu-tacked to the ceiling. It was just off a busy corridor, lifts pinging and trolley wheels rattling, and there was a sense of taking your rest on the banks of the dying. Craik got a coffee, poured in too much sugar, took a table beside a woman on a drip. She ignored the 'no mobile phones' sign, called into the office.

Obiri answered. 'What happened?'

'She's dead. Shot. The rest isn't clear. Who's with you?'

'Everyone's here. We're waiting for Homicide to get in touch.'

'We need to establish why she was in Leyton. There's a pile of paperwork on her desk. Look for any company that might connect to Argall Avenue Trading Estate. I want a full list, who's renting each unit.'

'Okay.'

'Before she went there, Josie was looking at an address in Harlesden – Flat A, sixty High Street. It may have been used as part of a trafficking operation. The building used to house the Royal Oak pub. It's now owned by a company called London Commercial Property Solutions. See if anyone can get hold of them, find out who was renting.'

'We're on it.'

'I'll coordinate with Homicide,' she said to Obiri. 'Let me know as soon as you have anything.'

She called Lawrence. 'Something terrible's happened. A colleague's been killed.'

There was a moment as Lawrence processed this, and she felt him calculating the acceptable limits of indignation. 'Are you okay?' he said.

'I'm just about okay. But I'm going to need to stay here.'

'Oh, for Christ's sake,' he muttered, very quietly.

'Lawrence?'

'We have everything prepared. My parents are incredibly excited.'

Craik searched for words. Bizarrely, what she found herself saying was 'Perhaps I can get there for Christmas Eve.' She could hear him breathing deeply.

'Prioritise what you need to prioritise,' he said.

The chief inspector emerged from the lifts. Craik lifted a hand as she hung up. Price sat down, stared at her coffee. 'Is it drinkable?'

'I don't know. Any news?'

'Nothing yet. You said you have possible companies used in the importation of the cocaine. What about after that? Who do they move it to? They must be working with people.'

'They use subsidiary gangs: Stephen Copeland, Danny Spiers. I sent you an email. They're all people who've been lying low, licking their wounds since the foreign crews crashed in. People we took our eye off.'

'Danny fucking Spiers.' Price groaned, staring at a dangling cardboard angel. 'Suggests the importers might be old-school too.'

'Right.'

'Figure out what you need and let me know. I'll take this to the bosses. I tried to call Scott Montgomery but there's no answer. I've called the nursing company that looks after him, in case they can get him to string a sentence together, but I wouldn't pin too much hope on it.'

The lifts pinged and Craik saw the Homicide team emerge. Price went to talk to them, and when he returned, he looked uncertain.

'Apparently they've just got someone for it,' he said.

'Who?'

'Some kid, nineteen years old.'

The Incident Room was a work in progress, a large office at the back of Leyton Custody Centre from which the investigation was being coordinated. The centre was new and huge. It looked like a leisure centre but contained thirty cells, built after they'd closed all the traditional police stations and realised they didn't have anywhere to take arrestees. A big-box Asda of policing on a patch of neglected wasteground.

When Craik explained who she was, she was led through to the white-walled room at the back where people were setting up tables and plugging in computers. The senior investigating officer was DI Greg Hannaway, whom Craik knew from her work on gangs in north-east London. Classic Homicide: arrogant, well-dressed, his silvering hair parted with a flourish. He'd asked her out on a couple of occasions, offering what he called 'steam-releasing drinks'. Homicide were notorious philanderers, both the men and the women. There was a logic to it, Craik sensed. But he did the job well, took it seriously, regardless of the victim, which was her test of character.

'Kirsty. Heard she's a colleague of yours.'

'That's right.'

'So sorry. Come through. Your chief inspector thinks this could be related to what you were working on.'

'Yes.'

'You know we've just arrested someone?'

'I was told. I'm curious about that.'

'He's being processed, but I wanted to chat to you first.'

'Who is he?'

'A gun for hire, so to speak. That's my reading. An unfortunate individual with a history of being used for other people's dirty work. My suspicion is that our man wasn't just walking around aimlessly, armed with a pistol, and happened upon Detective Constable Jocelyn Summer. Question is, who sent him and who gave him the gun?'

'And how they converged.'

'Right.'

Hannaway found a room at the side, bare but for a water-cooler and a locked cupboard. He brought in chairs. 'Coffee?'

'I'm okay, thanks.'

'Let me grab one.'

He came back a minute later, set his polystyrene cup on the floor, clicked a pen. 'So, the lad we're holding is Joshua Parish, nineteen years old, based nearby in south Tottenham. Like I say, he's well known to local police: dealing, possession of knives, car theft. Gang stuff. On CCTV you can see him sprinting south along Lea Bridge Road some time after she was killed. Got picked up half an hour later on Hackney marshes. He'd dumped a lot of his clothes near the river, all covered in blood.'

'Which gangs does he connect to?' she asked.

'Mostly the Stone Hill Boys. More recently Block 9, who usually stick to NE11. Obviously they're used as foot soldiers by the bigger dealers. I know you just put some nasty people away. Wondered if this could connect to that.'

'I don't think it's revenge. In the last couple of days we've been looking into an individual shipping cocaine from Mexico. It's very much a live operation. Highly sensitive.'

'Who are they?'

'We don't know.'

Hannaway paused with his pen over the pad. Craik told him about the flat in Harlesden. 'Josie Summer was there at around midday by my estimation.'

'That's interesting. Why did she then travel to Argall Avenue?'

'It's not clear. I'm curious about the businesses that operate there.'

'So far, it seems she didn't go into any of them.'

'Maybe she never got the chance.'

'Maybe. We estimate she was in the area approximately twenty minutes before it happened. So she must have been doing something.'

'Lured somehow?'

'Possibly. She didn't call in?'

'No.'

This troubled Hannaway. There was a rapid flicking of pen against notepad. 'That's unorthodox.'

'It is, but we work quite independently sometimes.'

He nodded, unconvinced. 'She hadn't been on the unit long.'

'A year.'

'Uncomfortable question, Kirsty, but did you have any concerns about her? Any connections you think we should look into?'

'No. She was a top detective.'

'Just being independent.'

'We know the Mexicans have contacts over here. They may have been involved in the shooting of Trevor Hart a couple of days ago. You need to liaise with the FBI officers on Operation Flyway.'

'You think?'

'It's something you need to be aware of. Was there anything among her possessions that might give us any clue why she went there?'

'We haven't had a chance to do a full check of anything yet. I know her phone was gone.'

'Really? I haven't been told that.'

'Yes. Possible that her pockets had been rifled.'

'Other valuables taken?'

'Not as far as I'm aware.'

'Notebook?'

'Let's have a look.'

He led her to the evidence room and unlocked it. The possessions found on Summer's person were bagged up, arranged on a table: pens, keys, wallet. At the end of the row was her notebook.

Hannaway held out a box of gloves and undid the seal on the evidence bag while Craik put them on. She removed the notebook and opened it. Old entries, routine stuff, all crossed through. Then one fresh entry, dated today.

It was a sketch of a road junction. She'd marked in a camera and drawn a cone out from it to represent coverage. It was Harlesden. In cramped handwriting beneath it, Summer had written: *Micro-CN4*.

'Mean anything?' Hannaway asked.

'This is the make of a CCTV camera,' Craik said. Summer had written down the settings for a CCTV system, then a time and date: 12 July, 1–3 p.m. The date of the *el jefe* meeting. At the very bottom she'd noted the make of the flash drive used to transfer footage.

'She got something,' Craik said. 'Transferred onto a USB.'

'Right.'

'Has any USB stick been found?'

Hannaway checked the evidence log and then the bags themselves. 'Nothing here.' He took the notebook, studied the notes, frowning. 'She got footage from July?'

'We think there was a meeting at the Harlesden flat on that day.'

'Where keeps footage that long?'

Craik looked at the sketch, then a map of Harlesden High Street on her phone. 'Banks,' she said.

SEVENTEEN

In the winter darkness, Harlesden was cold and hard, oblivious to its role in a young police officer's death. It felt as if this news would struggle to penetrate the ongoing business of survival. The white light of Chicken Cottage bleached the pavement; Alishba Food and Wine remained open; Silvertime Amusements twinkled. The corpse of the pub looked even more impenetrable, streetlight glaring dully off its protective metal, eyeless sockets of its windows staring out. The TSB sat across the road from it, lights still on. Craik saw the camera covering the entrance, plus two ATMs at the side, both with pinhole cameras, both facing across the road to number 60.

The bank displayed a 'closed' sign, but a woman was visible, hoovering beneath paper chains. Craik knocked, pressed her warrant card against the glass. The woman squinted at it, then disappeared into the back and returned with a balding man wearing a Christmas jumper over his shirt and tie.

'Another?' he said, as he unlocked the door. He looked respectful but inconvenienced. His one word gave Craik her first sense of progress.

'Yes. Can I confirm that my colleague, Detective Constable Jocelyn Summer, visited you earlier today?'

'That's correct.'

'Did she download security footage while here?'

'Yes. Why?'

'The situation's become considerably more serious. Detective Constable Jocelyn Summer was killed a few hours ago, and there's a possibility that her death connects to what she was investigating.'

The bank manager looked horrified. 'She's dead?'

'She was shot at approximately midday today in Leyton.'

'Right ... I see.'

'She never had a chance to tell us what happened when she visited here, so I'd appreciate if you could share exactly what she saw.'

'Of course. Come in. What is this in connection to? She only said organised crime.'

'That's right. I can't tell you much else right now.'

The manager locked the door again behind Craik, led her through, past adverts for mortgages and low-interest loans, to a secure staff door into a back office. Inside were several filing cabinets, a PC and a separate cupboard containing a hard drive and monitor exclusively for CCTV. The manager wheeled a chair in front of the monitor, brought his own from behind the desk. He talked her through Summer's visit. She had arrived at the bank at approximately 11 a.m., he said. She asked to see any security footage from 12 July.

'And you have it?'

'Yes, archived. But we can access that remotely.'

The manager set up the recording again. There were six cameras in total, two covering the front and back of the building, two internal, one for each of the cash machines.

'Was there a particular camera she was interested in?'

'This one, I think. The furthest cash machine.'

The manager expanded the window. It was a fish-eye lens,

installed to film whoever was using the machine and any potential shoulder surfers. The angle got the road in front and a fraction of the opposite pavement. You could just see the side gate of number 60. The quality was poor.

'What time frame did she ask for?'

'A window of two hours. Twelve thirty to two thirty.'

'How much did she watch?'

'Not more than ten minutes or so.'

'Then what happened?'

'She sped through the rest and downloaded the footage.'

'Onto a USB?'

'Yes.'

'Can you remember what the USB looked like?'

'It was black, I think. With a red cap. I didn't notice more than that.'

'Did she see something?'

'I think so.'

Craik checked the footage from the camera in question. Cars came and went, none very visible. Her excitement dissipated into a familiar sense of the trawl to be done. Whatever Summer had seen, it wasn't evident to her.

'Did she make any calls?' Craik asked.

'No.'

'Checks on any licence plates?'

'Not while here.'

'Did you get any idea of where she was going next?'

'None at all.'

'But you think she saw something.'

'That was certainly the impression I got.'

Craik copied the footage onto her own USB, then emailed it to herself and two of her colleagues to be on the safe side. She told the bank manager he'd need to wait to speak to Homicide, who would be on their way very shortly. Then she crossed the road to the shell of the Royal Oak and evaluated access.

Best Deal Hardware remained open, the same woman behind the till. Craik bought a foldable ladder and a pair of wire cutters. She took them to the pub's side gate. The ladder got her to the top easily. Clearing the barbed wire was trickier, but after a few minutes she was able to remove a section, leaving a gap wide enough for her to climb over. She balanced precariously at the top of the gate for a second before swinging her other leg over and dropping hard, down into a puddle of filthy water. But she was in.

The back stairs were icy. They led up, past a first-floor window obscured by cardboard, to a door on the second floor. Beside it was a pane of dirty glass that afforded a view into a small kitchen with bare shelves and peeling wallpaper. The door was locked. The window was single-glazed and already cracked in one corner.

Police need a warrant to enter premises unless a delay in obtaining one would be likely to defeat the ends of justice. That would do, Craik thought, as she removed her baton and smashed the glass. An alarm went off. She hadn't expected it, but she should have done, Craik thought, if the place still contained something sensitive. She blocked her ears with tissue, then cleared the remaining glass and climbed through.

The place stank of mould and neglect. She put her gloves on, took out her spray. The kitchen was the size of a cupboard, with a small fridge and a single-ring electric stove. But no one had used these for a long time. The fridge was unplugged and empty, the food stains on the cooker prehistoric. Dust and cobwebs lay thick on every surface. Next to the kitchen was a room only slightly bigger, with a single mattress on the floor and plastic hangers in a broken cupboard. But someone had been in recently. Craik studied the faintest disturbance of dirt on the floor, leading to the door out.

She followed it to a landing with a toilet at one end and stairs at the other. The toilet was bare and grimy: no soap or loo roll or toothbrush. Craik went to the stairs.

From here she could smell pub. She followed the stairs down to a ground floor, with signs for male and female toilets and a third door marked: *Back to the Bar.* At some point this door had been locked, but the locking mechanism had been forced through the wood of the frame and now the door swung freely.

Craik stepped in.

The ceiling of the main bar had collapsed, a heart-stopping waterfall of plasterwork, wooden struts and wiring frozen in mid-air. Plaster dust had coated the bar, rendering it ghostly white. Framed photographs of old Harlesden lay on the floor. Chairs and tables had been stacked to the side to make room for kegs and crates of empties. The alarm blinked blue beside a side door to the street. On the floor, next to this entrance, were boxes of surgical gloves, shoe covers and disposable overalls with hoods. Craik knew at once there wouldn't be a print in the place.

But the shoe covers hadn't prevented vague, anonymous steps being preserved, leading behind the bar itself. The door down to the cellar was protected by new insulation foam. Craik looked at the kegs again and wondered why someone had cleared out the cellar.

She stepped behind the bar to the cellar door. The stairs on the other side were narrow and uneven. She used the light from her phone as she descended slowly.

The sight took her breath.

The basement was filled with tall glass cylinders with bowls at the bottom like fish tanks. Alongside them were tubes held in clamps, and a lot of shining stainless steel. Metal and glass contraptions filled the space from floor to ceiling. An extractor fan had been rigged up. There were tubs of chemicals at the side, then a mound of bin bags. Craik slit one open and empty bottles for skin cream, toner and botulinum toxin spilled out.

They were trying to get in to retrieve their equipment. That was her theory with regard to the attempted break-in. They didn't want to be seen entering from the front. Something had made them paranoid: maybe the shooting of Trevor Hart, maybe the missing delivery. They thought police might be on to them and they needed to be as discreet as possible as they removed the evidence.

Sirens were now audible over the alarm, pulling up outside. Craik had a final look around, took some photos on her phone. She could hear police in the building, coming down the stairs, tracing her own route.

'Hello?' an officer called.

When she appeared behind the bar they pulled their Tasers. Craik showed her badge.

'No one else comes in the building,' she said. 'We need a full forensics team here immediately.'

EIGHTEEN

The Organised Crime team had left the Christmas party and gone straight back to the office, shaken. Now they were waiting for instructions. They watched Craik when she arrived. Ciaran Gibson sat limply; Jackie Weller gripped a packet of cigarettes; Obiri stood at the side, as if on guard.

Craik took a seat at Summer's desk. She didn't touch anything. This was a crime scene, she felt sure, the paperwork a labyrinth with a monster at its heart. 'Has anyone spoken to her family?' she asked.

'Price is with them now.'

Weller's voice was hoarse. Gibson blinked, red-eyed. Craik considered sending him home but that wasn't going to be a favour. 'Any more on Leyton?'

'The timing suggests she must have driven directly,' Weller said. 'We've got a list of businesses on the trading estate, seventy-three separate companies in total. We're starting to compile names of staff, figure out who was present.'

'The Harlesden pub,' Gibson said. 'I tried to contact the company that owns it, but they're based abroad and not currently answering. They own a lot of derelict properties, and have been in multiple disputes over planning permission. Three tenants have claimed for disrepair in the last couple of years. I'll keep chasing, but whoever chose them as landlord did it for a reason.

Forensics are there now, I believe. Homicide are arranging door-to-doors around Harlesden High Street.'

'Take a look at this.' Craik brought up the pictures of the lab on her phone, handed it to Gibson. The team gathered around. 'This is in the basement of the pub.'

'A fucking lab,' Gibson said.

'I think it's for extraction,' Craik said. 'I think they're moving the cocaine in liquid form.'

Obiri peered closely. 'That would confirm my suspicions.'

'Go on,' Craik said.

The tech specialist brought his MacBook over and loaded up the chemical analysis of the cocaine being distributed in the UK. He touched his pen to one of the rows in the table of data. 'Botulinum toxin is a protein that prevents the release of a neurotransmitter in the muscles. Causes paralysis. It's what they use in Botox.'

'That's what I figured.'

'It's showing microscopically in the coke itself. UK end only. Along with a bunch of other micro-traces of chemicals used in beauty treatments. So I think you're right. The drugs aren't hidden among the cargo – they're not swapped for the original products. They're inside them, dissolved.'

Craik had seen reports about this technique, but not many. The principle was simple: liquids evaporate, cocaine doesn't. Last year, Dutch police seized a couple of hundred T-shirts from Colombia that had been soaked in liquid cocaine. The receiver just had to know how to reverse the process. In Slovenia, they'd found a makeshift lab for extracting coke from Plexiglas, melting away the plastic using petrol and acetone. But it was difficult, and generated a lot of residue. Craik's syndicate seemed to have devised a neater solution.

She studied the photos again and felt the heat of ingenuity.

Of the creativity that arises when several million pounds is up for grabs. 'Can we be positive that's what the equipment is for?' she asked.

'These are evaporator systems,' Obiri said. 'They've got at least seven set up here, each with a section for heating, a section for collecting the waste water, one for the cocaine that's left at the end. I'm positive.'

Craik plugged in her USB and they watched the cash-machine footage on her computer. 'This is from the bank across the road, from July the twelfth when we believe there was a meeting at the property attended by whoever was running the UK end of this import operation. I think the meeting might have involved instructions for how to set up the lab. Josie seems to have got something from this footage, a lead to an individual, perhaps, but I've no idea what it was. It's going to be a trawl.'

Her colleagues leaned closer to the screen, studying the cars coming and going.

'She can't have run checks on all these vehicles,' Gibson said.

'I don't think she ran checks on any. I think she saw something.'

Craik tried to call Perez but the Mexican investigator's phone was off. She left a message asking her to call back urgently. Gibson began working through the cash-machine footage. Obiri opened an email and passed his MacBook back to Craik.

'Gangs Unit have sent this.' It was a mugshot of Joshua Parish from a couple of years ago; a boy acting as a man, with the usual combination of hostility and hopelessness in his eyes. 'Plenty of history.'

'Any idea what he's said so far?'

'Not much, by all accounts. According to Gangs, he was arrested in 2015 for carrying a knife, sent to Feltham a year later for involvement in the stabbing of a sixteen-year-old a kilometre or so away from Summer's crime scene. Sentenced on a joint enterprise charge, released eighteen months ago. Seems to have been lying low since then. Hasn't crossed the police radar.'

'It's like someone had been preserving him for this.'

'That's an interesting way of seeing it.'

Craik cleared the whiteboard. 'These are the gangs we believe had a connection with the person we were investigating, so start here. We know they all have access to firearms, all have been willing to kill or maim to protect their interests in the past.'

She drew up the speculative network of criminals buying from this new syndicate: Spiers, Copelands, Rafferty. Then she drew arrows up to a question mark at the top: the boss, *el jefe*. 'Someone guaranteed quantity and quality. They were able to reassure the Mexicans that this import route remained stable even after the shooting of Scott Montgomery, who was on to them. They're able to control a middle man or middle men sufficiently well to ensure they never have to reveal themselves to their buyers. I want people brought in. See about the Copelands and these robberies. Contact North West Regional and see if they can find a pretext to get them into an interview room.'

'Homicide are asking about someone called Nick Belsey,' Weller said.

'What are they saying?'

'Former police officer, may have been in contact with Joshua Parish. You come up as having worked with him.'

'That's right.'

Weller paused, assessed Craik's aggressive tone.

'Sounds like the FBI have connected Belsey to some pretty nasty players. If he didn't know Parish personally he'll certainly have connections to people in Parish's circle. Might have given the instruction to kill Josie before she got too close. It's an avenue of enquiry. We've been compiling lists of acquaintances.

He's certainly chequered, shall we say? I wondered if you had any suggestions.'

'My suggestion is to focus on the names I wrote up. Belsey's not the man we're looking for.'

'Seemed more complicated than that.'

'Do what you need to do. But look for concrete connections, not speculative ones.'

Craik ignored a message from Fraser Dunlop, the *Sun* journalist. She tried Perez again and this time got through.

'I heard about what happened,' Perez said. 'I'm sorry.'

The Mexican investigator sounded neither shocked nor intimidated. Craik imagined she had been on calls like this before.

'There's a possibility this importer is transferring the cocaine in liquid form. The Cancún safe house,' Craik said. 'Could it have been a place where they dissolved it before transportation to the airport?'

Perez considered this. 'What makes you say liquid?' she asked, after a moment. Craik ran her through the story so far, including the property in Harlesden. She explained about the evaporator system, said they'd send through the pictures.

'That sounds a strong possibility,' Perez said. 'We've looked into Farmaco Mondiales, and some people in the company have connections with ATO members. We know ATO have experimented with transporting liquid cocaine before.'

'I believe this property is where the meeting was held in July. The woman who was shot, Josie Summer, had just visited it.'

'I see. There is a suspect arrested, no?'

'There's a suspect. Maybe instructed to do the job. What I don't understand is why Josie went to the area where she was killed. Has Leyton come up in your investigation? Or an industrial park called Argall Avenue Trading Estate?'

'No. I don't know those names.'

'I'll send through what we've got. We're tracing connections for the man arrested. And I'm working on Summer's actions after collecting the footage. Hopefully something will give us an idea of what happened. People are still talking about Nick Belsey. Do you have more intelligence? I remain concerned that this is an unproductive tangent.'

'He has been on the move. That's all we know. Something is going on. It looks like he may be back in Europe.'

'Really?'

'I'll keep you updated. Inspector Craik ...' Perez paused. It was the first time Craik had noticed the investigator seeming hesitant or uncertain. 'Inspector Craik, I don't know you very well, but I want to say ... be careful. You understand, I'm sure.'

'I understand.'

'We make a decision as to where to go in an investigation, what risks are involved, and what we are willing to risk. Do you have a family?'

'Not really.'

'Well, you have a future. I want us to get to the bottom of this, but when an organised group decides the truth must not come out, when they have successfully established the upper hand, it is hard and dangerous. I do not believe in waste, I believe in strategy and calculation. That means deciding what to pursue when.'

'I'm not going to be intimidated out of doing my job.'

'Of course. But I am conscious that we may have set you on this particular path.'

'I appreciate your concern.'

'Please keep in touch.'

Craik promised she would and ended the call. Belsey in Europe, she thought. On the move. What did that mean?

Gibson came over. 'Bit of a result on the bank CCTV. Half result.'

'What is it?'

'A car parks up across the road just after twelve thirty. It has a false registration.'

'Show me.'

They went back to his PC, where he played the bank's security footage at one-eighth speed. At 12.38 p.m., a black saloon car inched into view, completed a reverse park manoeuvre, stopped beside the derelict pub. As it angled itself into the parking space you caught its front licence plate for a few seconds. Glare off the windscreen meant you couldn't see the driver. It parked with its nose jutting into the shot.

'I can't even see what make that is,' Craik said.

'Pretty sure it's either an Audi A8 or an S-class Merc, but that licence plate belongs to a school minibus in Stirling. No report that the originals have been stolen so I assume these are cloned.'

Cloned plates were usually used for a stolen vehicle, or to evade speeding fines. They could be put on, taken off, used if you knew the vehicle was going to be involved in criminal activity.

'Any shots of the driver?'

'Nothing. I've checked.' He skipped forward to 1.45 p.m. and showed her the same car driving off. You didn't even see the windscreen this time.

So what did Summer see? It was maddening. Craik wanted to grab the monitor and re-angle it. She felt sure this was the individual they were after, the one so important it had got Summer killed. Surely not Belsey. Gibson saw her frustration.

'I've had a look. There are two thousand seven hundred black Audi A8s licensed in the UK. Even more Mercs.'

'Have you checked if these fake plates have been recorded in connection with anything else?'

'There's nothing on the system.'

Craik watched the manoeuvre again. 'Zoom in,' she said, after a moment.

'What?'

'Look at the bodywork.'

Gibson enlarged the image. Beneath the handle of the left-hand passenger door, someone had begun to scratch a horizontal line. It stopped, then continued for sixty centimetres or so, undulating across the back door to above the rear wheel where they'd made a couple of vertical marks.

'It's been keyed,' Gibson said.

'Right.'

'You think Josie noticed that?'

'I don't see what else it might have been.'

A combination of scratches, like a signature. Distinctive, with a sense of having been done in anger: not one idle line but a brief attack on the car. On *this* car, by someone who didn't want to linger over their action. An identifying detail, but one that would have been erased by now, she felt sure. Owners of flash cars didn't go around with scratched bodywork for six months. Not when they were trying to move incognito. What that did mean, however, was that it was most likely scratched in the days immediately preceding the footage.

'What can we do with this?' Gibson asked.

'It might tell us something in itself. Maybe the driver's someone who attracts hostility. Parked carelessly, or pissed his neighbours off.'

'Okay.'

'Cross-check with records of vandalism in the preceding days, just in case. An insurance claim would need a crime reference number.'

'Would they report it? Someone using false plates?'

'It's worth a try.'

Craik studied it again. It was just possible that Summer might have recognised the car. Working on the principle that the vandalism was fresh, it would have to be something she'd come across around the same time. What had Summer been working on in July? Where had she been?

Craik clicked back through the unit calendar. The week preceding 12 July, Summer had been working on Goldmine. She'd gone to liaise with the surveillance units watching a couple of other gangs. It was possible she saw something with them, maybe off footage they collected. Nothing on the Friday, as she'd been arranging a community outreach event. That event occupied the first half of Saturday, and then Saturday afternoon she'd met with police translators, who'd been transcribing the tangle of dialects their phone taps had accumulated. Unlikely that it had brought her into conjunction with actual criminals but it would need to be checked out.

Price arrived as Craik began to gather contact details, conscious of how this was clutching at straws, but also knowing that this was what you did: turned every stone. Part of investigation, part of grief. The chief inspector shook his head as he came in.

'That was awful,' he said. He went to the plastic Christmas tree, unwrapped a bottle of Scotch and poured a generous measure into his coffee mug. When the whisky appeared to have calmed him, Craik talked through developments. She showed him the cash-machine footage, then the scratch.

'Okay,' Price said. 'This seems very speculative.'

'This is what we've got.'

'So Josie Summer saw this car, which had been keyed. Then what? Why did she go to Leyton?'

'I don't know.'

'We need to know. Keep looking.'

Gibson came back and announced that no similar vandalism had been reported to cars of those makes in the days either side of the meeting. So that was one potential avenue closed off.

'It's on the news,' someone said.

They switched on the office TV in time to see Summer's face.

A police detective from Scotland Yard's elite Organised Crime Command was found murdered today near a trading estate in east London ...

Shots of the tents and the trading estate; Hannaway appealing for information. They cut back to a picture of Summer from the community event she'd helped organise, beaming beside a young woman with an award. The sign behind her said *Inspire 2 Aspire*. It was an uncharacteristic photo, Craik thought. It didn't do justice to her brilliance. But she was glad they'd found one.

When it was over everyone remained staring at the TV for a moment, then went back into action with renewed vigour. At 8 p.m., Craik gave herself a break. She could feel her brain closing down. She walked to the river, head filled with dead ends.

When she got to the embankment she breathed, then brought up the news story on her phone, and looked at Summer's face from the event photo. It only reinforced the sense of how much had been lost. Craik hadn't attended the event, but Price had told her how good Summer had been, even defusing tensions when the chief inspector found his phone had been stolen by one of the less reformed of the invitees. Price had wanted to close the whole thing down and Josie had talked him round. She had a human touch as well as an eye for details. Craik thought of Perez's response: *I do not believe in waste.* That was the word for it: total waste, of a woman who would have been one of the Met's top detectives. There was no stepping back for herself now, Craik knew. She was prepared to risk everything to get justice.

As she was heading back into the office she passed Jackie Weller, smoking on the pavement. Weller considered her through a cloud of Lambert and Butler.

'Ma'am.'

'Yes?'

'We've had a tip-off that Nick Belsey ordered Summer's killing.'

Craik stopped. 'Tip-off from who?'

'Someone called it in.'

'People can call anything in.'

'This is someone who might know, apparently.'

'Any ID?'

'Protected. The report came through Criminal Intelligence.'

'I want to see it.'

Weller flicked away her cigarette and they returned to the office. The report had come in ten minutes ago, from DS Mark Regus in the National Criminal Intelligence Service: anonymised human intelligence source; contacted the police on a direct line, named Nick Belsey as the individual responsible for the shooting of Josie Summer.

The National Criminal Intelligence office was on the top floor of their own building. Craik walked straight in.

'Who is this from?' she said, dropping the report on Regus's desk. She'd liaised with Regus before. He was a reasonable detective, with the air of an accountant about him, but not the brightest spark in the building.

'It's not for me to release that,' Regus said.

'Come on, Mark. I worked with the victim every day for the last twelve months. I was just standing in a pathology lab staring at her corpse. Don't even try to fuck about.'

156

He took a breath, searched his papers. 'A guy called Eric Jackson.'

'Eric?' The name dropped into the scenario with an air of absurdity. Craik almost felt like laughing. 'And why do we think he's given this information, exactly?'

'For a reward maybe?' Regus said defensively.

'Let me see the details.'

According to their intelligence database, Eric Jackson had contacted a detective sergeant in Special Branch – Tony Cox – who had handled Eric as a source during his time in Southwark CID and still occasionally received intelligence from him in return for authorised payments.

In his call to Cox, Eric claimed to have spoken to someone who had put Belsey in touch with Joshua Parish. According to this middle man, Belsey's words were: *I need to nip something in the bud.* The hit apparently cost him fifty grand.

'You know this is most likely to be total bullshit,' Craik said.

'You haven't complained about using Eric Jackson's intel in the past.'

'Like what?'

'On the gangs you've been rolling up. Where do you think half the information we've supplied you has come from?'

Craik went back down to her own desk and brought up Eric's file on the system. She remembered the fear in his face the previous day: *There's no joy for you here.* Who did he connect to?

She searched back through a long record of a criminal life, but also a charmed life. Arrests were rare, which meant those that did occur stood out. Like selling five grams of cocaine to an undercover officer back in January 2018. That was careless, not his style.

Craik checked the date again, as something unnerving began

to connect. Then, feeling lightheaded, she went to Price's office and knocked. 'Can I have a moment?'

'Of course.'

She closed the door behind her.

'Eric Jackson's just given a tip-off that Belsey ordered Josie's killing'

'I saw,' Price said cautiously. 'What do you make of that?'

'It's a load of crap. He's dangerous. I was looking at his file. Eric Jackson was arrested the day before Scott Montgomery's shooting. Records suggest he was released in return for intelligence. You said Montgomery had just got a tip-off, the one that lured him to where he was shot. I think Eric Jackson let himself be arrested so he could be put in touch with Montgomery.'

Price looked over the records.

'You know this Jackson guy?' Price said.

'All too well,' she said. Then Craik saw what he was thinking.

'Via Belsey?' Price said. 'Did he introduce you?'

'Originally.'

'So if he's just come to us suggesting Belsey is indeed involved with this importing business, we should probably listen to him.'

'It's clear that Eric Jackson's not to be trusted. That he makes tip-offs under instruction.'

'From who?'

'The boss. The man we're looking for.'

'How long are we going to keep ignoring the name Nick Belsey?'

'You know it's not Belsey. Someone's setting him up.'

'*You* seem to know it's not him. I know our job is to follow evidence, and right now there's a lot pointing in his direction. I hate to say it, Kirsty, but you're being blinded by emotions.'

'You want it to be him.'

Price slammed the desk. 'I want to stop any more officers getting killed. Where was Belsey at this time?' He jabbed at Montgomery's old paperwork.

'I'm not sure,' Craik said, although she was wondering if it was when they worked together in Hampstead.

'Find out. Find out where he is now.'

She walked back to her desk, memories cascading: Belsey in Hampstead; Belsey when she first met him in Borough, her first day at the station, assigned him as a mentor, and wondering why people laughed at that. Waking up beside Belsey, seeing he was already awake, watching her, amused. Running home with him through the rain, drunk, 4 a.m., being stopped by the police.

Craik locked herself into a cubicle. She emailed Belsey a final time.

Nick, I don't know where you are or what you're doing ... And she tried to outline the situation. If it involved something he knew about, maybe he could help. If it didn't, he needed to get help himself. She gave him everything she had, and was glad of it, from the ATO and their missing cocaine, to Eric and *el jefe*. *I am trying very hard to establish the identity of this figure. I believe Eric Jackson not only knows who they are but is being used by them to frame you. If you know anything whatsoever about this situation please notify me ASAP. And be careful, Nick.*

It was only a few minutes later that a senior officer from the International Crime Bureau rushed into the office. They went straight to Price. A moment later both came out of his office. The chief inspector wore an odd expression, one that seemed to float between emotions. He gathered people's attention.

'We may have one kind of result.'

'What's that?'

'He's dead.'

'Who?'

'Nick Belsey. Apparently he was killed in Belgium a few hours ago.'

Craik found herself unable to move. The office felt very cold and bright, but not entirely in focus. A separate part of her mind continued to function, trying to think of something to say, to mask whatever emotions might surface. She was conscious of other officers watching her, alert to her response.

'Who's that from?' she eventually managed.

'Belgian police.'

'Why was he in Belgium?'

'I don't know.'

'Any details?'

'Not many. Something about a mass shooting. That's all we've got so far.' Price seemed uncertain how to react. She could see him forcing down a smile. 'Let's not open the champagne yet. Until we know how he connects to Josie's killing.'

And when everyone was back at their desks and Craik still stood there, he said, 'Sorry, Kirsty.'

NINETEEN

When Belsey woke that morning, the sun was already high, sending blazing stripes through the slat blind. He went to the window and peered out. A new guard sat on the terrace beneath him. Beyond the guard was a view out over the defensive fortifications of the compound to granite mountains. The perimeter fences were at least ten metres high, with watchtowers and cameras. A man patrolled them with a dog on a leash.

Where in Mexico was he? Thinking back to the drive, he had a sense he'd gone north. Belsey tried to remember a mountain range on the map. He couldn't smell the sea any more. The guard beneath him looked up. Belsey gave a salute and the man turned away. Belsey checked the door to the room and it was still locked. A second after he tried the handle, it opened.

'*Come esta?*'

This guard was taller and thinner. Belsey hadn't seen him before. 'Any chance of coffee? Maybe a toothbrush?'

The man closed the door again. A few minutes later a young woman in a pink housekeeper uniform brought in a silver tray with coffee and pastries and a cigarette in an ashtray. The toothbrush was in its pack. The coffee pot, the pastries and even the ashtray were on white cotton doilies.

'*Gracias,*' Belsey said. 'What's the time?'

She showed him a thin-strapped watch on her wrist: 10.15 a.m.

'*Gracias.*'

Belsey drank the coffee, then locked the bathroom and brushed his teeth. When he'd finished, he snapped the toothbrush in half and rubbed the broken end of the base against the stone tiles until it had sharpened to a point. He pressed the point against his throat. As a weapon of last resort, it could work. He'd seen them do the job. It was better than nothing.

He took a shower, then lay back on the bed in a robe, blowing smoke up at the turning blades. How was he doing? He was alive. He was trapped. Anything could happen. The only sure thing was that he had no idea what.

Shortly before noon the analyst appeared with a woman who was also in domestic uniform but appeared more senior. She carried suits and shirts in laundry bags, and had several ties draped over her arm.

'Sleep well?' the analyst said.

'Great.'

The woman laid the clothes on the bed, appraised Belsey, turned to the analyst and nodded. She collected the empty coffee cup and left again.

'These should be your size,' the analyst said. 'See which you prefer.'

'What's the event?'

'Going on a trip. The progress I mentioned, it's been very promising. There's still a lot to do, though. Your assistance is required.'

'You found the stuff that had been stolen?'

'Maybe. Please, choose a suit.'

'We've got a saying: beware all enterprises that require new clothes.'

'There is nothing to beware.'

'Where are we going?'

'We are taking you home.'

'That's what I'm worried about. We need to talk about how we do this.'

'Later. Please.' He gestured at the clothes. 'I'll be back in half an hour. We'll talk on the way.'

The suits were new, with price tags attached: Givenchy, Hermès, Ralph Lauren. There were ties, shirts and shoes as well. Belsey chose a narrow-cut charcoal grey Ralph Lauren suit with notched lapels, white shirt, dark tie. He transferred his possessions into the new jacket, slipped the broken toothbrush into a trouser pocket. In the mirror he looked smart, neat, dressed by someone else's hand. He looked ready for an open coffin.

A man with a white moustache came in with a bowl of water, a towel and a cut-throat razor. He arranged the towel on the floor, moved the chair on top of it and gestured for Belsey to sit down. He was old, his shirtsleeves rolled up on loose skin.

'They treat guests well here,' Belsey said, as the man lathered his stubble.

'*Sí, señor.*' The man was nervous. The blade danced in front of Belsey's throat.

'You stay on the grounds? Come in each day?'

'*Sí.*'

'Is that your job, the in-house barber? How many people do you shave?'

'*Sí.* Barber.'

'How should I look? Any idea where I'm going?'

'*No, señor.*'

When Belsey was clean-shaven and smelling citrussy, the analyst returned. He had his own jacket on, ready to go, holding a document wallet. He appraised Belsey, gave a thumbs-up. 'These are your papers. We can sort them out in the car.'

They walked back through the grounds. Tables and chairs from last night were being folded up, cigarette butts combed out of the hyperreal lawn. The cleaners and gardeners all averted their eyes as they passed.

The car was at the front gates: a glossy Chevrolet Suburban with pitch-black windows. Two men already sat up front, stiff in suits and shades. Belsey and the analyst got into the back. The gates opened and they set off.

Belsey was able to see the route this time: mountain roads, then roads through flat blank ground. They drove through a checkpoint, presumably the same one as yesterday, no stopping this time; a wave from the armed men. Occasionally, in the valley beneath, you could see scraggly looking towns. None looked like La Cada.

The analyst opened his folder and produced a Mexican passport and a driving licence, both in the name of Ricardo Orozco, both using the photo of Belsey they'd taken yesterday. Belsey took them, tilted the holograms. 'They look good.'

'They are authentic.'

For the first time Belsey allowed himself a flicker of hope. You didn't go to these lengths to kill someone.

'We're flying?'

'Yeah.'

'Which airport are we using in the UK?'

'You'll see. Just sit tight, trust us. Try to relax. You'll be given more instructions at the other end.'

TWENTY

After twenty minutes they turned off onto a narrow access road and Belsey saw a control tower ahead. It was a small airfield with one private jet on its runway, a Boeing Business Jet in the process of being refuelled. They drove right up to it.

'Good luck,' the analyst said.

'Not coming with?'

'No.'

Fuck you, Belsey thought. What was this? Some kind of muling? What was he providing cover for? One of the two guards from the car came with him – a squat, shaven-headed man with silver bristles in the folds of his neck. The set-up didn't fit muling. He followed Belsey up the steps into the plane, where a stewardess welcomed them aboard. It was luxurious inside: a commercial airliner that had been retrofitted with conference rooms and a bar, and space for eighteen passengers. There were ten or so men and two women, all looking business-like, all of whom studiously ignored Belsey and his companion as they made their way to the back. Were they all on clandestine operations? Did he blend in, in his new suit and tie? Belsey's chaperone kept his shades on as they sat down across the aisle from one another. He moved a holster around to his front, gazed out of the window.

Belsey knew the British airports where this kind of plane

landed: Farnborough, Biggin Hill, City. Low-key, exclusive, but still with border control; still with Customs and data-sharing and biometric technology. Maybe he was being passed off as part of an entourage, a diplomatic delegation, which could create some blur. But still.

The aeroplane doors closed and he felt himself sealed into whatever fate lay ahead. The captain said something in Spanish. He caught snatches. *Señoras y señores, en nombre de nuestro capitán y el resto de la tripulación . . . El tiempo de vuelo estimado será aproximadamente nueve horas . . .* No one demonstrated any emergency procedures. The seatbelt lights came on and then they took off.

Belsey watched the land beneath him becoming miniature. He looked for the coast, for the fishing village, saw mountains and what looked like factories and a river like a question mark. But not his village. *Adios* to that. Time to figure out the present. He had several dead hours in which to think and prepare. He was heading to the UK. Surely a home advantage would be something. There'd be a chance to slip off eventually. In a worst-case scenario, he had connections. To some extent. He spoke the language.

A stewardess came along with newspapers and drinks. He took an *El Universal* and a Jack Daniel's with Coke, flicked through the paper, thought about what he'd seen at the ranch. The evidence of the cartel's access to police data troubled him. It put good police officers in a dangerous position. There were people he needed to warn. He wanted to speak to Kirsty Craik before she walked into the line of fire.

Belsey handled his new passport: Ricardo Orozco. DoB 12/5/1980. Occupation: *Empresario.* That was a nice touch. He imagined being Señor Orozco, thinking of his family, off to a sales conference. Mexico disappeared beneath clouds.

Food arrived – ceviche and avocado, and seafood tacos. His guard tucked a napkin into his shirt, set about it hungrily, staring at a film about a superhero. Belsey ate, then ordered another JD and Coke. Two rows ahead, across the aisle, a guy in shirtsleeves fell asleep, his phone on the seat beside him. Belsey considered getting the phone, calling someone. When the trays had been cleared, he stood up. The guard glowered.

'Toilet,' Belsey said.

The guard watched him down the aisle. Once inside the cubicle, Belsey locked the door, leaned against it, took a breath. He checked the sharp stub of toothbrush, envisaged a scenario where it was one-on-one: a car park, maybe. Be the last to get into the car, catch the guard in the fleshy part of his throat, run like hell. Next to the toothbrush was the bag of coke from last night. He laughed when he felt the plastic. He'd need to ditch that before Customs. It was a shame. He did a line off the edge of the sink, listened to the rush of Atlantic air outside, thought of the ocean beneath him.

Back in his seat he ordered a large cognac and watched a couple of films. After a while the lights dimmed and he fell asleep. Occasionally he'd wake up and get more cognac. Eventually another meal came around, with wine and coffee. Next time he raised his window blind the cloud had thinned and he saw the edge of Europe: white lines of foam approaching rocky beaches.

They began to descend half an hour later. The captain's voice returned. *Señoras y señores, bienvenidos. La hora local es las tres menos diez, y la temperature es de quince grados ...* Ground appeared late, out of cloud: flat fields; blank water, anodyne clusters of small homes. But something was different. Belsey stared at the tiny cars and after a moment he realised they were driving on the wrong side of the road.

The runway lined up to meet them. The airport hugged the side of a lead-grey sea. It was bigger than a private airfield, but smaller than an international hub. As they touched down he saw a boxy terminal with a sign saying: OOSTENDE BRUGGE.

TWENTY-ONE

Belgium, Belsey thought, as they left the plane, walking across the tarmac into the grey terminal. He breathed Europe, crisp and wet beneath a dull, metallic sky. The terminal wasn't much cheerier inside: orange-carpeted corridors, posters for Belgium's tourist attractions. They were all escorted VIP-style to a dedicated desk for processing. Belsey realised, belatedly, that he still had the wrap, but there was no Customs attention, no dogs or anything, and he wondered if this was part of the play. Belsey's new paperwork got a cursory check, then he was back in Europe.

In Belgium.

The men and women from the front of the plane walked off without looking back at their fellow passengers. Belsey and his guard headed for the short-stay car park. Somewhere along the way a second man joined them, wearing a baseball cap and a Burberry scarf. He seemed to be leading them. Belsey hadn't clocked any exchange between the two men, but the new arrival led the way through the rows of cars to a silver people carrier with one sliding door open and a bald, bespectacled guy waiting behind the wheel.

'What are we doing in Belgium?' Belsey asked, as he was ordered into the back seat. But he was with the silent crew now: no answer, no conversation. The four of them drove away from the airport, away from the sea, through an area of anonymous warehouses onto a dual carriageway. It was late afternoon: crushed charcoal clouds against a blue like thick stained glass. The dashboard clock said 6 p.m. The flight had been at least nine hours. Eventually Belsey realised that he'd lost a day.

They moved fast now, overtaking articulated lorries. The industrial units became flooded fields. Belsey watched the signs as they flew by: Oudenburg, Jabbeke. He glimpsed the other drivers in their Fords and Fiats, oblivious to whatever was going on at Belsey's end. Why was he in Belgium? Pretty close to the UK, but the wrong side of a substantial body of water. And heading further away by the look of it. It started pissing down, rain streaking the windows. The driver handled the car recklessly, swinging around vehicles. There was a word from the guy in the baseball cap and he drove more carefully.

You didn't fly someone to Belgium to kill them, Belsey thought. But he didn't know what you flew them there for.

They were heading east towards Bruges, then turned off onto a quieter road. A few minutes later they pulled into a layby in front of a farm shop and he was told to get out. There was another car there, a slightly beaten-up red Citroën, one gaunt man smoking beneath an umbrella. Belsey was told to get into the Citroën. His guard came with him. The smoker folded his umbrella and got into the driver's seat. The baseball cap got into the front beside him. Then they were on the road again, doubling back at the junction and turning off towards the south.

The roads narrowed, past farming hamlets to a small town with a Carrefour supermarket and a tattoo parlour. On the edge of town, a few larger homes hid behind unsettlingly tall hedges. Their destination was one of these, it turned out: a detached brown-brick house on a slope. The driver made a call, and after a moment the door of its garage slid up and they parked under the lights beside a black BMW.

They entered the house directly from the garage, through a pink kitchen to a green living room filled with cigarette smoke, rain drumming against the windows. Five men sat across its sofas and armchairs and at a glass dining table, discordant with the antiquated furnishings. They'd been watching a laptop. Now they studied Belsey. A tanned, clean-shaven guy in a blue suit jacket seemed to be in charge. He wore a holster. He looked like someone who'd worn a gun professionally. Sticking close to him was a tall skinhead in a grey tracksuit and white trainers. A shorter guy sat on the sofa with his coat on, podgy and unshaven. There were ammo cases on the floor. Everyone was wearing blue latex gloves.

'Take a seat,' the boss man said.

Belsey took an armchair at the side. He read the set-up. Eight men in total, not including himself. An operations team, with a lot of adrenalin in their muscles. There was twitching, heavy smoking, checking of watches. No alcohol in sight. A carriage clock had been removed from the mantelpiece and set on the coffee table beside the laptop. Belsey could smell more weaponry about. It lent an edge of focus to the gathering. It was a prep house. Something was about to go down.

For a few moments they spoke among themselves and Belsey tried to discern the hierarchy. There were multiple languages going on. Baseball Cap and Tracksuit Man spoke an Eastern European language together. When Baseball Cap removed his scarf, he had a tattoo of a double-headed eagle on his neck. The boss was addressed as Luka. He spoke to the others in English. The podgy man didn't speak, but had leery, jaundiced eyes and smoked foul-smelling unfiltered cigarettes. They all knew each other.

Belsey had talked a good game in Mexico. He wondered what he'd bought his way into.

'You help us and you are free,' Luka said.

'Great.'

Luka gestured at the laptop. 'This woman, you have met her.'

There she was again: Esmerelda, with short, dark hair this time, beside a man in a thick jacket with the collar turned up.

'Yes.'

'The man?

'I don't think so.'

Luka clicked to another picture: the man alone this time, waiting to cross a road. Definitely not someone Belsey recognised.

'Never?' Luka said.

'No.'

'Is there any possibility he would know you? Recognise your voice?'

'Not as far as I'm aware.'

The next picture was from a security camera angled over a hotel reception desk, with the man filling out a form.

'He signed in to a hotel near here as Nick Belsey,' Luka said, and waited for Belsey's response. 'He had your passport.'

'Cheeky guy,' Belsey said. The paperwork wasn't visible. The guy bore a very approximate resemblance to himself. Was this who Esmerelda had seen when she looked at him? he wondered.

'Is the passport clean? Would it attract attention?'

'It got me to Mexico. I wouldn't necessarily have tried using it again. Who is he? Working with the girl? Got the coke?'

'You're going to call him. You're going to say you're Dean Gloster.' Luka typed the name on his phone and held it up, then deleted it.

'Who's Dean Gloster?'

'He's someone who's come to Belgium to do business with this man. To make a purchase.'

'Right. What does Dean sound like?'

'English, like you.'

'That's not very precise.'

The man considered for a moment, went to a room at the side and came back with a wallet. He removed all the cards and arranged them on the table. All were in the name of Dean Gloster: driving licence, bank card, reward schemes, gym membership. The name didn't mean anything, but Belsey was concerned for his wellbeing. The home address on the driving licence was in Wavertree, Liverpool. Age thirty-eight. Belsey looked at the personal effects and caught a whiff of cordite. Some of the tension in the room, he now suspected, reflected crimes already committed.

Luka thrust an iPhone at Belsey. The number was already punched in.

'Say you're here. You've just got off the ferry. You have the money and you're ready to meet. That's all. Don't say anything else.'

'Do I get gloves?'

Luka shrugged. Belsey sensed general amusement at this request, which felt a bit sickening. Someone produced a box of surgical gloves and Belsey put them on, more in an attempt to show them he wasn't someone to fuck around. For what that was worth. The phone was on speaker. Belsey hit the call button and everyone went silent. Smoke drifted around the sea-green ornaments. The man at the other end answered immediately.

'Yes?'

'I'm here,' Belsey said. 'I just got off the ferry.'

'Where are you?' The man sounded Spanish or maybe Mexican, and tense as fuck.

'Belgium. That's all you need to know.'

'You have the money?'

'Of course.'

'Are you alone?'

'Yes.'

'Got a car?'

Belsey glanced to the boss. The man nodded.

'Yes.'

'What car?'

Luka picked up a notebook and scribbled 'Citroën'.

'Citroën,' Belsey said.

'Who does it belong to?'

'People. Do you want to do this or not?'

'Have you had any problems with the police?'

'No.'

'The E40 runs from Ostend to Ghent. About halfway, turn south onto the N32. Follow signs for Zevenkerken Abbey. Just before you get to the abbey there's a motorbike dealership and a small road that runs past it into the woods, where it splits. Go to that split, nine p.m., then call this number again.'

Luka winced, shook his head.

'That's not going to work,' Belsey said.

'That or nothing.'

The men around Belsey looked at one another, communicating with their eyes. The tracksuit leaned over to the laptop and typed something in. Luka waited a beat then gave a weary thumbs-up before the silence got conspicuous.

'Okay,' Belsey said.

'You can make it by nine?'

'I can try.'

'You will come alone?'

'Who do you think is going to come with me?'

'If you're not alone, it's off.'

'I understand that.'

'What is the money in?'

The boss looked around, found a bag and lifted it.

'An Adidas holdall.'

'Is there someone with you?'

'I've already answered that question.'

'Nine o'clock. And I'm serious.' He hung up. The carriage clock said seven fifteen. Everyone gathered around the laptop. There was a map up. They discussed possible places they'd be led from the initial location. The boss and the grey tracksuit pored over the map, checking their watches, pointing with cigarettes. Belsey had a feeling he wasn't going to be turning up on his own.

When they'd exhausted the logistics of the meet, the boss opened a new file and showed the man with the eagle tattoo pictures of a fishing boat and a map of Ostend's royal marina. In another window he had information on tides and daylight. This seemed to be the jaundiced man's area of expertise and he talked Eagle Tattoo through something involving the boat.

The idea, evidently, was to retrieve the drugs and then get the hell out of there as quickly as possible. Everyone in different directions: drugs across the Channel, most of the men across the border into France or Germany. Occasionally they glanced at Belsey. There was no suggestion of where he was meant to go.

'Am I going to the UK?' Belsey said. 'That was the agreement.'

'We will see.'

Belsey sighed. 'This isn't going to work.'

'We'll get the stuff back for your Mexican friends. Don't worry.'

The tracksuited skinhead popped a pill and started stretching, cracking his knuckles.

'Is there a bathroom?' Belsey asked.

He went upstairs, saw another man sitting on the bed in a darkened room across the hallway, watching the street at the front of the house. He glanced at Belsey without expression, then turned back to his lookout. The bathroom was crowded with ornaments, window too small to get through. When Belsey came back downstairs two suitcases were open on the dining table and the man with the eagle tattoo was slotting together an assault rifle. The men passed kit between themselves: ammunition, radios, night-vision equipment. They put Kevlar vests on under their shirts. Outside, the rain had stopped. There was something unnerving about it, as if nature was holding its breath.

Belsey spoke to the boss. 'What if they have the same idea?'

'We have numbers.'

'They're setting the plan. They're telling you where to go.'

'These are not professionals.'

'You don't need to be professional. You don't know what numbers he will bring. You think *he*'s coming alone?'

'Just do your bit. You mess this up, we kill you.' He slipped spare magazines into his jacket pockets. People removed the batteries from their phones. Eagle Tattoo rolled a balaclava onto the top of his head, flexed his fingers.

At 8 p.m. they got into the two cars: Belsey in the Citroën with the boss and the two Eastern Europeans, the others in the BMW. They held the weapons on their laps covered with coats. Belsey couldn't see any money. He was given the holdall, but no one filled it.

TWENTY-TWO

They barrelled down the E40 in convoy. Indeterminate agriculture alternated with poker-faced villages, sinister in their peace. There was a two-way radio connection with the rear vehicle but no one spoke now. Forest gathered along one side. Belsey saw signs for St Andrew's Abbey, Zevenkerken. *Before you get to the abbey there's a motorbike dealership and a road that runs past it into the woods . . .* Someone pointed out the bike dealer and they turned fast, without signalling. A few seconds later the road forked and the driver stopped.

Rain dripped from tall, leafless trees on each side, pungent and hushed. They peered into the darkness, then Luka handed Belsey the phone again.

'Tell him you're here.'

The skinhead twisted round in the front passenger seat and put a gun on him.

'Take the gun off me,' Belsey said.

'Don't do anything stupid.'

'How about none of us do anything stupid?' Belsey said. The gunman was instructed to put away his weapon. Belsey hit the call button. The same man answered.

'I'm here,' Belsey said.

'Take the next right, keep going until you see a bench. Step out of the car.' He hung up. The boss lifted his radio and passed on the message. When they set off, the second car dropped back, headlights off.

Next right was a dirt track. Belsey felt the men tense. The rain began again, reducing the senses. They stopped just short of the meeting point. One man lifted night-vision binoculars, confirmed something.

'Walk,' the boss said to Belsey. 'Go a few metres.'

'Empty-handed?'

'With the bag.'

'With the empty bag?'

'Go see. Don't worry, we're here. See what they have.'

Belsey sighed. The gun pointed at his head again. He got out, into the rain, into the moonlit air, among the resinous pines. Took a lungful. How many breaths did he have left? What a fucking freefall. Belsey walked along the beam of the headlights. A figure stepped into the road in front of him.

He was young. Not the man Belsey had spoken with on the phone – a teenager with a blond fringe, half terrified, getting soaked. At first, Belsey wondered if he'd stumbled into this scene by accident.

'You are Dean?' the boy said.

'That's right. Where's the stuff?'

The kid sensed something was up. He glanced behind Belsey at the blinding headlights.

'Put the money on the ground,' he said.

'Not until you show me the drugs.'

'Follow me.'

'It's not going to work like that.'

Something moved behind the kid. A man appeared out of the darkness, shotgun beneath his arm. There were others, shifting, close to vehicles parked up among the trees. The kid was jittery. Belsey leaned closer, dropped his voice.

'Run away. Fast. Just get out of here.'

The kid stared at him, rain in his eyes. The man took another step towards Belsey. It was the one who'd been using Belsey's passport.

'Show us the money.' He cocked the gun. Someone else did the same thing behind him. Belsey grabbed the kid, pulled him towards the trees. Then all hell broke loose.

The first shots smashed the headlights. Belsey hit the ground with the boy beside him. People fired from all directions. Someone gave a hideous cry. Bullets pinged off metal. Belsey rolled sideways, then dragged himself through mud into the forest. He heard a second man cry out, then someone shouting instructions in a language he didn't understand. A separate firefight had broken out in the trees beside him. When that went silent he got to his feet. Someone was running ahead of him. It was the kid.

Belsey followed. A few hundred metres into the trees there was a clearing with picnic tables and a Land Rover, all four doors open. An individual sat in the passenger seat with half their skull missing. Something moved on the ground and Belsey began to spin away then saw it was a man with his guts coming out of his stomach. The kid stepped over him, reached into the car. Belsey thought he was going to get in and drive, but he hauled out two heavy bags. He turned to Belsey, and Belsey could just make out his eyes as the boy seemed to hesitate for a final second. Belsey nodded. The kid ran, fifty kilograms of cocaine skimming the forest floor.

TWENTY-THREE

The sirens started. Belsey stumbled through the woods, into ditches, over fallen branches, following the sound of traffic until he was on a path with halogen lights visible ahead of him. He emerged beside a dual carriageway. No sign of the kid. No more shots behind him. Flashing blues in the distance, gathering.

He was conspicuous beside the road, but a sign suggested there was a place called Vijvers just a kilometre away and Belsey decided that Vijvers might be somewhere he could gather himself together, plan his next move. He was finally free, to some extent, and needed to use that freedom wisely if it was going to last. He kept in the shelter of the trees, following the road until it reached a roundabout, waited for a gap in the traffic, then crossed and walked down a slip road, using the rain to wash the soil from his face and hands, ears still ringing with gunfire. He passed a sign for the village, then a lot of neat red-brick houses coiling away into cul-de-sacs. A modern concrete church sat next to a small school. A few blocks further in he found a shuttered convenience store, then a bar with its windows glowing.

The sirens behind him were continuous now, alongside the new buzz of a police helicopter, its searchlight creating a cone of rain in the distance.

Belsey entered the bar.

It was very quiet and beautiful, with wood panelling and old posters for beer and chewing tobacco. A small TV in the corner showed pundits analysing a football match. Three customers in total: a young couple in the corner, a man standing at the bar, one hand on his glass, shopping bags at his feet. The owner leaned low on the counter beside him, angled towards the TV. They were both middle-aged, grey-stubbled. The owner glanced at Belsey.

'*Goeienavond meneer,*' he said without lifting himself. He eyed the state of Belsey sympathetically.

'Evening. I'm soaked. I need to call a cab.' Belsey gestured at his clothes, mimed a phone call. The barman reached under the counter and placed a phone on the bar.

'Please,' he said, then went back to watching the football. Belsey lifted the phone, considered his options. A third man burst into the bar as he was trying to decide what to do, removing his rain-speckled glasses and gesticulating. He spoke in Flemish. Belsey heard a word that sounded like 'incident' – with the man crossing his hands in an X and pointing at the outside world in a way that seemed to suggest things were getting closed: roads, exit points maybe. Belsey wasn't one hundred per cent sure what he was saying but he got the gist of it. The customer at the bar inflated his cheeks.

'*Hoe erg is het?*'

'*Ik weet het niet, er werd geschoten.*' 'Geschoten' came accompanied by gun fingers. Belsey punched in the code for the UK, then the number for Special Operations. He got through to a switchboard, turned away from the other men.

'Could you put me through to DI Kirsty Craik? I don't have her extension number.'

'Kirsty Craik?' the man at the other end said. 'Which department?'

'Unit Seven, Organised Crime Command.'

'Okay, I've got her extension here.'

It rang. No answer. When it went to voice message Belsey killed the call, then tried one of the few other numbers he knew by heart. A man answered tipsily in the Wishing Well.

'Who's that?' Belsey said.

'Who am I? You call a phone and ask who it is? Who are you?'

'Eric?'

There was a long pause.

'Nick? Fucking hell.'

Belsey was glad to have a familiar voice on the line. Even if Eric was a shifty bastard. Useful didn't have to mean trustworthy.

'Where are you?' Eric said.

'Abroad. I need to get a message to Kirsty Craik.'

Again, the dealer went silent. Belsey sensed something guilty or uncertain going on, but didn't have the luxury of alternative contacts.

'She was in here.'

'When?'

'Yesterday. She was asking about you.'

'Asking what exactly?'

'Just if I'd heard from you.'

'Why?'

'No idea.'

'Is she okay?'

'Doubt it. Sticking her nose in the wrong places, Nick.'

'What does that mean?'

'You know how it goes. You choose your battles, don't you?'

'What makes you think she's chosen the wrong battle?'

'There's a hell of a lot going on around here. I can't help any more. I tried. No one listens to me anyway.'

'Tell me what's happened.'

'You know her colleague was killed?'

'No. Who?'

'Girl called Josie Summer. It's fucking bananas over here, Nicky. Where've you got to?'

'Who killed her?'

'People who wanted her dead.'

'Did Kirsty think she was in danger when you saw her?'

'Probably.'

'Is it anything to do with me?'

'I'm not the man to ask, Nick. You know what you're to do with.'

'Eric, I need to speak to her. Do me a favour: find Kirsty, tell her I'm trying to get in touch. She can pass a message through you, through the pub, whatever. Ask how I can contact her. I'll sort you out. I've got money now.'

'I don't know, Nick.'

'I'd owe you a large one.'

Belsey hung up before he drew attention. The TV had been switched to news. A reporter stood in the rain outside the motorbike dealership. You could see the lights of police activity in the trees beyond him. The barman turned to Belsey, saw he was off the phone.

'No taxis.' Belsey shrugged. 'This weather – it's all busy. Thanks, though.'

'Where do you need to go?' the drinker at the bar said. He spoke English with careful exactness. It was a good question.

'Into town. Ostend,' Belsey said.

With a final glance at the news report, the man drained the remains of his beer and picked up his shopping.

'Come with me. I am going there.'

'Really? That's very kind.'

The man nodded to the barman.

'Saluut.'

'Hou je haaks.'

They stepped outside and Belsey flinched: two armed-response-unit vans sat across the road. A chorus of dogs barked in the distance. The man muttered as they crossed to a blue Peugeot.

'What happened?' Belsey said.

'A shooting. I don't know. Where in Ostend do you want to go?'

'Just the centre. Anywhere.'

'The station?'

'The station would do.'

The man put the radio on news as he drove, shaking his head. 'This is very serious.'

'Wonder what it was about,' Belsey said.

'It will be immigrants,' the man said.

The railway station was built of imperial granite. It looked like a forbidding nineteenth-century hotel. The man pulled up in front. 'Here okay?'

'Perfect, thanks.'

Belsey got out, walked into the light of the station and dried off. People hurried past. A cluster of uniformed police entered and walked towards the ticket barriers, spreading themselves out so they could intercept passengers. Belsey went to a map of Ostend on the wall. He was already close to the water, he saw. He located the main dock a few hundred metres away, got his bearings and headed towards it.

More police patrolled heavily over the wet paving stones. People stopped to watch the news through bar windows. Belsey kept his head down, got to the seafront.

A thicket of yachts' masts obscured the glistening sea. The harbour was overlooked by high apartment blocks that gave it a feeling of seclusion. The boats shifted in the high water like restless animals, keels knocking. Belsey breathed salt water, petrol and algae, and the traces of fish, old fish, like a stain in the air. There was no one in sight.

According to what he'd seen on the laptop, the area he needed was the fishing port, on the east side of the main shipping channel. He passed the fish market – a long brick building with its shutters down – to the business end of the marina, where the moored vessels became more functional, with winches and beam trawls.

He walked along the jetty, trying to remember what he'd overheard, looking for the boat they'd described, which seemed ambitious now he was faced by the hundred or so options before him. He reached the end of the jetty. As he stood there, wondering what to do next, he became aware of being watched. Belsey turned to see someone flicking a cigarette as they got up from a bench. Two men emerged from the darkness, glancing up and down the dock. They could have been father and son, both in oilskin waterproofs. The younger man was taller and more thickly built. The older man had a bottle in a carrier bag, which he rammed into the pocket of his jacket.

'Hey,' Belsey said. The older man gave a nod. It looked like they were waiting for something.

'You're the guys?' Belsey said.

They stared.

'I'm from Luka. We need to go fast. You know Luka? I represent the Mexicans. *Mexique.*'

The word earned him a closer appraisal. They beckoned for him to step towards them out of the security lights. They reeked of spirits and tobacco.

'You?' the younger man said.

'Yes, me. We go now.'

'Vous êtes seul?'

'Just me now. We need to move. There's been a bit of a situation.'

They looked puzzled. Belsey realised what was confusing them.

'It's in my car. If you're ready I can get it.'

'Ready, yes.'

Belsey walked back to the shuttered fish market to some large wheelie bins at the side, checked around, then opened a bin and removed a few sacks of rubbish. He found one that didn't stink, and didn't clang with metal or glass, and returned. The men eyed the bag.

'Quick,' he said. 'There's no time for fucking about.'

They led him along the jetty to a ten-metre trawler with a rusted hull. He climbed aboard. There was a row of three seats at the back, two up by the controls. While the older man got the engines started, the younger one unlocked a panel in the deck and shone a torch. Inside there were lifejackets and flares. Beneath these another panel opened to reveal an empty space big enough for at least a tonne of coke. Belsey had come light-handed. He put the bag down there and the man handed him a lifejacket, then went to untie the boat from its mooring. A moment later the engines started with a growl and they manoeuvred out and set off.

It was freezing. Belsey took the bench at the back of the boat, shoved his hands into the lifejacket. They slid past industrial docks, gantry cranes, container cranes, out into open, infinite water. The boat was faster than it looked, bouncing over the waves so Belsey was forced to grip the edge. There was a lot of headwind. He twisted to see their wake crossing itself as it spread in moonlight. Belgium receded behind him. He imagined the scene currently going on in the forest and knew he was heading in the right direction.

The men sat up front, one handling the wheel, the other beside him occasionally passing the bottle. A solemn pair, out of their depth, perhaps. How much were they getting for this? Belsey saw himself alone at the back, like an emperor, or someone recently deceased, carried on their last journey. They left the harbour into the open sea and he wondered where exactly they were aimed for. An astonishing immensity of darkness stretched around them. The glow of their GPS monitor seemed to be the only light in the universe.

Belsey clambered to the front. 'Where are we going?'

'England.'

'Where in England?'

They had coordinates, but nothing that told him clearly whether he was going to turn up in Dover, Brighton or anywhere else. He assumed they were aiming for a quiet stretch of coast. Smuggler terrain. As a child he'd read a book about smugglers and it said they'd wrap the hoofs of their horses in wool to muffle them. That was the mentality he needed. He went back to his seat and prepared.

The men took turns on watch, half-hour shifts. Belsey watched clouds crossing the moon. He studied the occasional lights out in the shipping lanes: ferries and freighters. Eventually the wind died away to give a flat, calm sea. They passed a container ship, tall as a mountain range, like a chunk of continent that had come adrift. They didn't see anything else until the lights of Britain appeared on the horizon.

They appeared around 3 a.m., very faint, gradually becoming attached to a low hump of darkness. English waters now. The men killed the engine. The younger one came back, opened the hold and brought out a small square orange device and a spherical white fishing buoy, then some roll-top waterproof stuff sacks. He unlocked the second panel and gestured for Belsey to bring up the bag. The orange device he held was a locator beacon. Belsey got the idea. You drop the drugs into the sea tied to the buoy, with the beacon attached. They're collected by someone coming from the UK side, another fishing boat on a supposedly routine trip out. Half a tonne of drugs arrives in the UK and no one's had to pass Customs. Smooth, if it worked.

'Jetez le pacquet,' the man explained.

'Where is this?'

The man shrugged.

'What happens after I jeter le pacquet? Where do I go then?'

The man gestured back towards Belgium.

'How close to the coast can you go?'

'Coast?'

'I want to go all the way. Go to England.' Belsey pointed.

'Trop dangereux.'

'Luka wants me to walk it in. You not get the message? Me and the pacquet, we go in.'

The men looked at one another. Then the older of the two spat into the sea. They spoke together, away from Belsey, checked watches, came back.

'Where?'

'Just up to the land, somewhere I can get ashore. Anywhere. Then you go back to Belgium. Easy.'

They consulted the screen again. The younger one went to the hatch and came back with a white box the size of a carry-on suitcase. He tied it to the railing, then tossed it overboard. When the white box was floating on the sea he pulled the cord and in an astonishing moment it expanded, hissing and unfolding into an inflatable lifeboat.

188

The man proceeded to unroll a rope ladder down the side of the boat, then he fetched an outboard motor from the hold. With this under one arm he went down the ladder and dropped into the lifeboat. Belsey passed him the bag, then followed, almost tipping the craft before steadying himself and sitting down.

'Traceur?' The man held up the GPS beacon.

'No. We're good.'

The man started the motor and they moved fast, low. Really bouncing now. He kept peering into the water. When they were a kilometre further into shore he stopped, pointed what looked like a yellow torch down at the sea, and checked a reading.

'Ici.'

'Are you sure?'

He showed Belsey the reading on the depth finder. It didn't mean much. It looked like there was still a couple of hundred metres of sea until you got to dry land. Not many lights on shore. A pale glow along the coast, one or two brighter lights from buildings on higher ground. Whichever stretch of the British coast lay ahead of them it wasn't a big port.

'I can go in? Stand up?'

'Oui.'

Belsey took off his shoes and socks, stuffed them into his jacket. He took the bin bag, swung his legs over, released himself, expecting to sink. The water was freezing but only went up to his thighs. The seabed was grainy beneath his feet. The man watched this with the look of incredulity it deserved. There was a flash of torch from the fishing boat and he turned the lifeboat and sped off, splashing Belsey with his wake.

Belsey stood for a moment, alone. It was cold but very peaceful, and walking towards land didn't seem the only option. The moon hung to his left, a familiar English moon, watching over him, and that was all the company he sought for now. He took a final breath, savouring the unhuman emptiness, then began to force his numb legs through the water towards England.

TWENTY-FOUR

The Met's International Liaison team got the news first: four dead, three critically injured after a shooting near Zevenkerken Abbey at approximately 9 p.m. Terrorism had been ruled out. A major possibility seemed to be that it was a drugs deal gone wrong.

Craik called her own contacts. Eventually a colleague in Narcotics, who'd been working closely with the Belgian authorities, said he had some details. She went up to the fourth-floor office, where DI Patrick Westerman was sifting a lot of paperwork, his phone ringing. He silenced the receiver when he saw Craik approach, told her to pull up a chair.

'It was one hell of a mess, that's all we've got for sure. Looks like a consignment was being touted, worth several million. From Mexico, originally. But no one wanted to play nice.'

'One hundred kilograms?'

'Possibly. Was it stolen?'

'Yes.'

'I think whoever stole it tried to shift it, and the original owners got word. Names emerging connect to our records of Serbian Mafia known to be working with the ATO cartel. They've operated in Belgium before.'

He showed her names and faces, taken from an assortment of police records and surveillance shots.

191

'This is Luka Mitrić, former Serbian intelligence officer, believed to have been an important link in the trafficking network in the Balkans. Connected to the killing of three detectives in Amsterdam in 2012. He would have been able to get a team together. One of those who survived is this guy, Gerard Reubben. He's in custody now. His previous includes a five-year sentence in the nineties for smuggling heroin in fishing trawlers. Still has connections on the British east coast. It looks like there'd been a plan to move the drugs off the Continent ASAP.'

'And a police officer from the UK? Nick Belsey?'

'Yes. There's speculation that Nick Belsey stepped in on behalf of the cartel to whom the cocaine rightfully belonged, or possibly he tried to step in between, get the drugs himself.'

'But he was definitely there.'

'He was there. Belgian police have emailed this. It was on him when his body was found.'

Winterburn showed her a photograph of Belsey's passport, covered with blood. One corner appeared to have been lost to a bullet.

'He was shot about twenty times, by all accounts.'

Craik hadn't been braced for these details. A sense of loss now contended with horror, by an image of a body torn apart.

Apparently there was no sign of the missing cocaine.

As soon as she was back at her desk, Craik dialled Perez's personal number.

'You're calling about Belgium,' Perez said.

'Do you know what happened?'

'It seems the ATO located their missing shipment. Martinez and her accomplices were trying to sell it fast, and a gang with ATO affiliations attempted to step in and take it back.'

'I'm told Belsey was there.'

'So it appears. The men who were meant to have been buying

the stolen load are called Joel Speed and Dean Gloster. Do you know of them?'

'I don't think so.'

'Their bodies have just turned up in the basement of an Airbnb in a village called Oudenburg.'

Perez stayed on the line while Craik checked their entries on the system. There were plenty. Joel Speed and Dean Gloster had been minor-league gangsters based in Merseyside. Speed was a one-time yacht dealer and suspect for the unsolved murder of his Spanish girlfriend. Dean Gloster had been an army recruit and drugs courier at various points in his life. At the time of their deaths, both had been out of prison on licence for offences linked to the Mackenzie-Boyne crime family, which worked Liverpool and the north-west. Craik came across the Liverpudlian mafias often enough: an informal grouping of traffickers, less territorial than London gangs, more internationally active. She imagined this had been the logic of approaching them.

'Your colleagues in the Border Force have located footage of the two men travelling to Belgium in a Mercedes-Benz Sprinter,' Perez said. 'Driving onto the Eurotunnel Le Shuttle train at ten a.m. on the morning of December the nineteenth. The van's been found a few miles away from the Airbnb. It has false panels in the base for smuggling but they never got the chance. Looks like they'd been kidnapped and executed.'

'How did they get involved in the first place?'

'A mutual friend, perhaps, connected to the production of MDMA and amphetamines. My theory is that Martinez and her accomplice were trying to sell the stolen cocaine fast and this friend put them in touch with the gang in Liverpool, who they'd worked with before. Gloster and Speed were sent over to collect it. On CCTV, you can see the men's van leave the Euroshuttle in Calais. They then drive straight to Tournai, over the Belgian border, where they make a call and are never seen alive again.'

'And how is Belsey meant to have been involved?'

'I would very much like to know. Whatever he was up to, he had a small army with him. I suspect there was a plan to overwhelm their targets with superior firepower. Perhaps they thought it was going to be easy, retrieving what was theirs. Only their target wasn't going down without a fight.'

'And the drugs?'

'No word of them yet. We need to ascertain who exactly was there, then whether any drugs were taken to the meeting in the first place. Nothing is clear right now.'

'Any suggestion how Belsey got over there?'

'I understand his passport was used recently to travel to Europe but I'm still chasing the details.'

Craik got a call from the journalist at the *Sun*.

'Is it true? Nick Belsey's dead?'

'Nothing's confirmed.'

'Hearing he was in a gunfight in Belgium. Can you just say yes or no to that?'

'You tell me. What's the story out there?'

'People are saying he'd got involved in some pretty heavy business. Major league. Robbing the cartels.'

She hung up.

'You okay, Kirsty?' Obiri watched her with concern.

'Yeah.'

He glanced at the desk where Summer should have been sitting, misunderstanding the object of Craik's grief. 'She looked up to you. That doesn't mean you need to hold yourself responsible.'

'No.'

'We'll get to the bottom of this.'

It was 10 p.m. Craik needed a drink. She told people she was going home, and they nodded understandingly. Then she went to the Wishing Well.

TWENTY-FIVE

Almost last orders. How long since she had done this? Slipping into the Well at 10.30 p.m., like stepping through a secret door into a night-time world. *You've got to know the night, Kirsty. It's where the answers lie. It makes the day worth surviving.*

The usual late crowd at the bar: Fat John, Mike the mechanic, Elizabeth on her stool. A couple of the older regulars in the darker corners: Brendan McCarthy, Dell Patterson; Steve Locke by the jukebox. No Eric.

Craik felt numb, oddly weightless with unprocessed grief. But she'd made the right decision in coming here. Death demanded rituals. Being in the Well was like wearing his shirt, breathing in the last pungent, human, hedonistic scent of the man.

She could tell by the solemnity with which they watched her enter that they'd heard the news. Rod fixed a double Jameson's, slid it across the bar.

'Is it true?'

'Seems to be.'

'Shit,' Mike said, more in awe than regret. 'Wow.'

She shouldn't have been surprised by their knowledge. The Well was a paradox: hidden corner and hub of all grapevines. Craik wondered when Eric Jackson would hear, and if he'd then come to the Well, driven by the same instinct that had brought her to its refuge. Eric, who seemed increasingly likely to be in contact with *el jefe*. He would be on his rounds now. This time of night he would have moved on to the hipster bars, the private customers in expensive apartments. She'd be very interested to talk to him if he showed up. If she could do that discreetly.

Locke stepped away from the jukebox without putting any music on. He stood there for a moment, tattooed muscle rippling, then returned to the bar.

'Nicky,' he said.

'Nicholas fucking Belsey,' Mike said. 'You wouldn't have thought the bastard was mortal.'

Mike Jarrow stole cars and car parts. She'd last seen his name in conjunction with the large-scale theft of catalytic converters. The corpulent John Holmes beside him had been a solicitor specialising in family law before losing his job for stealing from the practice to bet on horses. He still dressed as a solicitor, with a briefcase containing God knew what. Elizabeth, the queen of the Well, remained regal on her stool. Always immaculately presented, she was a compendium of local knowledge, of indeterminate age and profound alcoholism, a fixture treated deferentially by the largely male clientele who destroyed themselves around her.

Locke took a suck on his vape and exhaled slowly. He was a nasty character, all Rolex and creatine, boss of a door-security mafia, now running his own gym. Craik had crossed paths with him before, over some domestic violence and the possession of a weapon. At one point he had used far-right football firms for a drugs ring that was eventually capsized by its own greed. The deals he dabbled in now weren't profitable enough to cross Craik's desk, but not for want of trying.

'What's the story?' he said, in his rasping voice. 'I've just heard rumours, none of which I'm minded to believe myself.'

'What are the rumours?' Craik asked.

'The godfather,' Locke said. 'Taking on all sides. A one-man cartel.'

'Shot in Belgium,' John added.

'How did you hear?'

'Some people have already had police around asking what they know about his gangland connections,' Locke said. 'Where he's hiding his money. All that.'

'Which police?'

'Someone from the Yard. Hour or so ago.'

'And the press,' Mike said.

'Yeah?'

'Your friend from the *Sun*, Fraser. Posh lad, used to drink in here sometimes. Says some Scousers went over to Belgium to collect a load of drugs. Belsey killed them and impersonated them and almost got away with about two tonnes of marching powder. Fraser wanted a quote on Belsey. I said: "Nick Belsey had balls the size of a fucking cathedral. Quote that. Lived his best life. Blaze of glory."'

'He established himself in Mexico, apparently,' Elizabeth said.

'You know what they called him in Mexico?' Mike said. 'The Scorpion.' He looked awestruck.

'Santa Muerte,' Locke said. 'That's what they called him. Know what that means? Saint fucking Death.'

The others nodded. Vape mist coiled like fantasy around them.

Craik downed her whisky and tried to ignore the bullshit while sensing it was all that was stopping a flood of real memories bursting its banks. She got a round in.

John looked contemplatively at the fresh pint beside the dregs of his previous one. 'There will be money about.'

'For sure,' Locke said.

'He made about two hundred mill over there,' John said.

'Is that right?' Craik said. John seemed to think he knew a lot about this.

'Word is he stored a lot of it here, though. Probably just a few minutes away. Rainy day. You know what Belsey was like.'

'Not a big saver in my experience,' Craik said.

'When he had money he was a generous guy,' Elizabeth offered.

'Squirrelled, Kirsty,' Mike added. 'He had a brain on him when he wanted to. And he was chivalrous, had his code of honour. He wouldn't leave friends out of pocket.'

'You think you can get money out of this?'

Mike breathed a sigh of wonder. 'You never know.' He finished his old pint, drank the new one fast. 'I'd have another, Kirsty, if you're buying. It's helping. For Nick. For the road he's on now.'

'You know he killed five people before they got him?' John said, when she set down more drinks.

'Five?'

'Single-handed, with an M16 rifle,' John said. 'Can you believe it? Hard to get that picture, I know.'

'It's the effect of drugs,' Mike suggested. 'I've seen a girl who was still at school do someone with a machete while under the influence. Doing well at school and all. Nick fucking Belsey.' He shook his head.

'The least he could have done was pay off his debts,' Rod suggested, from behind the bar.

'Nicky always said you can't take it with you,' Elizabeth said. 'You wait. He won't have left us empty-handed.'

John turned to her, nodding in agreement.

'Wouldn't be surprised if there was a payday soon. A little bird says he passed some of his earnings to a trusted person, with instructions to distribute it all if anything happened.'

'Who said that?' Craik asked.

'Someone heard it. You remember that time Vince Gaffney passed away, and it was happy days all round. Everyone had been saying what a cunt he was and had to wipe the smile off their faces quick smart.'

Vincent Gaffney was a successful fence whose sidekick had turned up at his memorial with bags of cash. Memories of that night had become legendary, a rare flash of luck in lives short on it.

'Vince Gaffney.' Someone sighed. Then the pub door opened and Eric Jackson walked in.

There was a beat as he saw Craik and seemed to consider turning on his heel, but he checked himself and proceeded to the bar.

'It's true, then,' he said.

She nodded.

He leaned his weight against the sticky woodwork, shook his head. 'Fuck me. What happened?'

'What have you heard?'

'Nothing.'

She caught herself staring at him as he laid a note down. 'Jameson's all round?'

'Cheers, Eric.'

'Reckon I was the last to speak to him,' Eric said quietly, when the shots were poured.

'You spoke to Nick?'

'That's right. On the phone.'

'When?'

'Just this evening. Must have been before it all happened.'

He turned to Craik, eyes wide with the dawning significance of this missed connection. 'He wanted to speak to you.'

She checked his pupils for any clues as to which narcotics were currently flooding his brain. 'What else did he say?' she asked warily.

'That I'd get paid.'

'For what?'

'Finding you.'

'What time was this exactly?'

'Not sure. Fucking freaks me out, Kirsty. He *sounded* dead and all.'

'Called on what?'

'The public.' He nodded at the phone.

'Did he sound in danger?'

'Yes, exactly. In danger, and worried about you. Your well-being, Kirsty. If I could have done something . . .'

She turned instinctively to the phone. The others regarded Eric with varying levels of scepticism.

'Told anyone?' she asked. He watched her carefully before replying.

'Who would I tell?'

'Give me a better time estimation,' she said.

'Nine p.m.'

'That doesn't make sense.'

'Told you,' Mike muttered.

'Swear on my mother's life.'

'Well, if he calls again, tell him to check his emails,' Craik said.

Locke laughed. The others studied her, wearing cautious smiles, trying to gauge if she was taking the piss. Craik watched Eric down his drink, wondering how to have a word with him in private. She wanted him to cast his mind back to 2018 and a dangerous tip-off. For a second she even entertained the idea of inviting him to a game of pool. Then her own phone rang. Everyone stared at the screen when she brought it out, as if Belsey's name might appear.

It was Lawrence.

'Hey,' she said, moving to a quiet corner.

'Kirsty?' His voice had a wild, strangled air. 'What have you done?'

'What do you mean?'

'Why are there police at my parents' home asking when I was last with you?'

'I don't know.' Her heart began racing. 'What are they saying?'

'They want to know timings of when I spoke to you, where you've been, details of any mobile phones you have. Can you please tell me what's going on?'

'It's a mistake.'

'I'll say. Are you able to sort this out? It's not exactly what my parents need.'

Her phone beeped: Price calling on the other line.

'I'll sort this out. Leave it with me.' She hung up, answered Price's call.

'Where are you?' he said.

'What's going on?'

'Homicide are at the office. They want a chat.'

'They think I've got something to do with it?'

'I don't know what they think.'

'I'll come in.'

'Kirsty, is there anything you haven't told me that I need to know about?'

'Like what?'

'Like things I could do with knowing before Homicide do.'

TWENTY-SIX

Price ushered her towards his office as soon as she got to HQ.

'You smell like you've been in a pub,' he said, incredulously.

'That's because I was in a pub.'

'You're not drunk, are you?'

'No. What's going on?'

'We're about to find out.'

Waiting in the office were DI Greg Hannaway and a woman with short blonde hair who introduced herself as DCI Eve Pawlowski. Hannaway smiled at Craik. He looked more focused and intent than he had in their previous encounter. Pawlowski looked serious and short on time. Price took a seat at the side.

'Thanks for coming in,' Hannaway said. 'Obviously this is just a voluntary interview, but we'll stick a tape on, if that's okay.'

'What am I suspected of?'

'It's just some oddities that we need to clear up. Want a police rep? Anything like that?'

'Am I being charged?'

'No.'

'Then I'll be fine.'

Hannaway pressed record, gave the spiel and they began.

'I spoke to you earlier and you suggested the murder may be related to your work.'

'That's right.'

'You were working with Jocelyn Summer on Mexico-to-UK drug trafficking.'

'Correct.'

'Part of an ongoing operation?'

'Not yet.'

'You hadn't, technically, been tasked with it.'

'We're experienced officers. We use our initiative.'

'True.'

Hannaway opened the cover of an iPad, switched it on and slid it across the table. The screen showed a photo from a birthday party, *circa* 2008. Amid a crowd of sweaty men and under-dressed women, Craik was sitting on Belsey's knee drinking from a bottle of cava. It was the legendary Vagabonds. She looked young and happy. She wondered where this image had surfaced from. Price tore his gaze slowly from the iPad. So this was it, she thought. What a ridiculous waste of resources in the initial few hours after a murder.

'Do you remember this night?' Hannaway asked.

'Yes.'

'Can you tell us when and where it was?'

'Roughly. It was a club called Vagabonds. Around 2008, I reckon.'

'The man on whose lap you're sitting is Detective Constable Nick Belsey. Can you confirm that's correct?'

'Yes.'

'You were close,' Pawlowski said.

'That picture's not entirely representative. It was a party.'

This didn't do much to soften their stares. Price looked sickened, as if he'd tried to defend her and now felt he'd been played. He looked like he wanted her to say something to show this was a big mistake.

'Belsey was a chancer,' Craik said. 'Cut a few corners, knew a few tricks. He wasn't a gang boss. Nor did he have any aspirations to become one. It would have been too much responsibility.'

'You recently put an alert on his name,' Hannaway continued. 'Requesting updates on information about him stored on the police databases. That was the morning of December the twentieth.'

'That's correct.'

'The alert was put on a day *before* you were informed by the FBI and their Mexican colleagues that he was involved in Mexico.'

Craik knew how interviews worked. You had to stay close to the truth. Venturing out, even in small steps, led you onto thin ice.

'I got a call, an anonymous call, threatening me but relating to Belsey. That prompted my concern.'

'You didn't inform anyone about this call the following day?'

'No. It could have been a prank. I spoke to one woman who'd had a similar call, also an acquaintance of Belsey. It was only gradually that I realised the situation was more serious. There was a possibility it connected to the shooting of Trevor Hart.'

'When did you last have contact with Nick Belsey?' Pawlowski asked.

'A long time ago. We're talking years. I'm not sure.'

'Have you *attempted* to contact him?' Hannaway asked.

'I tried. In case he was in trouble. I didn't succeed.'

'Did you know he was in Mexico?'

'No.'

They waited a beat before continuing, watching her carefully.

'You're a senior officer,' Pawlowski said. 'Would it not have been better for someone of lower rank to be interviewing Samantha Topping? Like Detective Constable Summer?'

'No. This was entirely speculative on my part.'

'Relating to the calls you'd both received.'

'Exactly.'

'You also left a message for the FBI.'

'I saw on the system that they were interested in him. I tried to get in touch.'

'And at this point, it's still just you, working off your own bat.'

'Yes.'

None of this was cutting through. The mood darkened with every word she said. Pawlowski continued: 'You visited a pub yesterday.' She checked her notes. 'The Wishing Well in SE1.' Craik wondered how she knew that, but police liked intimidating interviewees with surprising knowledge.

'Yes, and I was there just now. What would you like to know about it?'

'On that first visit to the Wishing Well, who did you speak to?'

'A man called Eric Jackson.'

Price stared at Craik, then turned to the Homicide detectives. 'You said this was just a chat.'

The investigating officers took a breath. Pawlowski leaned to Hannaway and whispered something. Hannaway nodded.

'I'd like to reiterate that Detective Inspector Kirsty Craik is here answering questions voluntarily, but for the sake of clarity, Detective Inspector Craik, you do not have to say anything but it may harm your defence if you do not mention when questioned something which you later rely on in court. Anything you do say may be given in evidence. Do you understand?'

'Of course.'

'As mentioned, you're entitled to a police representative, and a solicitor. Would you like to request those now?'

'Whoever killed Josie Summer is out there, and I'd like to clear this up so you can readjust the focus of this investigation as quickly as possible.'

'Okay. To continue then. You met Eric Jackson at the Wishing Well pub in SE1.'

'Yes.'

'What did that involve?'

'Eric Jackson is a drug dealer and I wanted information about the cocaine that appeared to have gone missing, and which people believe may connect to Nick Belsey.'

'Did you ask about Belsey himself?'

'Yes.'

'And what did he say?'

'He didn't know where he was.'

Pawlowski opened her wallet file and removed another sheet.

'This is from an investigation in 2018, led by Detective Inspector Scott Montgomery. In it, he draws upon Eric Jackson as a covert human intelligence source. In return for the waiving of a charge, Jackson gave DI Montgomery false information. It's believed this information is the reason Montgomery visited the area where he was shot the following day.'

'Yes.'

'You're familiar with it.'

'We were the ones who discovered it.'

'When did you become aware of this connection?'

'Yesterday.'

'Too late to ask Eric Jackson about it?'

'If I'd known about it earlier I wouldn't have approached him.'

'So what did Mr Jackson say when you did approach?'

'Not much. He clearly knew something but felt intimidated.'

'Was anyone else privy to your conversation?'

'No.'

'Where did it take place?'

'There's a back room.'

'A back room.'

'With a pool table.'

Slow nods all round, as if this detail was the most damning yet. Pawlowski produced another piece of paper. What now? Craik thought. It was a photocopy of a smaller scrap, which looked like a torn-out page of a lined A7 notebook. On it was an address in Josie Summer's handwriting.

290 Childs Hill, SE14.

'Is this address familiar to you?' Pawlowski asked.

'Two hundred and ninety Childs Hill? No. I don't think so.' What area was SE14? Craik wondered. Greenwich? Beyond Greenwich?

'This was found in Josie Summer's jacket pocket.'

'What is it?'

'Scott Montgomery's current address.'

Craik studied the scrap. So Josie had tracked him down. Even now, she continued to impress.

'She didn't tell you about this?' Hannaway said.

'No.'

'She did some digging to get it. Through the police pension scheme. Why do you think she wanted it?'

'She wanted to speak to him.'

'About?'

'The UK end of the cocaine-trafficking operation.'

'Right. That's very much what we believe. I need to ask you directly: are you protecting Nick Belsey?' Hannaway said.

'No.'

'Can you tell us where you were between eleven a.m. and one p.m. yesterday?' Pawlowski asked.

'I was here, at the office in the morning. There was a press conference. When it got to eleven thirty and Josie still wasn't answering her phone, I established that she'd gone to Harlesden and went there myself.'

'She wasn't answering.'

'No.'

'But you tried to call her.'

'Yes.'

'What did you think she might have found?'

'An identity for the importer.'

'Who may have been Nick Belsey. That was a possibility raised by the FBI, was it not?'

'A possibility.'

'Any other reason she might not have informed you of her visit to Harlesden?'

'We'd had a small disagreement. Nothing work-related.'

'About what?'

'Personal matters.' She felt Price shift uncomfortably.

'Okay,' Hannaway said. 'Personal matters. What time were you in Harlesden?'

'Just after midday. Then there was the Christmas lunch.'

'You got there late.'

'Yes.'

'Anyone see you at the property in Harlesden?'

'I spoke to a neighbour, the woman in the store next door.'

'What time was that?'

'I'm not sure. Around midday, like I said.'

'You didn't note a time.'

'No.'

'As you know, it's proving difficult to establish the exact time of Detective Constable Summer's death,' Hannaway said. 'Apparently loud music was playing, but it has to have been between eleven fifty-seven a.m. when her car's seen on a security camera a few hundred metres away, arriving in the area, and ten past one when her body was found.'

'Did you tell Josie Summer to drive to the trading estate?' Pawlowski asked.

'No.'

She slid a picture across. Fresh from Forensics: a photograph of a car's chassis from beneath. Attached to it was a small black box with two round silver magnets on one side.

'Know what this is?' she asked.

'It's a tracker. Is this Josie Summer's car?'

'That's right. It was found beneath the chassis of DC Summer's car. Doesn't look like it's been there too long, either. Any idea how it might have got there?'

Craik studied it. The tracker was a standard type, battery-operated, easily available online. The GPS location would be sent straight to a phone or laptop. She hoped someone was looking into that. It filled in a big gap of the narrative, at least, explaining how the syndicate might have traced her to Leyton, even if it left the question of what she was doing there even more mysterious.

'No.' Craik said. 'You need to look into where she's been parked recently.'

'Good idea,' Hannaway said. 'Now, Joshua Parish. You hadn't crossed paths with him? A gang member?'

'We deal with the higher echelons.'

'Anything that might suggest a connection to Belsey?'

'Not as far as I'm aware.'

'We think Belsey may have had connections with people who knew him. People who could pass on an instruction to kill Josie Summer. Parish appears in a rap-music video with several individuals we've got on the gangs matrix, including George Downey, who is now in Pentonville but used to deal drugs on behalf of someone called Craig Smith. We've been told that Belsey had been drinking partners with Smith on occasion.'

'On that kind of principle you could connect him to pretty much anyone in London.'

'That's our point.'

'Belsey wouldn't arrange someone's death.'

They nodded, but not in agreement. As if she was saying exactly what they expected.

'You're a very successful detective,' Pawlowski said.

'Have we finished?'

'You've taken down . . .' she checked her list '. . . Artem Boyko, the Guliyevs, Curtis Atkinson. Is that right?'

'I work in Organised Crime Command. That's what we do.'

'All of whom previously controlled a significant chunk of the UK's cocaine trade.'

Craik sat back.

'This is ridiculous,' Price said.

'You can see how it looks,' Hannaway said.

'You're accusing me of clearing the way for this new importer?'

'That's precisely what's happened. I'm curious why.'

'It's one thing asking about her previous associations,' Price said. 'Casting aspersions on the work we do as a team in Organised Crime Command is disgusting. You're barking up the wrong tree.'

'Why didn't Jocelyn Summer answer your calls?' Pawlowski asked.

'I don't know.'

She checked her notes again. 'According to the records, you tried five times between ten a.m. and twelve p.m. Why didn't she answer them? Because of a falling out?'

'Maybe.'

'I don't think DI Craik should answer any further questions without a lawyer,' Price said weakly.

They looked at her. 'Your decision, Detective Inspector.'

'How many more questions do you have?'

'One,' Pawlowski said. 'For now.'

'Go for it.'

'Do you have any personal contacts in Belgium?'

'Belgium? No.'

'Okay, we're done.' She collected up her papers. Hannaway went to stop the recording.

'Why?' Craik said.

Hannaway hesitated with his finger over the button.

'There was a call from Belgium to your direct line in the office at nine fifteen UK time,' Pawlowski said.

'From Belgium?'

'Yes. Nine fifteen p.m. Ten fifteen in Belgium. From a phone less than a kilometre from where Nick Belsey was killed.'

Was it true? It was around the same time as Eric claimed to have got a call from Belsey.

'I don't know anything about that.'

The Homicide detectives watched her.

'We're not saying the call was from Nick Belsey,' Hannaway said. 'But it raises questions.'

'I'm sure.'

This time, no one broke the silence until Price cleared his throat. Hannaway said he was terminating the interview and stopped the tape.

'What the fuck was that?' Price exploded at the detectives.

'We're doing our job.'

Craik stood up. 'I really hope this isn't your best line of enquiry,' she said. She turned to Price. 'I'll be in the office.'

'Wait for me there.'

TWENTY-SEVEN

Craik left the room, feeling like she'd been punched, sat down at her desk, saw her paperwork had been searched. Only a handful of colleagues remained in the office. They kept their heads down.

Did Homicide have reasonable grounds for her arrest? Surely not. And what would she be charged with? Arresting a senior officer in an elite squad for involvement in organised crime was a nuclear option. There was no going back from that. You needed more than hearsay.

A call from Belgium.

One to her, one to the Well. Trying to communicate something. A warning, perhaps, before he died. A last message. She put in a request to the switchboard. 'Apparently I got an international call to my direct line around quarter past nine last night. Can you get me details?'

'I'm afraid that's not possible.'

'Why?'

'I'm not sure, but you're coming up on the system as temporarily unauthorised.'

'Since when?'

'A couple of hours ago.'

Craik put the phone down, then emailed BT's police liaison department, assuming it wouldn't have received notice of her fall from grace yet. Accessing data for personal phones required a warrant but public phones were a grey area she'd exploited before. She put in a request for call records to the public telephone in the Wishing Well.

Hannaway and Pawlowski left Price's office, heading to the lifts. Price emerged a moment later.

'What are they saying?' Craik asked. For a moment he just stared at her. She realised he was searching for words. 'Are they going to charge?'

'Not yet. They want you in their offices nine a.m. tomorrow. I've done what I can. What's going on, Kirsty?'

A new cold front had appeared. Police survival instincts: protect yourself from colleagues' disasters.

'Do you believe me?' she said.

'Right now, I don't know what to believe.'

It was like shutters coming down with a crash. So she was alone. The realisation hit Craik hard. No one on her side now. Apart from the dead.

She drove home. One a.m. The driving calmed her a little. As the fear receded, her operational mind kicked in. The method you were taught for approaching any investigation was to begin with four questions: what do I know? What are the hypotheses of what happened? What do I *need* to know? Finally: how can I find out? The last was going to be increasingly problematic as her resources were stripped away. Craik's knowledge of what had happened was straightforward enough – she'd seen the body. What she needed to know was *how* it could have happened. There had been something in the interview that had caught her attention then got lost amid the swirl of accusations. She drove, trying to remember what it was, but it had gone.

When she got to her street, Craik paused before getting out of the car. She thought she saw movement near her home, but the street was empty. She checked all her mirrors before leaving the vehicle slowly, then moved to her front door fast.

Inside, she sat on the sofa and worked through the tangle of information she had, replaying the interview again, knowing she had sounded too defensive. She considered drinking, then thought of the 9 a.m. appointment with Homicide. She needed to be on the ball for that. Messaging Lawrence seemed an obvious thing to do, but to say what? Sorry, I'm now a murder suspect so your mum's going to have to buy her own gardening gloves. That world seemed to be vanishing rapidly behind her.

She wasn't going to sleep, so Craik put the kettle on. Then she sat in the kitchen with the pot of coffee and a pad of paper. Keep calm, she thought. Take it back to basics. You're a detective.

She wrote down the facts she had, then the questions remaining, including what had made Summer drive fifteen miles from Harlesden to Argall Avenue Trading Estate. That was where her investigation needed to focus. On a more practical level she needed to establish her own solid alibi. The lack of precise timing was a frustration. Usually, you'd hope that was one benefit of gunshots: they were noticeable and precise. This kind of uncertainty created gaps through which innocent lives could fall.

What kind of music was playing in a trading estate anyway? Both the officer at the scene and Hannaway had mentioned loud music playing nearby. Craik thought through the units she'd seen on the trading estate and wondered who was playing music loud enough to drown out gunshots. There had been another mention of music, and it was this, she realised, that had seeded itself in her mind as a detail needing further examination. Her pen hovered over the pad of paper as she tried to recall why. Then she put the pen down and opened her laptop.

Parish appears in a rap-music video, someone had said. And she realised how little she knew of the young man currently sitting in his cell or an interview room, going through an ordeal somewhat like her own but very different. Her supposed accomplice.

She typed Joshua Parish's name into the search bar. He came up in local news articles around the time of his sentencing: 'notorious gang terrorises community', 'fourteen-year-old connected to string of assaults'. Then the eighth result, from the other side of his incarceration: *Aspiring music producer and videographer reflects on gang past*. That was the *Hackney Gazette*. It ran an interview with Parish as part of a local talent column: *Joshua, now 18, helps out regularly at a charity called Fresh Direction, working with young people perceived to be at risk of gang culture.*

The picture here showed Parish in a recording studio wearing a blue tracksuit with a boy and girl of around twelve, headphones on, close to a microphone.

This was at odds with the impression she'd been given of the young man. If she'd been allowed to investigate, Fresh Direction would have been where she'd gone next. She found their website.

Our mission is to prevent re-offending, raise aspirations and provide positive role models. We unpack myths and de-glamorise the lifestyle related to crime, prisons, gangs and weapons . . .

Craik looked to see where they were based. It was Argall Avenue Trading Estate.

Their drop-in centre was a few metres away from where Josie Summer had been killed.

Here in our Leyton hub we provide classes ranging from dance and music production, to interview skills and money management . . .

She'd been racking her brains, trying to figure out why Josie Summer had gone to Leyton, but what if the answer was staring her in the face? She'd gone to meet Joshua Parish.

Craik brought up a map. Parish had been found hiding on

Hackney marshes at 1.50 p.m., taken straight to Leyton Custody Centre. He was covered with blood. He had a history of violence. But not recently.

It was now deep into the small hours. Police had twenty-four hours before they had to charge or release him. They'd be interviewing through the night, possibly trying to find connections to herself. Craik dialled the Defence Solicitor Call Centre. They confirmed that Parish had requested a lawyer, and had been assigned the solicitor at the top of the rota that afternoon: Gavin Andrews of Aschcott Criminal Solicitors. He was in attendance now. Craik got a number for the law firm and they, in turn, supplied her with a contact number for Andrews. His phone was off, presumably in interviews.

Craik checked she had her Taser and baton, then put her coat back on. On the other side of the night was her own formal interview. Whatever the outcome of that, the implications would tangle her into immobility. She had one night. Summer had gone to meet Joshua Parish, Craik felt sure. But why?

TWENTY-EIGHT

Four thirty a.m. Dawn raid time. The hour every detective associated with catching the world unawares. Craik kept the baton on the passenger seat as she drove. When she'd gone a few hundred metres, she stopped and checked her mirrors, and when she was sure she was alone she continued towards Leyton Custody Centre.

The area at night was sinister. The silhouettes of the Olympic Park loomed over a low-rise kingdom of auto repairs and MOT centres. The air was freezing. When Craik arrived at the custody centre she stayed in her car, called the solicitor's mobile again. This time he answered.

'Are you representing Joshua Parish?' Craik asked.

'That's correct.'

'I worked with the victim in Organised Crime Command. I'm outside the custody centre now and wanted to speak to you.'

'To speak to me?'

'Yes. It may be of importance to your client.'

'This sounds somewhat unorthodox.'

'It is. Are you able to meet me in front of the centre?'

Andrews came out a few moments later, pulling on a parka over his grey suit. He was tall, young, visibly exhausted, eyes blinking behind glasses. He slung a rucksack over his shoulder, saw Craik beside her car and walked over to her.

'How's it going in there?' Craik said.

'How's it going? Well, that depends whose seat you're sitting in, I suppose. What was it you wanted to say?'

'There are some aspects of the events yesterday that I'd like to get more information about, with a degree of urgency. It involves the role of Joshua Parish in the whole thing.'

'What do you know?'

'Let's sit down and talk properly.'

Andrews checked his watch.

'I've got twenty minutes. I need a coffee. Are you coming into the custody centre?'

'No.'

'I got a feeling perhaps you weren't. May I ask who you are?'

'Detective Inspector Kirsty Craik.' She could see a reaction.

'Your name's come up.'

'In what capacity?'

'He was asked whether he knew you.'

'He doesn't know me, but I'd like to help. Give me five minutes.'

The only place open was a twenty-four-hour McDonald's close to the railway station. It was huge, the largest facility on the street, and crowded even at this hour.

Two security guards afforded you admission to a messy scene. The restaurant appeared to serve as both refuge and field hospital, filled with the nocturnal: post-clubbers, post-pubbers, post-brawlers. One man in white shirtsleeves had a bandage around his head. Another clung to a touchscreen menu to steady himself. The homeless kept to the corners, charging phones and laptops, watching the transient customers with subdued disdain.

Andrews looked around uncertainly. 'I guess there's not many other places open,' he said.

'I guess not.'

219

'I don't suppose they're doing the breakfasts, are they?' Andrews said.

'I've no idea. Grab a seat, I'll get coffees.'

He squinted at the menu.

'I need something to eat. A burger, anything. Thanks.'

Craik got a burger and two coffees. She found Andrews in a booth at the back. Under the bright lights he looked older than she'd first thought.

'What's the situation?' Craik asked.

He peered at her as he stirred three sugars into his coffee. 'I'm meant to be talking first?'

'Give me an idea of where things are at.'

'Where things are at is my client's facing a life sentence without parole for the murder of a police officer.'

'Any doubts about his guilt?'

'On whose part? He's on CCTV running from the scene, found an hour later with the victim's blood on him, strands of her hair on his clothes. He's got a record as long as my arm for violent crime. Joshua seems a reasonably bright young man,' Andrews continued. 'He knows the system, been through it before. I've explained what's going to happen.'

'What does he say?'

'That he didn't do it.'

'What's his explanation?'

'He was going to help the victim.'

'After she'd been shot?'

'Before she'd been shot. She wanted to speak to him.'

'About what?'

'It's not clear.'

'What does he say happened?'

'She came to the centre and asked for him. It was too loud to talk – there was a dance session on – so they went to her car.

220

Before she could explain anything she saw someone or something and got out again. That was when she was shot. Joshua says it happened just out of sight. He heard the shots and he ran and found her bleeding. That's how the blood got on him. Then someone shouted and he ran, panicked. He's not sure if it was the killer or someone else. They chased him. That's his account. On the CCTV, there's only one person running, and that's Joshua himself.' Andrews raised his eyebrows, as if to say: Would *you* believe it?

'What else does he say about this other person?'

'He didn't see them.'

'But what did they shout?'

'"Stop." Something like that. "What have you done? Stop there." Words to that effect.'

'Do you have any idea why Jocelyn Summer would have wanted to speak to him?'

'Possibly so he could help with an investigation, he says. Only, from what I understand, your colleague wasn't investigating anything to do with Mr Parish, so this argument is proving unconvincing.'

'I think she may have been investigating something to do with Joshua Parish.'

Andrews fixed Craik with a puzzled stare. 'Shouldn't you know one way or another?' the solicitor said.

'Ideally.'

Andrews unwrapped the burger, bit into it, pinched a napkin.

'When was your client last in trouble?' Craik asked.

'When he got sent to Feltham.'

'He's been behaving since then?'

'As far as we know.'

'He's involved with a charity called Fresh Direction. Has he mentioned that?'

'Yes. That's where he was before coming to meet the victim.'

'He was at work.'

'More a voluntary place he drops into.'

'He leaves this voluntary place and shoots someone.'

'That's the police line.' Andrews stuffed the rest of the burger into his mouth and sat back. He took the lid off the coffee and blew on it.

'Possessions were taken from the victim: a phone, a flash drive. Have they turned up?'

'Not yet. I believe police are still searching. Look, what's going on here?'

'What would Joshua's motivation be for killing her?'

'Police are speculating he got instructions. Apparently Organised Crime Command think it was connected to what Detective Constable Summer was working on.'

'Organised Crime are no longer so sure.'

Andrews nodded. 'It was your idea,' he said.

'That's right. Has anyone from Fresh Direction said anything?'

'Someone from the organisation turned up at the police station yesterday, wanting to see Joshua.'

'Why?'

'I think it was more in shock. Couldn't believe he'd do it. All that.'

'And his family?'

'Not seen them. I don't believe they're on the scene very much.'

'What exactly does Joshua do at the centre?'

'Bits of everything. A mentor. I'm not sure.'

'Sounds like he was doing okay.'

The solicitor shrugged. 'Fresh Direction appear to get results. You guys gave them an award so you can't think they're total fraudsters.'

'An award?'

'In the summer.'

It took a moment to think what he might mean. Then Craik brought her phone out and found the Fresh Direction website again. She went to the 'events' page, scrolled down to last July.

Fresh Direction at Met Police's Inspire 2 Aspire Party in recognition of our work turning lives around.

Craik clicked the link, saw Josie Summer's face. It was the photo they'd used on the news: Summer with her arm around the shoulders of a teenage girl holding a sheet of engraved Perspex.

Several of our helpers were honoured to be invited to the inaugural community awards ceremony, sponsored by the Metropolitan Police's Specialist Operations Department ...

Now Craik cast her mind back more thoroughly. The idea for the event had come after the unit had shot someone during a botched raid. When the negative headlines began to mount up, Price suggested doing something with the community, sponsoring awards for recovered gang members. They hired a venue, got in touch with charities, found people who had turned their lives around: dealers transformed into life coaches, robbers into personal trainers. Craik had been too busy to attend, and hadn't spared much thought to missing what most officers were too polite to call a waste of investigative time.

'What do you infer from this?' Andrews said, trying to see the phone.

'Josie Summer might have met Parish before. He was at an event she helped arrange.'

'Okay.' Andrews looked disappointed at this vagueness. He checked his watch. 'I need to go back. How should I advise my client?'

223

'I don't believe he's guilty.'

The solicitor looked exasperated. 'What am I meant to do with that?'

TWENTY-NINE

The trading estate was open again but you could see police still present. A-frame murder boards appealed for witnesses; loose strands of crime-scene tape dangled among the fencing. A few bouquets had been left beside it, petals frozen, ice in the folds of the cellophane.

According to the list of companies at the entrance, Fresh Direction occupied Unit 17 of the blue zone, among the industrial kitchens, a couple of Baptist churches and a media company. The estate map indicated its proximity to where Summer had parked.

Craik glimpsed the crime-scene tent in the distance as she walked through, taking a wide approach to avoid the ongoing investigation. She left the bigger grey hangars, went into an area of smaller red-brick units with concertina loading doors beneath long stretches of window.

Unit 17 had its lights on, a slice of gold in the darkness. Craik watched a short, sturdy woman carrying boxes from her car. She recognised her from the website as one of the founders, Gabriella Santos. Santos turned towards Craik cautiously as she approached, and Craik realised how she must appear: unslept, on the run. In need of a fresh direction.

'I'm from the police,' Craik said. 'I wanted to talk to you about Joshua Parish.'

The woman set the box down, wiped her hands on her front. She wore a look of wariness that was held deep in the muscles of her face. Craik saw someone else inside the building, a boy no older than twelve or thirteen, unpacking the boxes.

'What do you want to know?' the woman asked. 'I don't have much time.'

'I'm not sure Joshua is responsible.'

'I know Joshua is not responsible. Who are you? Police don't turn up trying to prove people innocent.'

Craik showed her badge. The woman eyed it as if its authenticity was no indication of anything good about to happen. Then she studied Craik. 'I know people in a corner as well. What's up with you?'

'I worked with the victim. I'm very keen to find out what really happened.'

'What do you expect me to be able to do? They wouldn't even let me speak to him.'

'I'd like to know about an event the charity attended in July. My colleague was there.'

'I think she was here too, yesterday?'

'That's what I'd like to know about.'

'Well, come in.'

The unit was an open space beneath a glass roof, with a pool table in the centre and photographs on the brick walls. There was a café area in one corner, PCs along the wall. Upstairs, a mezzanine area had mirrors and dance barres. The boxes that the woman had brought in contained food and drink.

Santos put the kettle on, set up two mugs. She instructed the boy with regard to peeling and chopping potatoes.

'How do you take it?' she asked Craik.

'Milk, no sugar.'

226

Craik looked around while the woman made the tea. The photographs on display showed visits from various celebrities and sports people. A timetable listed CV workshops, boxing, IT, music. The music session coincided with Summer's shooting.

'You keep them busy,' Craik said, when the woman came over with the mugs.

'That's the idea.'

'Must make a big difference.'

'Sometimes. If they bring the right mentality. For some it's a success if they just show their face.'

'Seems like Joshua's pretty helpful to have around.'

'Joshua's a star. A good person, who's lived through more than you or I ever will.'

'Did you see my colleague before she was killed?'

'No. I didn't see anything. I was out, collecting some donations.'

'How much do you know about what happened?'

'I believe she came here and asked for him. Someone saw him walk off and he said he'd been asked to help with something.'

'Can you think what that might have been?'

'No.'

'Did Joshua attend the police awards event in July?'

'Yes.'

'Did you?'

'Of course.'

'Do you remember him meeting Josie Summer there?'

'No. But, then, I wasn't paying Joshua much attention. He won an award, by the way.'

'For what?'

'His work here.'

'What kind of work?'

'Filming, music, everything. He uses the studio here. He teaches the other kids how to use it.'

'Can I see it?'

'Why?'

'I don't know. But something might tell us what's going on.'

The woman regarded Craik warily. Finally, she said: 'Are we about to get shot?'

'I hope not,' Craik said. 'But maybe lock the front.'

Santos checked to see if she was joking, then walked to the front and drew the shutters down. The boy looked up, glanced between the two women, went back to chopping.

They climbed the stairs to a side room off the dance area, which Santos unlocked with a key attached to her belt. Inside was an Apple Mac and what looked like a small mixing desk and editing suite. A certificate had been framed: *Joshua Parish: BTEC Level 2 Certificate in Creative Media Skills.* Awarded when he'd still been in Feltham Young Offenders Institute. Craik had been inside Feltham. If you got out with your sanity let alone a qualification you were doing well. You deserved more than a certificate.

'Joshua overthinks things,' Santos said. 'He has anxiety. Soon as we got him a camera he was happy. He's done courses. Raised his own money for them. You think he'd throw all that away?'

'Do you mind if I check the computer?'

'Please.'

Craik turned it on. Files were arranged alphabetically. She was working her way down the list, wondering what she was looking for, when she saw the name: *Inspire 2 Aspire Festival.*

'Joshua filmed it?'

'Yes.'

It was the day before the Harlesden meeting, Craik now

realised, staring at the date on the file. Had Josie connected the scratched car to this event? It was possible. The awards were for supposedly reformed criminals. *El jefe* used criminals who were supposedly out of the game.

Craik opened the file and began to watch. Someone in this video connected to the traffickers, she was beginning to feel sure. But there was a lot of video to get through. Parish had filmed the whole day, dawn to dusk: setting up the stage, the sound system, the arrival of people. You saw the police arrive, you saw Josie Summer.

Summer smiled at the camera and Craik felt a stab of anguish. The young detective constable reappeared again a bit later, helping set up drinks, then mingling with the guests as they took them. The woman was dead, yet here she was, still trying to tell Craik something. Still communicating with Craik if she could only hear.

Craik skipped through the video. She watched the ceremony, a couple of musical performances, the presentation of awards, then a talk from Price. As he spoke, the camera panned across the crowd and she leaned closer to the screen to see each face. Price savoured his own voice: 'We, as police, know that we arrive too late. We turn up once the damage is done. We cannot intervene early enough to prevent the harm occurring in the first place, but you can.'

It was after the speech that the chief inspector discovered someone had nicked his phone and the whole thing descended into grouchy chaos. When Price requested that people empty their pockets there were jeers, a few mischievous cries of 'Fuck the police'.

Santos stood in the doorway, arms folded, shaking her head. 'It was a good day. I still think he overreacted. These are people with negative experiences of police enforcement.'

'I'm interested in people here who feel negative towards the police because they're still breaking the law.' Craik said. 'Someone with a nice car, maybe.'

'I've no idea about that.'

'Maybe someone using this whole rehabilitated thing as cover.'

'You're asking the wrong person.'

Craik sensed mounting impatience. The centre would be receiving its young people soon. There were several hours of footage to trawl and no sense of what she was looking for.

'This footage connects to my colleague's death.'

'If you say so.'

'I need a list of attendees from your charity,' Craik said. 'Everyone who was present that day.'

The woman sighed.

'The murdered police officer was investigating an organised criminal, a senior one. We need to think if anyone here could connect to them.'

'Please, Inspector. These kids, if they were organised criminals they wouldn't have been getting awards that day.'

'But there were adults involved.'

The woman closed her eyes briefly and inhaled. 'Right.'

'I'm just trying to understand why my colleague was killed. Right now, police think Joshua was responsible. If we can show it was something Joshua filmed that my colleague wanted, if we can show that Joshua is as much a victim of this as she is, we can do something for him. But I need to understand what was of significance about this footage.'

'Okay.'

'Was there any kind of guest list I could see? An invite list showing who was there?'

'Do police not have it?'

'It may be quicker if you can access one,' Craik said. If Santos registered anything suspicious about this, it didn't show.

'I'll see if I can find anything.' Santos turned and left. Craik could feel herself losing time and good will. She rewound and watched Summer again, smiling, chatting, disappearing out of shot. Then she skipped ahead, through the speeches and awards, looking for cars. It was only at the very end that the camera followed the sound of a commotion out to the car park.

At 4.35 p.m. Parish had caught a small upheaval on the fringes of the main event. He focused on Gabriella Santos reprimanding a handful of young people about something. You saw Robert Price close by, looking weary, restraining his anger. The shot angled in on Price's Audi where a mess of fresh scratches decorated the bodywork. Then the video cut.

Craik stared. Then she rewound and watched it again, trying to see the pattern of the scratched lines, then she called Santos back. 'Do you remember this?' She showed her the closing scene.

'Yes.'

'The chief inspector got his car keyed.'

'Apparently. Like I said, he didn't make himself very popular. I'm not saying it's right . . .' Santos noticed Craik's expression. 'I don't think it was one of our kids,' she said nervously. 'And how does that have anything to do with Joshua?'

THIRTY

The file was too large to email to herself. Craik found a USB stick in a drawer and copied it. She thanked Santos, who looked at her, puzzled. 'Did you see something?'

'Possibly.'

'Are you going to be able to help Joshua?'

'I'm going to try very hard to.'

Craik hid the drive inside her jacket and walked out. Surely not, she was thinking. But something icy had begun to trickle into her veins, making her feel dizzy and unreal.

The chief inspector, she thought. *El jefe*, meaning the chief . . .

It was too big, with too many implications to compute. Robert Price the committed, the careerist. Her lover. Some advice of Belsey's returned to Craik. *Always ask yourself about your colleagues: what the fuck are they doing here? It's them you need to worry about.* She stood for a moment watching the scene-of-crime officers in the distance. It was past 7 a.m., first light approaching. Summer's car was still there, in its Forensics shelter. She'd driven straight from Harlesden to here. She'd seen the cash-machine footage, seen the tell-tale scratch, had gone to the only person with evidence of who that car might belong to, a young man who'd filmed it the day before its visit to the abandoned pub.

She did one other thing, Craik remembered now, between seeing the footage and meeting Parish. She'd established Scott Montgomery's current address.

290 Childs Hill.

Craik was at the edge of the trading estate now. She turned slowly, watchfully, before moving back towards her car, then checked no one was already in it, hiding in the back seat.

She put *Childs Hill* into the satnav.

Childs Hill was a seemingly endless road, a tentacle reaching out of the city from the Greenwich peninsula towards Kent. After a mile or so, detached cottage-style homes gave way to bigger buildings, sheltered housing and care homes behind shrubbery and giant pines. Everything was silent, empty, suspended in the urine-yellow glow of the streetlights.

Number 290 was a pebble-dashed bungalow. A very dim light shone from inside. Craik parked across the road and considered how she would appear, turning up at this address now, out of the dawn. *He's not compos mentis. Last I heard.*

For Josie, Craik thought. She would do this to complete her journey, if nothing else. Craik gathered herself, then went and rang the bell. A woman answered, wearing a sweatshirt with the logo of a private nursing company.

'I need to speak to Scott.'

'It's very early.'

'Who is it?' a man asked from the shadows behind her.

'DI Kirsty Craik.' She held up her warrant card so both could see it. 'I don't know if you've heard – an officer was killed yesterday. I worked with her. You may be able to help.'

Silence.

'I believe she was going to visit you before she died,' Craik said.

The nurse frowned, turning between them.

'Why?' Montgomery said.

'Because the thing she was working on may connect to what happened to you. To the people who shot you. You may know something.'

'I don't know anything, these days,' Montgomery said. Craik could just about see movement of a smile. The nurse looked at her as if this last statement should be conclusive.

'Can I come in?'

'Come in,' he said. The woman continued to stare at Craik as she entered.

Craik followed Montgomery as he wheeled himself into the living room, where the light caught his new face. The skin had a plastic sheen, younger than the white hair that remained. A line of scars ran from the ear to the jaw, like the edge of a mask, then continued over the bridge of the nose. The nose itself was very perfect, quite feminine.

Maybe the mind also had a plastic sheen. He seemed okay but there were different kinds of madness, ones like a mask, ones like a cliff edge. Pills were lined up on the coffee table beside a mug with a straw in it. A solitary Christmas card sat beside them. At the centre of the room an armchair was arranged with everything in reach: three packs of Rothmans, three disposable lighters, the medication. The sofa was made up as a bed. Spaces on the wall remained where pictures and mirrors had hung.

'Please. Make yourself comfortable.' Montgomery shook a cigarette pack, took a Rothmans and lit it. She focused on his eyes. 'They got someone, I heard,' he said.

'They've got a suspect.'

'How can I help?'

'We were looking into a company that used to own High

Class Fashion, importing shirts from Mexico. Am I right that that's what you were investigating when you were attacked?'

Montgomery didn't move. Craik tried to discern the thoughts going on behind his scars. Finally he nodded. 'The clothing company,' he said. 'That's right.'

'I know it must be strange to think back to that time now. But did you have a suspicion of who your target might be? Who had arranged this system for smuggling drugs?'

The former detective shook his head. 'Sadly not.'

'But someone had information. They said they knew about a meeting.'

'Do you know what, my love? I can't even remember. Isn't that ridiculous?'

'It's not ridiculous, after what you've been through.'

He ashed the cigarette into his mug. 'I should have asked if you minded me smoking,' he said.

'Not at all. I believe the tip-off came from a man called Eric Jackson.'

Montgomery nodded. He looked surprised to hear the name. 'Eric. That's right.'

'Worked with him before?'

'No.'

'Just came to you out of the blue.'

'Apparently. Stupid of me, wasn't it.'

'But you didn't want to go alone.'

'Didn't have the balls, did I? I knew Rob would be up for it.'

'Ask anyone else?'

'I think Rob asked a lad called Geoff Cooper, but he said Geoff wasn't happy with the set-up. Smelt something, didn't he?'

'Smelt what?'

'Trouble.'

'Rob didn't?'

'Rob trusted me. That was his problem. I let him down on that one.'

'He seems to have got off lightly,' Craik said.

'No. Not lightly.' Montgomery shook his head again. 'I wouldn't say that.'

The icy shell of astonishment continued to enclose Craik. Yet it felt better than the raw unknown. Her voice was steadier in her ears. 'You were close, you and Rob,' Craik said.

'Yeah.'

'So what happened? You got to this place ...'

'I can't, sweetheart. I can't go there. Do you want to know about the man this face belonged to? I'm acquainted with his mother now. She says he was someone who had always been overwhelmed by questions. Do you understand that? You get a chance for a second life, you have to let the first one go.'

'I understand.'

Craik sat back. For a second she saw the young man who had donated his face, also present, watching all this. And beneath his gift, for all the surgical ingenuity, a moment of violence preserved, a shattering blast from the side, from someone who hadn't been able to look Montgomery in the eye. 'What about Eric Jackson?' she said. 'I could do with knowing a bit more about him. Seems he's more than just a drug dealer.'

'I'm sure he's many things. That's all I can say about Eric. Connects to the top.'

'Robert ever talk about that night?'

'It's hard for him too.'

'I imagine so.'

Montgomery watched her. 'Are you okay?'

'Excuse me for one second.' Craik found the number for Fresh Direction and dialled. Gabriella Santos answered. 'I need you to take that file to the police.'

'They've already got it.'

'What do you mean?'

'Someone came and took it. About ten minutes ago.'

'Did they say who they were?'

'Just police.'

'How many?'

'Two.'

'Uniformed?'

'No.'

'Did you see their names?'

'I saw their badges. I don't remember their names.'

Craik hung up. So the only evidence now occupied a USB that rested against her heart. Montgomery stubbed his cigarette. Craik realised she had run out of words.

'Sounds like you've had better luck against the Eastern Europeans,' Montgomery said finally.

'Yeah.'

'Different kettle of fish.'

She stood, to get out of the smoke. Montgomery saw her staring at the solitary card.

'Robert still visits,' he said carefully.

'Yeah?'

'Pretty much the only one who does.'

She nodded, tried to meet his eyes, but he wouldn't look at her now. Was it possible that he knew? she wondered. Surely not. How much could the mind refuse to acknowledge?

'Is there a computer I could use?' she asked. 'I'd like to try emailing some evidence to my colleagues, for security reasons.'

'I'm not sure you should be doing that,' Montgomery said. His tone had changed. There was something in the air now.

'Why's that?'

'People saying things about you, Detective Inspector. Thought I should be upfront about that. You probably know already.'

'What are they saying?'

'About Josie Summer. Question marks. That's all I know.'

'Question marks?'

'Always the way, isn't it?'

'Who said that?' Craik asked. She became aware of the nurse standing in the doorway.

'He was just here, Kirsty,' Montgomery said.

'Robert?'

'About an hour ago. Said to call him if you turned up.'

'He told you that?'

'Told us.'

Craik looked over to the nurse and understood now why she looked nervous. She had her mobile in her hand.

'How long ago did you call them?' Craik asked.

'I think you should stay here,' the nurse said.

'Did they tell you to say that?'

Craik checked the front windows. No one there yet. She left the bungalow fast, without any goodbyes, back to her car. Certain now. And everything fell into place.

Now she knew why Josie had stopped taking her calls. Just the previous night she'd seen that moment of intimacy in Price's office, followed by Craik suggesting she move away from the case. Maybe she'd thought they were in it together. She had to be cautious. Price had left the press conference early, which would have given him two hours before the Christmas party. The tracker told him precisely where Summer had been, and where she was heading.

He had recruited Craik to close down his rivals. He had seduced her when he sensed she was a threat.

Craik drove away from the property fast, out to where

London ended and the pines took over. When she was secluded enough, Craik stopped at the side of the road but kept the engine running.

Where to go with this life-threatening information? Instinct was to get back onto home territory, but that was sometimes the most dangerous direction. Could she access an untainted section of the Yard? Find someone who would listen to what she had to say without prejudice?

She set off, back past Montgomery's bungalow, mind filled with a rush of sudden comprehension, flooded with so many insights that she didn't see the white Mondeo pull into the road behind her.

THIRTY-ONE

Belsey sank to his knees on the beach, starting to shiver violently. He worked his hands into the coarse sand. The wooden stumps of a groyne rotted in the moonlight beside him. Hardy grasses grew wild in the stones around it, blown crooked by salt winds. Where was he? There was a defensive concrete wall at the back of the beach, then a promenade. Keep moving, he thought. He got up, clapped his hands, walked away from the sea.

A row of beach huts stood like sentinels in front of the wall. He found one that opened. Inside was a stale towel and trunks on a hook. He stripped off his wet trousers, dried himself, tied the towel around his waist and searched the hut. There was a barbecue in the corner, a box of Cook's matches, no briquettes. He took the matches and a couple of old *Puzzler* magazines, picked up his trousers and walked to the promenade.

A row of seaside diversions greeted him in the darkness: Pie and Mash, Tea Room, Bingo, then amusement arcades with children's rides chained to bollards at the front: *Las Vegas, Fun Factory, Playtime.* He'd arrived back in the 1970s. The arcades stood across the road from a patch of balding grass with a bandstand and trestle tables. Coin-operated telescopes faced the sea. At the end of the promenade was a newsagent, its window display showing faded magazines and a bucket and spade. The handwritten adverts Blu-tacked to the glass carried a 01795 prefix. Not an area code he recognised. Belsey pulled some protruding envelopes from the letterbox and the address was 9 Leysdown Road, Leysdown-on-Sea, Sheerness, Kent.

So it was the east coast. Sheerness, on the Isle of Sheppey. Odd bit of the country. But the right country, at least. He could progress from here but he needed warmth and dry clothes. He wasn't going to get far with hypothermia.

Belsey put an eye to one of the telescopes, checked the coin return, then walked on, uphill, past signs for sewage works, a retail park, holiday villages. Caravans and chalets appeared, filling fields like a crop. Everything was still sunk in the depths of night, with barely a light on. A dog barked but he didn't see anyone. Further along he could make out the dark forms of trees. That spelled shelter at least. He rattled the box of matches in his pocket, looked for a route towards the trees and found himself at the entrance to a golf club.

No one around. Belsey climbed the fence and set off across the course. He felt conspicuous on the fairways, so kept to the trees at the side, past a couple of holes, alongside a bunker to where the woods thickened. He continued into the darkness of the trees until there was no direct sightline to the road, then collected up all the dead wood he could find. When he'd amassed branches from the ground, Belsey went to the edge of the course and removed some fence poles and a No Trespassing sign. He stripped the bark from a fallen birch and piled it up with the smaller pieces of wood.

Eight matches. The first two crumbled when he tried to strike them. The third lit. He used the flame to light a *Puzzler* magazine, then the magazine to light the smaller twigs and the bark from the birch. Slowly he added twigs one by one until there was heat. When the flames were large enough, he threw on the No Trespassing sign then stripped down to his necklace. He emptied his pockets and almost laughed when he saw the bag of cocaine. A lot of trouble to smuggle three grams into the country. But it had been preserved by the plastic. Potentially useful as a fix of last resort, if he could go absolutely no further without; a class A defibrillation. But that would be his final roll of the dice. He was hungry, light-headed, and remembered his last flirtation with narcotic life-support. He didn't want to burn another hole through himself.

He propped his shoes close to the fire with the socks draped over them and watched the steam rise, then held up his clothes to the flames, feeling the heat licking his bare skin. Eventually his shirt dried, and then his trousers were warm enough to ignore the residual damp. He put them back on, fetched more wood and built the fire back up.

The ground around it had baked dry. He lay down, warming one side, then the other. Eventually his eyes closed. When he opened them there was a bruised luminescence to the sky, across which his smoke fanned out, like a smudge. The fire's embers winked. There would be golfers soon. He needed to move.

Belsey scattered the charred remains, stamped the last glowing fragments into the cold earth, clapped the ash off his hands and set off back across the course.

THIRTY-TWO

Mist coiled around the fairways, seeming to lift as he passed through it. When Belsey got to the road, the dawn had pulled back the curtains on Sheerness, revealing more tiered holiday homes, a rusted Ferris wheel and austere, soggy marshland beneath vast skies. Birds of prey wheeled over the marshes. The air was so still and cold it seemed about to shatter.

He walked past bungalows and cottages, past the bare salt flats, feeling hallucinogenically empty, on the lookout for clothes or food or drinkable water. Steam rose from vents, like signals. Seagulls screamed. When he couldn't walk any further Belsey sat on a bench at the edge of a playing field and admired the herons feeding in a drainage ditch. A rubbish-collection van cruised past. Then a fellow human appeared, walking a bull terrier, the breath of man and animal forming around them. The dog-walker lifted a hand at Belsey and Belsey returned the gesture. He felt it was the UK waving at him. He got slowly to his feet and continued past the Ferris wheel and a merry-go-round wrapped in mouldy tarpaulin.

The shops at the front were still closed, but there'd been a delivery to the chippy. Belsey took a broken bottle from the gutter, and used it to slit open a box. He removed a packet of white baps, crammed one into his mouth, one into his pocket, silently thanked Woody's Fish and Chips, then went to the newsagent and sliced open the stack of today's papers.

Kirsty Craik stared up from the front page. *Elite Detective Questioned over Colleague's Murder.*

Belsey blinked. He had to read the article three times before it began to make any sense. He looked at the smiling picture of Jocelyn Summer, 'killed in execution-style hit'. They had aerial shots of the crime scene, a picture of Kirsty and Josie Summer together at the Organised Crime Command HQ, then a picture of Kirsty at a recent press conference, standing in front of an Uzi.

The paper ran through what it knew of the killing: a targeted assassination in broad daylight; a young officer believed to have got too close to uncomfortable truths. *It is understood her own boss, Detective Inspector Kirsty Craik, is being questioned over possible connections with the criminal underworld . . .*

Belsey put the paper back. A seagull swooped against the new blue sky, a sight so peaceful and empty of horror he wondered if he'd just read a work of fiction, and how he was going to believe in it sufficiently to respond.

He stuffed the paper into his pocket and walked back to Chalet World Holiday Village. The situation was slightly more urgent than he'd realised. He needed to get to London, but he also needed to establish more details before he got there.

Chalet World Holiday Village was, in fact, fifty static caravans, all beige, some on blocks as if the wheels had been stolen. Orange propane gas tanks sat brightly among them. Reception was a large beige caravan with a flag on top saying 'Welcome'. Its opening hours were from 10 a.m. until 3 p.m., Monday to Saturday. It was not yet 8 a.m., according to the clock inside. Peering through the window, Belsey could see a small wooden desk with a cordless phone on it. No evident security system. He went around to the back.

The windows were held only by plastic handles. Belsey found his Mexican driver's licence, slipped it up to the locks and less than three minutes later he was inside.

The caravan smelt of carpet and instant coffee. A bed was made up with a floral cover but didn't look like it got used. There was a kitchen area that did get used, with kettle and fridge and microwave. The fridge contained half a bagel, milk and some pasta salad in Tupperware. He put the pasta salad into the microwave, and ate it sitting on the bed. Then he made a coffee and went to the desk at the front.

The desk contained maps of the holiday park, a reservations book and the telephone. Belsey opened the drawers and found a Lenovo laptop, which he turned on. It was slow but connected to Wi-Fi. Belsey checked the webpages of a few police units until he had the names he needed. He lifted the phone and dialled the number for the Frontline Policing Directorate, asked for Homicide and was put through.

'Hi. Yes, this is Ciaran Gibson from Organised Crime Command. Is that Darren?'

'It's Philip.'

'Darren Oakes about?'

'Not yet.'

'No worries. I was speaking to him last night about files you need connected to the Josie Summer investigation. I've got her annual reviews and the forensic swabs and wondered which department exactly they should be sent to.'

'It's Greg Hannaway running the investigation. Incident Room is in Leyton Custody Centre.'

'What's the state of play with Kirsty Craik? People here are asking.'

'She was being questioned. I'm not sure where she is now. We're trying to track her down. I heard she's not with you guys.'

245

'Not right now. So she's not in custody?'

'No.'

'We want to secure what we can at this end. Wondered if you could you give me any more details of what's going on, and what evidence we should be looking to protect. What was she questioned about?'

'Connections with a guy called Nicholas Belsey, also CID. The lead investigators think she's closer to him than she's saying. Might be something going on, connects to the Summer murder. The guy's got form. Has he come up anywhere recently?'

'I'll take a look. Nicholas Belsey comes up most places. I'm sure we've got something.'

Belsey hung up. It was 8.30 a.m., but he called the Well just in case he could get through. After a minute or so, someone lifted the receiver, swore and slammed it down again. Thanks, Rod, Belsey thought.

Craik was still in operation, he felt. She wasn't in custody. She had connections, and she was brilliant. If he could just think of some way to help her . . .

Belsey wiped the search history, returned the laptop to the drawer. As he was putting it away he hit the jackpot: an old pay-as-you-go Nokia 130 with charger. It didn't look like it got used much any more, but came alive when he plugged it in. Belsey waited for the battery to hit 10 per cent then slipped it into his pocket and walked out.

Now he headed towards the main road. He needed to get to London and present himself, clarify that Kirsty had had nothing to do with anything. Clarify that she was the one in danger, and that sensitive intel had somehow made its way to Mexico. A police car with Kent Police insignia cruised past. It was too late to hide. Belsey walked casually onwards, got a glance from them, but nothing more. He wondered who or what they were looking for.

By his estimation, north-west would take him to the mainland, so he continued, past a turn-off for HM Prison Swaleside, trying to envisage what lay ahead. If helping Kirsty involved handing himself in, that was fine, but what charges was he looking at? Evasion, fraud, Mafia involvement, accomplice to murder. He decided to enjoy freedom while it lasted, filled his lungs with the sea air. A few minutes past Minster-on-Sea, he reached a sign: 'Thank you for visiting Sheppey, London 42 miles'. He stuck a thumb out, and eventually a couple towing a caravan slowed to a stop. A man with a round, reddened face leaned out, grinning cautiously.

'Where are you off to, buddy?'

'London.'

'London?' the man said. 'You're in luck. Jump in. So long as you're not in a hurry.' He laughed. There was something cherubic about him, in a balding way, his wife cut from the same cloth, both giving off positive, well-fucked energy.

'You smell like campfire,' the man said, as Belsey climbed in. 'What were up to in Sheppey that left you in need of an early-morning lift?'

'It was a stag night gone wrong.'

'Oh, I see.'

'Are you the lucky man?' the woman asked, as they pulled back onto the road.

'Yes. They left me on the beach. But my phone's died and I can't find them.'

'It can go too far, things like that,' the man said.

'I can barely remember it.'

'When's the wedding?'

'Not until February.'

'Never go to bed on an argument, that's my advice for married life,' the woman said.

'Remember she's always right,' the man added, and they laughed.

'Don't let the romance die.'

'Were you on holiday in Sheppey?' Belsey asked.

'That's right. We visit every year. I grew up there. Don't hold that against me.' The man laughed again. 'Couldn't wait to leave the place and now I'm back there every chance I get. Why do we do that?'

'I know what you mean.'

'Where did you go on the stag do? Bet it was the Cavern.'

'Definitely the Cavern at some point.'

'Meet Gilbert? He can't have been happy seeing you lot walk in.'

'Everyone was happy, as I remember it.'

'That place has been a hole since I was a teenager and we used to get served snakebite by the litre. The Bay View's nicer. Bit of a walk, but it's a B-and-B as well. You should take your missus.'

'I will.'

'But maybe not for a honeymoon,' the wife said.

They drove through Sittingbourne onto the M2, then up through Gravesend into Dartford. London closed around him like a trap. Like he was winding a clock back, winding himself back into his own heart, into the Blackwall tunnel, into a web.

THIRTY-THREE

They dropped him around 10 a.m., once they were north of the river, before the Poplar roundabout. Belsey thanked them, took some final advice on how to make a marriage work, then set off along Commercial Road dressed in the remnants of a dream. Back so soon. Where to go first? He had no real plan, that was the problem. When a destination finally occurred to him it seemed so obvious it was inevitable. He needed shelter, a moment to think and prepare. He needed a drink. He wouldn't be the first man to rack up a tab at the Wishing Well before disappearing. Maybe he could sell the wrap.

Elephant and Castle was a sight for sore eyes. The grimy street-level business gave him plenty of cover, as did the London crowd, everyone walking fast and oblivious like they were late to meet their dealer. But not everyone looking at their last few moments of freedom.

As he got to the Well, he saw the lights were still off. The clock in Mario's Café said five minutes to eleven. Belsey waited where he had sat a thousand times before, at the bus stop across the road, savouring the moment. This was where he'd be, coming off night shifts of one sort or another, the world going in one direction, him in another. Having to wait a little felt right. It lent a sense of commitment. Of appointment. And Belsey respected the arcane law that declared drinking acceptable from 11 a.m. You have made it through most of the morning, society seemed to say, enough of that. But don't kid yourself it's the afternoon, either. You stand the brave side of midday. Face that as you choose.

Rod Thompson emerged, spat into the gutter, secured the outer door open, and disappeared back inside. The lights came on. Belsey gave it another thirty seconds, for appearance's sake, then walked in.

For a moment he stood savouring the cold, bleach-scented interior; the sober, censorious morning light. He could hear Rod in the back room moving boxes.

'With you in a minute,' the landlord called.

Belsey gazed around, soaking it in. Then he saw his own name across the top of the bar. Someone had stuck up A4 sheets with handwriting across them: NICK BELSEY. RIP.

Belsey stared, feeling a cold sensation travelling up from his shoes to his stomach. He walked to the bar, picked up a photo frame containing a Polaroid of him that used to be stuck on the bar's woodwork. The words *In Memory* had been written on the photograph, alongside a sad face. A price sticker remained on the frame. Belsey removed the sticker, then set it back.

'Fuck me,' he said softly.

THIRTY-FOUR

He took a step backwards towards the door. Then, with a shiver still running up his spine, he moved sideways into the corridor just as Rod emerged.

'Hello?'

The landlord cursed under his breath, dropped a box of glass bottles on the bar and began loading the fridge. A woman called into the pub.

'Are you open, Rod?'

'Am now, love.'

The woman's arrival blocked Belsey's route out. She would see him when she passed the side corridor. Belsey backed into the loos, into a graffiti-riddled cubicle, locked it, sat down.

It sounded like the woman had brought a crowd.

'Good to see you, Rod,' a man said. 'Wish it was in happier circumstances.'

'It's a shock. Or half a shock, at least.'

'Barry told me,' a second man said.

'He'll know more about it than I do.'

'Came as soon as we heard.'

'Fine fellow.'

'A lively one for sure.'

Belsey didn't recognise anyone's voice. Were they there for him? For his death? He felt an awkwardness, as if the mistake

251

was his own. The longer it went on the more absurd he felt, and the more trapped.

'When did you last see him?'

'Been a while, to be honest. But feels like only yesterday. Feel he never left this place.'

'Someone said something about Mexico.'

'That's right. Long way from Elephant, that's for sure.'

He couldn't stay in the cubicle. It was the only functioning sit-down toilet in the Gents. He imagined people, a few hours deeper into honouring his memory, prising open the door to find him there, unflushed. When he felt confident that the coast was clear, he eased the door open, checked the corridor and moved to the stairs. There was no way he could leave through the pub. He went to the storage room on the first floor, through the boxes of J2O and broken fruit machines, lifted the blind an inch and looked down to the street. More people were arriving, some in dark clothes: men, women, regulars, people he had never met.

He closed the door to the room, sat on a box, then stood, opened the door a crack and listened to the voices beneath him, trying to untangle his mourners from one another. There was Sue from the café across the road, and a loud man – Richie Kendall, Belsey eventually decided, the obese manager of a dodgy sauna. Jesus Christ. The other man was Barry Turner, an acquaintance from the local Ladbrokes. Belsey wasn't sure whether to listen or to stuff his ears with blue roll.

'To Nicky.' A chink of glasses.

A younger woman said: 'He was a guy you could have a laugh with.'

'Knew everyone, didn't he? There'll be a crowd today.'

'Didn't surprise me when I heard. He was never going out in his own bed, was he?'

'Did he have one?'

Everyone laughed. Was that Eric Jackson?

'There were sides to him.'

'Twenty sides.'

'He was a fool at times.'

'Ah, he was all right.'

'No one like him, that's for sure.'

'No one as sly.'

'Come on, Eric,' Barry said.

'Who was he?' someone said. 'A copper?'

Belsey began to plan his escape. Somewhere down the line he'd need to arrange his resurrection, but that could wait. He'd been up on this floor before, avoiding all sorts of unwelcome visitations. There was a door to a fire escape somewhere, through a room that had briefly served as a kitchen.

'But what a way to go,' someone said.

'Fucking Rambo.'

Belsey opened the door wider, suddenly curious.

'So where's this money?'

'Stashed it all, didn't he? Buried treasure.'

'Owed me two hundred,' Eric said. 'So I could do with some of that treasure being found.'

'He owed everyone money, Eric. Get in line.'

'Speaking of which, I thought these were on the house.'

'I never said that,' Rod said.

'I thought there was some kind of gift.'

More people arrived. Belsey heard sarcastic laughter.

'Look what the cat dragged in.'

'Come on, Shauna.'

'People crawling out of the woodwork, isn't it?'

'We're here in memory. Let's have a bit of respect.'

'Is it true?' a man said. 'About the will?'

Someone put Oasis on the jukebox. One of the assembled mourners wandered into the corridor, speaking on his phone. 'Can you hear me?' Belsey tensed as the man came halfway up the stairs, then stopped.

'That's better ... Yeah, I'm there now. Nick Belsey. He's dead. Shot ... No, he *was* in Mexico – became, like, a godfather or something.' It sounded like Steve Locke: security boss, mixed martial artist and drug dealer. 'No, I'm not having a laugh, Michelle. It's true. Got shot in Belgium ... Sort of a party, yeah, a memorial. Rod said Nick had millions around the place and there'd be cash behind the bar. There's not even a tray of sandwiches, sweetheart. You know what Rod's like. Anyway ... Yeah, Belgium because he was in on some deal. All went messy, though, and now no one knows where the gear's gone. That's what I heard anyway. You should come down, gorgeous, it's a laugh.'

Steve Locke returned to the party. Belsey stood by the boxes for a minute, then left the storage room and went along the first-floor corridor to the old kitchen. A refrigerator remained beside a fire door: *Do Not Open*. He opened it and stepped out to the concrete stairs that twisted down to a bin store. The gate to the street was locked but he dragged a bin over and climbed up. More people were heading to the pub, some with flowers, so he had to wait. There was a cheer from inside. Someone began to sing 'Wonderwall'.

THIRTY-FIVE

Eventually the street was clear again. Belsey dropped to the pavement and walked fast, away from his memorial. Who had he become in his absence? When he got to the corner he took the Nokia out, dialled the pub. It took a minute for someone to answer.

'Hello?' a woman said. It was raucous in the background.

'Hello,' he said. 'Can you get Eric?'

'Speak up.' The woman who'd answered the phone laughed. She was struggling to hear him over the general hilarity that seemed to have developed.

'I need to speak to Eric Jackson.'

'Eric?' she shouted into the crowd. 'Is there an Eric?' More laughter. Eventually Eric took the receiver.

'Hello?'

'Walk out,' Belsey said.

'Who is this?'

'You know who this is. Walk out of the pub. Go to the old Dairy Crest depot.'

'Jesus fucking Christ. Is that really you?'

'The depot. I'll be there. Don't tell anyone, just do it. Now.'

Belsey hung up and continued to the brown bricks and broken glass of the derelict milk depot, hidden away behind the Old Kent Road. He shifted the locked gates as much as their padlocked chain allowed and squeezed himself through the gap. He still fitted.

The place had been derelict for as long as he remembered, victim of a planning dispute, the floor littered with a decade's worth of cans and broken bottles, inner walls graffitied, even evidence of a fire in the far corner. But no one here now, just the rats. He watched the front through a frame of broken shards. After a few minutes Eric appeared, looking around nervously. He squeezed through the gate. A moment later Belsey heard footsteps shuffling through the darkness. Eric turned his phone torch on.

'Nick?'

'Kill the light.'

Eric turned the phone off, peering through the gloom. He stepped closer, then saw Belsey and stopped, mouth open.

'Thanks for coming, Eric.'

'You're alive.'

'No, I'm dead. I came back to haunt you for your ingratitude. You think I owe you two hundred quid?'

Eric touched his face.

Belsey sighed. 'What's going on?' he said.

'You tell me, Nicky. Sixty people in the Well right now trying to lay claim to your inheritance. Grief, not of the right kind.'

'How did I die?'

'Shot in Belgium. Mike says you were trying to buy some drugs. Deal of the century, gone wrong. Steve says you crashed into someone else's business, trying to rob it.'

'So what happened to the drugs?'

'No one seems to know. One hundred kilos gone walking.'

'Seized?'

'Not seized. Word is no one knows what happened – not police, not the gangs, no one.'

Belsey tried to see the dealer's face in the abandoned light. He sounded sincere.

'What's the situation with Kirsty Craik?' Belsey said.

'She's in trouble, Nick.'

'What kind of trouble? What's this crap about her murdering a colleague?'

'She's been questioned for it. That's all I know.'

'When did you last see her?'

'She was in the Well last night. I told her I spoke to you. Said I couldn't believe it.'

'What did she say?'

Eric gazed into the shadows as he tried to remember.

'She said check your emails.'

'She's emailed me?'

'I don't know.'

'Give me your phone.'

Eric hesitated, entered his PIN, cleared his notifications then handed over the phone. Belsey logged in to his emails. Four hundred unread. Only one he cared about. The email from Kirsty Craik had come in at 8.17 p.m. yesterday. He opened it, heart beating fast. It was a long email, clearly trying to communicate a lot of information. *Nick, I don't know where you are or what you're doing . . .*

He read it at speed. The gist was clear enough: a big trafficker causing trouble, Belsey himself in the frame. Then he got to the bit about Eric Jackson and stopped. Craik had written that whoever was importing, they'd used Eric to lure an officer to his death. Eric knew the Mr Big. The Mr Mysterious. *I am trying very hard to establish the identity of this figure. I believe Eric Jackson not only knows who he is but is being used by them to frame you . . .*

'What's she say?' Eric asked, studying Belsey's face in the light of the screen.

'Basically just saying hello,' Belsey said. 'Checking I'm okay.' He walked over to a broken window, still clutching the phone, feeling Eric's eyes on him. Slippery as a greased pig, Belsey thought, but that didn't surprise him. Buying his nine lives with whatever stratagems and alliances came his way. Belsey breathed in the old sour-milk smell, thinking up a plan. Kirsty Craik was adamant: what they needed was the man at the top. She was also adamant that Eric knew him. But Eric would be a lot more afraid of the boss than he was of the police, and there was no way he was going to talk. Finally, Belsey said: 'Want to make some money?'

'What's that, then?'

'Got a situation. Need your help.'

'Yeah?' There was a long pause. 'Go on,' Eric said.

'Got a fair bit of product I need to shift fast. You see, the drugs didn't entirely vanish.'

The dealer stared at him. 'Seriously?'

'Yeah.'

Eric gave a low whistle. 'Nicholas Belsey, you astonishing bastard. How did you pull that one off?'

'Magic. That's why I had to die. But I've been granted twenty-four hours back on earth to do some business.'

'How much are we talking?' Eric said, a new brightness in his eyes.

'Fifty kilos for now. Very pure.'

'Fifty? How did you get it over?

'Boat to Sheppey.'

'Fuck me.'

'I could do with a wingman.'

'Yeah?'

'Someone who can make sure this goes smoothly, knows how to keep their mouth shut. You'd get a nice Christmas present, of course.'

'What are we talking?'

'Say a grand per kilo.'

Eric nodded. 'Think I'd be in for that.'

'But you've got to understand: this is retire-happy money. It's a lottery win. People will do silly things if they get the slightest word of this.'

'No one would believe me anyway, Nicky. You're dead and buried. Can I have my phone back?'

'One moment.'

Belsey pressed reply, typed quickly: *Hi, Kirsty. I'm alive. I very much hope you're at liberty and able to operate. Perhaps you will see this while you are still in a position to do something. I'm going to try smoking them out. Watch Eric, see what he does next. See who tries to rob me.*

He clicked send, logged out, returned the phone.

'See if you can find a van. I'm going to secure the load, make sure it's safe. Five million quid's worth of coke – it gives me the shivers. Sooner I'm rid of it the better.'

'What are you going to do now?'

'See if Steve Locke's interested.'

Eric went silent for a moment. 'Will Steve have the dough?'

'Maybe. He can get it, I reckon.'

'This would be big for Steve.'

'Steve's always wanted to be big. Now's his chance.'

'Right.' Belsey saw Eric's cogs turning. 'How will I contact you?' he said.

'I've got this.' Belsey produced the Nokia.

'What is that?'

'A phone.'

'What's the number?'

'I don't know.' Belsey gave him a missed call. 'That's the number.'

'Got it.'

'But, Eric, this has to be tight.' Belsey met Eric Jackson's bright, hungry, fearful eyes. 'The things people would do . . .'

THIRTY-SIX

The attack happened at 8.47 a.m. by the Angerstein round-about, in the shadows of the Woolwich flyover. Craik was still processing her encounter with Montgomery so she didn't notice the Ford Mondeo until it cut in front of her and suddenly stopped.

Craik hit the brakes, but not in time to prevent herself ramming it. She jolted back in her seat, dragged her handbrake on, swore. The very last thing she needed. Horns blared in every direction. A passenger got out of the vehicle. He wore a grey hoody with the hood up. So now she had some south London boy racers to deal with. Craik sighed. Then she saw the gun in his hand.

Craik wrenched her car into reverse but she was blocked in. The man came around to her side window. Craik ducked as he fired. Shards rained down on her.

She found the handle for the door and threw it open, hitting the man as he aimed again, making him stumble backwards. Then she grabbed her baton, climbed out, swung straight at his mouth. He spun away, spitting teeth.

She was peripherally aware of other vehicles stopping, people watching this unfold. Craik brought the baton down hard across the back of the attacker's skull as two more men emerged from the Mondeo. The first man went down, writhing on the ground, and she prised the gun from his fingers. One of his companions had gone for the passenger door of her car. The other, in a leather jacket, came straight towards her, holding a bottle of what might have been petrol or acid.

'Stop,' Craik said. 'Or I'll shoot.'

He hesitated, then kept coming. She shot. The bullet went through his collarbone. Blood misted the air. He dropped the bottle and someone screamed. Now the third man legged it, weaving through traffic. The shot man collapsed to his knees, clutching his shoulder. He gazed in apparent fascination at the blood pouring down his arm onto the tarmac. Craik wasn't going to hang about watching him bleed. Wasn't going to give him a lift to A and E either.

She threw the gun into her car, got in and managed to manoeuvre out, driving up onto the verge, around the other vehicles, then slamming the accelerator down.

No one tried to stop her. She saw blood on her hands, looked in the mirror and saw blood on her face. She'd cut herself on the broken glass. It was hard to tell where exactly. She was numb with adrenalin.

Driving across London in a car with a smashed side window and a gun on the passenger seat wasn't an option. Nor was driving with blood dripping down your face. Craik got as far as Peckham, then pulled up behind a row of cage trolleys at the side of a Tesco Express. She cleared up as much blood as possible. Then she realised her jacket with the flash drive was missing.

Craik punched the steering wheel. They'd got into her car, taken her bag and jacket. Phone and wallet gone, police ID, USB, evidence.

Fuck. She needed somewhere to get her head together, somewhere she could get a modicum of medical treatment. The car

262

was a liability. She got out. She didn't want to carry the gun around, didn't want anyone else coming across it, so she emptied it of bullets, wrapped it in an old carrier bag and locked it into the boot. She kept her own Taser and spray, then marched away from the high street.

Craik stuck to residential roads, deciding where to go. Not many choices of refuge around here, but she'd been policing London for a while and a few options came to mind. She turned off Southampton Way into the depths of the Willowbrook Estate, climbed to a top-floor walkway, to a door with a Buddha statue outside, and knocked.

The chemist answered, dressing-gowned, long hair down, wreathed in smoke. He looked at Craik, then at the blood.

'Come in,' he said.

She followed him inside. Belsey had introduced Jamie Bowles to Craik as a doctor. Later, she learned that he was specifically an anaesthetist. But everyone called him the chemist, because the chemicals he supplied were all they cared about. The flat was a shrine to psychedelic experimentation, with mandala hangings and sagging shelves of esoteric works. All of which lent his prescriptive behaviour a spiritual air, though he wasn't much more than a refined form of drug dealer. Craik used his bathroom to wash the blood from her wounds. There was a cut on the back of her neck that was still bleeding heavily and she held a compress on it. The scratches on her scalp had started to scab, leaving her hair a bloody mess.

The chemist stuck butterfly stitches on her neck, picked the glass out of her hair and gave her some painkillers. Then a selection of relatively gender-neutral clothes: T-shirt, tracksuit bottoms. He brought her a pint of water and told her to drink it all. Craik leaned back against a bean bag, tried to focus on her game plan and passed out.

When she came to it was with a start. She felt the stitches, saw the chemist at his kitchen table, smoking, watching her.

'How long was I gone?' she asked.

'Couple of hours.'

'What did you give me?'

'Nothing extreme. You're on the news.'

'What are they saying?'

'Wanted for questioning. On the run.'

He showed Craik the news reports on his phone. Finally she said: 'I need something for energy.'

'Coffee?'

'That would be a start.'

He made coffee, and gave it to her with some old Dexedrine. 'These might still work. What happened?'

'I'm not sure where to begin.'

'I heard something about Nick.'

'Yeah. There's a lot going on. Do you have a phone I can use?'

The chemist passed her his phone. Craik called the office and felt relief when Gibson answered.

'Where are you?' Gibson said. He spoke very quietly.

'Somewhere safe.'

'Right. Well, that's good. People have just found your car in south London.' Craik walked over to the window, eased the curtains to the side. She couldn't see any search team, but it wouldn't be long. 'Were you just involved in a road rage incident?'

'That's one way of putting it. I was attacked. I need you to run a check for me.'

'Kirsty, there's a lot of people after you. I'm not saying I know what's going on ...'

'Don't worry about them. Are you able to see if there's been property seized from an organisation called Fresh Direction as part of the investigation into Joshua Parish?'

'I can ask.'

'I'll stay on the line.'

Gibson came back a few minutes later.

'No,' he said.

'Okay.'

'Kirsty, Homicide are after you.'

'What do they say about the people who just tried to kill me?'

'I don't know. What happened?'

'I've got to go, Ciaran. I appreciate the help.'

'Wait. Did you put in a request to BT last night?' he said. 'Something about a pub phone?'

'Yes.'

'They've sent call records for the Wishing Well.'

'Can you access them?'

'I've got them here. One's a Belgian landline.'

'What time?'

'Nine fifteen p.m.'

So it was true, she thought. Was it Belsey? Just before his death? The thought was too poignant to contemplate. What had he wanted to say?

'Okay. Thank you.'

'There's one other,' he said. 'A call to the pub in the last few hours. It came from within the UK, but I didn't recognise the dialling code. When I checked online, the number came up as a holiday-chalet management company on the Isle of Sheppey.'

'What?'

'Chalet World Holiday Village in Leysdown. They tried to call the Wishing Well this morning. I wondered if that meant anything to you.'

'What time?'

'Five past eight. I've got to go, Kirsty. I haven't spoken to you.'

He hung up. Too bizarre, Craik thought. She used the

chemist's phone to look up Chalet World, then searched for the number of a police station in the area. Closest station to Chalet World was in Sittingbourne, across the bridge to the mainland. Craik dialled their direct line and the phone was answered brightly. She pictured the station: small, under-staffed but well run.

'Morning,' she said. 'I'm calling from Specialist Crime. Got a strange question for you. There was a call made from a phone in your area this morning. The phone belongs to a chalet company—'

The officer interrupted her: 'Dodgy-looking guy, dark hair, bit of a state?'

'I'm not sure. Is this something you know about?'

'Not much. Just that he broke into the Chalet World office.'

'Right. Any idea why? Or who he is?'

'No. But we've got a decent shot from CCTV. You can look at that if you want.'

'Could you send it direct to this phone? Our system's down.'

He sent it through while she stayed on the line. Craik looked at the image for a long time, reluctant to let herself believe what she was seeing. She told herself that, with all the chaos and medication, she must have lost the plot entirely, and was now compensating with wish-fulfilment fantasies. The CCTV came from the entrance to the holiday chalet village. At 7.50 a.m. on the morning of 21 December, ten hours after he was shot to death, Nick Belsey wandered into view. He did look a state: clothes filthy, skin streaked with something like ash or mud. But he looked alive. Craik felt a confused elation.

'What do you know about this man?' she asked the officer in Sittingbourne.

'Turns up out of nowhere, broke into a beach hut, wandered

around a golf course, robbed the chalet marketing office and helped himself to a phone and some food.'

'Do you have a number for that phone?'

'No. It wasn't a particularly valuable one, from what I can gather.'

'Any idea what this man was doing in the area?'

'None at all. Causing trouble as far as we can tell. Seems a rough sleeper, a vagrant, but I'm curious now because you're not the first person asking about him. So I'm thinking someone knows more about this than I do.'

'Who else was asking about him?'

She heard the rustling of papers. 'A woman called Perez. International Crime put her through.'

'What did she say?'

'She wanted to know if anything suspicious had been observed around here in the last few hours, so I told her about the break-in and it just took off from there. Then she asked where this man had come from, about the guys with boats around here, smuggling, stuff like that. I told her this was a little beyond our day-to-day concerns, said she'd be better off talking to the NCA.'

Craik thanked him and rang off. She called Perez. The investigator sounded cautious when Craik was finally put through to her.

'Where are you?'

'Why?'

'What do you want?'

'Nick Belsey,' Craik said. 'Looks like he's been in Sheppey very recently.'

'How did you establish that?'

'Call records.'

'You are in your office?'

'I'm out and about.' There was another pause.

'Any suggestion where Nick Belsey is now?' Perez asked.

'I don't know. I doubt he stayed in Sheppey.'

'What is he up to?'

'I'd like to find out.'

'Wait one moment.'

Perez put her on hold. Craik imagined the debate going on. A call from a murder suspect on the run. How do you treat that?

'Let's meet,' Perez said, when she came back.

'That would be good.'

'Who are you with?'

'No one.'

'Come to the barracks beside the embassy. I will meet you there.'

'I'm on my way.'

Craik gave the phone back, checked herself in the mirror again. She was going to have to work with the look.

'I've got a meeting,' she said to the chemist. 'Have you got any drugs to make me sharp, persuasive, able to convince other people I'm not an organised criminal?'

'I just gave you coffee and Dexedrine.' He checked his watch. 'They haven't kicked in yet. Take it slowly.'

'Okay.'

'I'm going to assume this is on a tab.'

'What do I owe you?'

'It's a joke. Anything else I can help with?'

'I need a car,' Craik said.

THIRTY-SEVEN

Belsey watched Eric disappear, back towards the Well, then walked away from the depot, away from his old stamping ground, and crossed Waterloo Bridge to the north of the river. He was still thinking through Craik's message.

He stole the rest of the day's newspapers, scouring them for any more information, but the story had gone quiet. At 3 p.m., as the first dullness appeared in the sky, he made his way to Bermondsey.

Back in the day, Steve Locke had used intimidation and bribery to corner the door-supervisor market. He'd had an army of steroid-pumped hooligans from his gym, Legend's. When raves began popping up, they saw the cash being made and got involved. Locke's men used to roll up and announce themselves as security, start working the doors and getting their own dealers in, hospitalising the competition. Promoters knew the chaos that would unfold if they rubbed Locke up the wrong way. So did police. Steve used to get Belsey in free to their venues. For a while, a certain peace was established, then the clubs started to shut and Locke hit hard times. He still shifted wholesale narcotics where he could, but struggled to compete. He was a notorious gambling addict as well, which was what Belsey needed right now.

Legend's Gym was above a row of shops, entered through a

269

doorway it shared with the minicab company next door. From the pavement, you could see lights on in the gym and the chain of a punchbag swinging. A large guy in a bomber jacket stood attentively inside the doorway.

'Steve in?' Belsey said, as he approached.

'Why?' the bomber jacket asked.

'Need to speak to him.'

'Who are you?'

'My name's Nick. I'm an old friend.'

The guy appraised him unenthusiastically. Belsey opened his jacket, showed he wasn't armed, and the man walked him up a narrow staircase to the gym. As they went in, Belsey pulled the necklace from his shirt, let it hang in front.

Neon strips cast an unforgiving light on the gym's white-painted breeze blocks. The austere decor and chipped equipment generated an atmosphere of low-paid industry, faintly institutional. There was a resemblance to the prison gyms with which many of the clientele were familiar. Belsey had never been sure if it was open to the public, as such. It was hard to imagine membership schemes, timetables for Pilates. Two men stood by the Smith machine, both in weightlifting belts, watching Belsey pass with unambiguous hostility.

One corner of the gym led to a dingy corridor, then a door signed 'Office'. A security camera had been affixed to the frame. The guard knocked and someone inside said, 'Come in.'

Inside, three men sat in a windowless room filled with dope smoke, lit by a single Anglepoise lamp. Steve Locke, his cousin Paul Whitehead, and a man called Gary Tait, who Belsey knew as a neo-Nazi troublemaker. They sat at a low table with brandy in plastic cups, a deck of playing cards and bags of weed. The room was made considerably tighter by a lot of cardboard boxes around the side, labelled *Powergirl AI Robot*. The three men looked up at Belsey. There was a second as they just stared at him, then Locke rose to his feet. Tait moved for the door. Paul stumbled backwards to the desk, where he found a handgun and levelled it. Belsey saw himself in a mirror behind the desk. He looked tanned, surprisingly healthy. The necklace was a good touch. The scene was ridiculous.

'Steve, Paul, Gary. Hi.'

'I thought you were dead,' Steve said.

'Yet here I am.'

'What the fuck are you up to?'

'I got to hell and they said bring your friends, more the merrier. Can I take a seat?'

Belsey sat down. The gun remained pointing at him, shaking slightly. He took a fresh cup and helped himself to a brandy. Steve ordered the security guard away. When the office door was shut, he said, 'What is this?'

'How were the memorial drinks?'

'What do you want?'

'Did anyone cry? That's what I want to know. Did anyone give a speech? Or was it just a good laugh? Maybe that's a nice thing.'

'Is the rest true?'

'The rest of what?'

'You were a boss in Mexico. You killed people.'

'I didn't kill people, for fuck's sake.'

'Why does everyone think you're dead?'

Belsey sipped his brandy, looked around, up at the light fitting, back at the door. 'Ever sweep this place for bugs?'

'No one's bugged it,' Steve said, but he seemed less certain now.

Belsey sat back in his seat. 'People think I'm dead because

that's what I want them to think. I need them to think that to get away with what I'm about to do.'

He took out the freezer bag of coke, tossed it onto the table. 'Have a go at that. See what you think.'

It drew them back to the table at least. The gun disappeared. Paul picked the bag up warily, studied the powder, did a small dab and passed it. Steve tried, passed it to Gary, then brought a small mirror out from beneath the boxes. Paul flexed his debit card. They shook some out and combed the ever-finer powder, watching it obscure their reflections. Paul rolled a twenty. Steve set up three lines and they did them, then sat back. Gary lit a cigarette, blew smoke at the ceiling. Metal clanged against metal outside. A weightlifter let out a roar.

'Not bad,' Paul said, grinning.

'You've never seen coke like this,' Belsey said. 'It will cut to three times that and still be the best powder anyone's tried.'

'Is this anything to do with the drought?'

'No, total coincidence.' Belsey winked. He found the Rizlas and started to skin up. His companions were momentarily speechless.

'Who knows you're here?' Steve said.

'I barely know I'm here.'

'Seriously.'

'No one.'

'How much do you have?'

'Fifty kilos for now.'

The men looked at each other, wide-eyed.

'How did you do that?'

'It crossed my path. I picked it up. Bit much for personal use, though. You can see my situation.'

'And you came to us?'

'You deliver. I know you. I trust you more than the other

options in front of me.' Belsey finished rolling the joint and lit it. 'Remember that time I was short of money for a birthday present and you lent me fifty quid, Steve? I thought about that a lot over in Mexico.' He turned to Paul. 'You were banged up all that time in ... Brixton, wasn't it? You didn't grass, didn't talk about our acquaintance. I'm sure there was pressure. Enough people have used my name to win favours. I don't forget things like that. Gary, I don't know you well, but I know you've got British values: a sense of honour, self-respect. Not like a lot of the crews out there. You guys are solid.'

The men stared at Belsey.

'What are you looking to shift it for?' Steve asked.

'How much can you get together? I need cash now. Say I sell you a couple of keys, before I find someone to take the rest. Fifty grand each.'

'How much for all of it?'

'All fifty? You couldn't afford it.'

'How much?'

'I wouldn't do it for less than a million.'

'By when?'

'Tomorrow. Then I'm out of here. That's what I'm saying. You don't have those resources.' He passed the joint to Gary.

'You don't know what we've got,' Paul said. They were wired now, ambition rushing through their muscles.

'Business been good, has it? The old Powergirl market?'

'You just tell us what you're looking for.'

'It's the whole infrastructure, Steve. That's a lot of gear. How are you going to carry it, let alone shift it?' He saw their eyes widen with further possibility. 'Don't get out of your depth.'

'Give us a moment.'

'Where?'

'Outside.'

'I'll go pump some iron.'

Belsey went out to the gym. The weightlifters watched him. He sat on a bench and studied a poster of flayed men working out, thinking what a miracle the human body was. After fifteen minutes, Locke called him back.

'Three hundred K for the lot,' he said.

Belsey laughed. He saw the freezer bag had emptied further. 'I risked my life for this.'

'Who else are you going to go to?'

'There's people. You can't get that together in twenty-four hours anyway.'

'That would be our problem. Do you want it or not? I thought you were in a rush.'

'Not that much of a rush.'

'All right. Well, merry Christmas, Nick.'

'Five hundred.'

'We're doing you a favour. Three fifty.'

'Three fifty for fifty kilograms of pure? You're absolute jokers.'

'You're here begging as a man in a corner, Nick. Look at yourself.'

Belsey massaged his neck. 'You're treating me like a cunt, Steve.'

'You walk out of this situation with three fifty in your pocket, I think you'll be a very lucky man. So don't fuck around playing Mr Hard Business. We can get the cash, but you piss us about . . . You know what I'm saying.'

'You're threatening me.'

'We'd be putting a lot of trust in you.'

Belsey poured another brandy. It was warming him now. 'How would we do it?' he said.

'What's it in?'

'Bags. A lot of bags.'

274

'You're driving, presumably.'

'No, I'm wheeling it about in a shopping trolley. Of course I'm driving.'

'We'll think.'

'Here?'

'Too hot. I'm not having fifty keys in here.'

'It needs to be somewhere I can check the money.'

'You're not going to be the only one wanting to check what they're getting.'

'We've got storage under one of the arches on Tanner Street,' Paul chipped in. 'It's secure.'

Tanner Street was a mile north towards the river. Getting very central.

'A storage unit?'

'It will be quiet,' Steve said. 'We can see what you've brought. You can count the money. We'll confirm a time once we've got the cash together. I reckon eight p.m., when all the businesses are shut and the traffic wardens have knocked off.'

'It's a bit central, isn't it?' Belsey said.

'Perfect cover. There's a Christmas market just up the road, people coming and going all hours.'

'Okay.' Belsey checked his watch. 'Confirm by the end of tonight. Otherwise I'm going elsewhere.'

He gave Eric a call from outside the gym. 'They're up for it.'

'Yeah?'

'I need that vehicle.'

'What's the plan?'

'Get me something to transport it with and I'll tell you the plan.'

'I'll call you ASAP.'

Belsey walked back to the high street and considered his progress. Locke might have a hundred grand stashed away but he'd need to go to other people to raise the rest. Belsey could imagine the characters who'd be willing to chip in. In normal circumstances that kind of incendiary rumour mill would be a nightmare, but right now it was precisely what he wanted. *Smoke them out.*

Two calls came into the Nokia over the next hour, both making him jump, both enquiring about holiday chalets. Then Eric called.

'We're on.'

Belsey met him at Lambeth North, followed him down the crevices between housing association blocks to a back road where a grimy three-ton van was parked, the words 'Baros Removals' across its side. Eric gave Belsey the key.

'Mr Baros know you've got this?' Belsey asked.

'It's all above board. This is what I could get.' He looked anxious. Belsey opened the cab and got in. He checked the parking permit, then the tax, then the petrol. He turned the key and listened to the engine, then switched it off again.

He opened the back. There were straps and old blankets, the floor protected by soggy cardboard. He closed it again and crawled underneath the vehicle. There it was: a tracker. Sophisticated. But not that sophisticated. He crawled out again.

'All ship-shape?' Eric asked, nervously.

'It's a beauty.'

'Know where you'll be going?'

'They're saying they've got storage on Tanner Street,' Belsey said.

'Tanner Street?' Belsey could see Eric thinking through the geography. 'One of the arches?'

'Probably.'

'When?'

'Eight p.m. tomorrow.'

'Where's the gear now?'

'Come on, Eric. You know I can't tell you that.'

'When are you going to load up?'

'Last minute.'

There was no request for his cut, Belsey noticed. Eric looked up and down the street, then started away.

'Eric,' Belsey said. 'What am I meant to do with the van when I'm done?'

Eric froze, then turned.

'Just park it somewhere and let me know. Unless you think it's hot. Just let me know where it is or get rid of it.'

'Okay.'

'Nick?'

'Yeah?'

'If this goes to plan we're going to be knee deep in vans, aren't we?' Eric grinned. 'We can get Mr Baros a whole new fleet.'

Belsey cut up a side road then doubled back in time to see Eric heading into a phone box. The call lasted a matter of seconds. When Eric emerged he hailed a cab.

That was interesting. Belsey watched the cab drive off. He was turning to go, feeling a plan progress, when something caught his eye: a boxy black Jeep Wrangler parked across the road. He'd seen the same vehicle earlier, near the Well. It pulled out, U-turned and drove slowly towards him. A man in a grey baseball cap stared out of the passenger side, trying to see Belsey. He looked familiar. Then he turned to speak to the driver and Belsey saw the eagle tattoo on his neck.

Belsey stepped back into the side road before the car could stop, then he began to run.

THIRTY-EIGHT

Craik's impression of US embassies was that they didn't like random vehicles parked outside, so she stuck the chemist's beloved VW camper van a few blocks away and walked. His prescription had started to kick in. That helped. Still, she felt uneasy being back beside the Thames, so close to her HQ, a fugitive on home ground. She was almost relieved by the heavily guarded shadows of the embassy. Security seemed to be expecting her. A marine of senior rank walked her through the metal detector, patted her down, removed the Taser and CS spray, then led her into the barracks.

Perez was waiting in the centre of the entrance lobby, flanked by the FBI attaché, Doug Brown, and a guard with a holster beneath his jacket. Perez saw Craik's wounds. 'You're injured,' she said.

'That's right.'

'Do you need treatment?'

'No. I need to talk.'

'She's clean,' the marine said. 'All yours.'

They took a lift up to the tenth floor to double doors signed 'Roosevelt Suite'. Inside was a penthouse operations room where four people were hard at work on laptops surrounded by a lot of elegant furniture. They included Perez's American colleague, DeLuca. Craik saw newspapers on the bed carrying her own face. The door locked behind her.

'Were you involved in a shooting earlier today?' Perez asked.

'Yes, I was ambushed. Do you know what happened to the other individuals involved?'

'No. I just know you're currently wanted in relation to that and in relation to Josie Summer's death, based on your association with Nick Belsey. Is it true? You're lovers?'

'No, it's not true. Not currently. Belsey's definitely alive?'

'For now. Please, have a seat.'

Craik sat down. They were going to do this methodically, it seemed. That was fair enough. She had no doubt that the FBI would hand her over, but they'd want to skim their own intel first.

'Tell us about Nick Belsey turning up on the Isle of Sheppey,' Brown said. 'What's that about?'

'I don't know. What I do know is that Chief Inspector Robert Price was the individual at the Harlesden meeting in July.'

The team remained motionless.

'And Belsey?'

'He's been misrepresented for the sake of distraction. I've been framed, and then attacked. One way or another they're going to try to silence me.'

'This is your boss you're talking about,' Perez said.

'Yes. That was why Josie Summer was in Leyton: to get footage that incriminated him.'

'Do you have that footage?'

'It was taken when I was attacked.'

Again, they studied her with caution. Craik didn't feel much trust. But it was possible that the flash drive's absence proved more than its presence would have done.

'What did it contain exactly?'

She began again from the start, explaining in as much detail as she could: the Fresh Direction event, the keying of Price's Audi, the subsequent attack on herself. She pointed out how the attempted break-in at the derelict pub came on the night after Perez had communicated her knowledge of a meeting in Harlesden. There hadn't been many people privy to that information. The FBI officers consulted then came back to her.

'Where were you two hours ago?' DeLuca asked.

'Peckham.'

'Do you have your phone with you?'

'It was taken.'

'Have you been in the Organised Crime office today?'

'No. I'm not able to be in the office.'

'Do you know if Robert Price was?'

'I imagine so.'

There was more consultation, and when they came back it seemed they wanted her onside.

'Let's see what you make of this. Whatever happened in Belgium, Belsey managed to escape. No one's sure where the drugs are, but it's possible Belsey got away with a considerable amount in his possession. Only a few other people made it out of that scene. One of them was a seventeen-year-old boy who was arrested at his home the following morning. He claims he saw an Englishman removing the drugs from a car nearby. We know that two fishermen employed by the gang took a man fitting Belsey's description from Ostend marina to a location just off the English coast. He had a large quantity of something with him. And he's now in London, we believe.'

'Nick Belsey's in London?'

'Yes. Alive, but possibly not for long. Belsey got collected by a couple towing a caravan on the edge of Sheppey – that was how he travelled to London. The vehicle's owner is a retired train engineer who'd just been on holiday with his wife. A few hours after Belsey got to London, the caravan was stolen and dismantled before being abandoned. Which suggests someone's managed to track Belsey's movements and is looking very intently for the drugs.'

'Where would Belsey hide the drugs?' Brown asked. 'Who would he trust? What properties does he have access to?'

'None, as far as I'm aware. I don't think he would trust anyone, either.'

'Family?'

'No.'

'What's wrong with this guy?' the attaché muttered. Perez beckoned Craik over to her laptop. On the screen was a still from a CCTV camera: two men on a seaside promenade, one suited, the other in a baseball cap and windbreaker. Beside them was the lurid façade of Fun Factory Amusements.

'The individual in the cap is Dragutin Savic. He was at the ill-fated handover in Belgium. When the surviving members of the gang got confirmation from the boatmen that Belsey went over to the UK they made them take the boat back out, all the way to Sheppey, searching for him. That's what Savic is doing here. The guy on the right is Carlos Mendoza, a known ATO enforcer, now based in the UK, which is more worrying. Our intelligence suggests he was the one who shot Trevor Hart. He's worked before as a bounty hunter of sorts, linked to killings in France, Spain and Morocco. We believe he has recourse to a network of people already over here. There are rumours he's been offered a million euros to get Belsey, more if he gets the drugs as well.'

'The fact they located the caravan –' Craik said.

'– means they have access to CCTV and vehicle registration records. That's right. Who knows what else? So, Belsey's in

London now, presumably to sell whatever he's got, but I'm not sure he knows what he's up against.'

The investigator clicked to another image. A Jeep.

'If we're correct that the vehicle his pursuers are using is this black Jeep Wrangler, they're closing in.'

Craik studied the car, wondering exactly which CCTV systems the FBI had hacked. Then she saw Mario's Café behind it. 'This is opposite a pub called the Wishing Well,' she said.

'Yes. Savic and Mendoza were present around the time a fight broke out in the pub, although it doesn't seem they were directly connected. But they just missed Belsey. Look at this. It's from a camera just a block away, twenty minutes later.'

The next shot made Craik swear. It showed Belsey and Eric Jackson emerging from the old milk depot.

'He's with Eric Jackson,' Craik said.

'You're familiar with this man?'

'More familiar by the day.'

'What do you know about him?'

'I think he works with Robert Price. He's a drug dealer but I recently discovered that he connects to the earlier shooting of a police detective called Scott Montgomery – an officer who was very close to breaking this import gang a couple of years ago.'

'Okay. That's interesting. Directly after the meeting, Mr Jackson goes and uses a public phone on the corner of Southwark Bridge Road and Gaunt Street to make a ten-second phone call to an encrypted cell phone located somewhere within the office block housing Organised Crime Command.'

'Not yours?' DeLuca asked Craik.

'Not mine.'

Deep breaths. More glances between them.

'Thankfully this encryption isn't quite as secure as some people believe,' DeLuca said. 'Not to us, at least. So we're able to establish that this cell phone then messages a number in the Manchester area, asking about the procurement of a large amount of guns at very short notice. Eight messages in total are exchanged, over the course of which the initial caller establishes a budget of up to several thousand pounds and confirms he has men for the job.'

'I'm afraid Nick Belsey's walking into a trap,' Perez said.

Craik felt the dread return. She'd been given hope, only to lose him again. He hadn't seen her message.

Or he had.

'Can I check my emails?' Craik asked. Perez fetched a clean laptop and let her log on. There was a new email received from Nick Belsey a few hours ago, a reply to her warning:

Hi Kirsty. I'm alive ...

She read it with increasing astonishment and trepidation. *I'm going to try smoking them out. Watch Eric, see what he does next ...*

'It's Nick who's setting up a trap,' Craik said. She showed them the email. The scepticism on their faces didn't shift. 'He knows Eric connects to the importer. I told him. He's luring them out.'

'He's trying to sell several kilograms of cocaine,' DeLuca said, as if by way of clarification.

'He's involved Eric for a reason.'

'So that the whole thing fucks up, you're saying.'

'Exactly.'

'Why would he do that?'

'Because he's clever.'

It wasn't the line to seal the argument, but she was glad she'd said it.

'So you are in contact with him,' Perez said, reading through the emails.

'I tried to warn him about what was going on, before I was told he was dead.'

They stared at her. Craik couldn't tell what calculations were being made. Finally DeLuca stood up, thrust his hands into his pockets and walked over to the window.

'Even if all this is true, there's not much we can do on UK soil,' he said. 'We don't even know where we're meant to be looking. We don't know their whereabouts, we don't know the plan, except that at least two groups of criminals are set to attempt to retrieve the drugs for themselves.'

'We can find out,' Craik said.

'How?'

'Eric.'

'How are you going to find him?'

'I know his hangouts. I can find him.'

'I don't think it's safe for you to go,' the Mexican officer said. 'You will be arrested or worse.'

'With all due respect,' Craik said, 'that's my problem, not yours.'

THIRTY-NINE

In the end they agreed to let her try locating Eric Jackson, on the understanding that Craik would take a new phone installed with tracking and recording technology. They would keep surveillance on her as far as that was possible but would have to step back in the event of UK police action. Craik asked for her personal protection equipment to be returned and a few moments later the Taser and CS spray were delivered to the suite.

They dropped her at Elephant. You didn't get many FBI convoys slipping into south-east London, but they were discreet and got in and out quickly enough. She waited for them to go before heading to the Wishing Well.

The pub was a mess. Spilled drinks, broken glass, Rod sweeping up. The landlord did a double take when he saw her, then his poker-face returned.

'What happened?' Craik said.

'Nick Belsey's memorial. People couldn't contain their sorrow.'

'Was Eric there?'

'Briefly. He said he had to see someone about a van.'

'Who?'

'No idea.'

'Any idea where he is now?'

Rod rested on his broom. She had always wondered how much the landlord knew about the lives his customers lived beyond the confines of his establishment.

'Lying low.'

'Where does he go when he lies low?'

'There's a flat on the Ivy Gardens estate, East Block. Not sure the number. It's not somewhere you'd want to go unless you had to, Kirsty. You know what I mean?'

'A crackhouse.'

'A party house, I believe they call it. You won't want to try getting in there alone.'

'Which floor of East Block?'

'First.'

The estate was only five minutes away. Craik walked over. She looked rough enough to pass as a crackhead, she thought. Certainly not looking very obviously like a police officer.

The building was ten floors of grey concrete, with external walkways on each floor. The flat she was looking for had made itself conspicuous with paranoia: metal outer door, grated windows. She could see why Eric had holed up there. Craik knocked and the viewing screen opened.

'Nothing today,' a man said. The shutter closed.

'I need to speak to Eric.'

'Fuck off.'

'I've got information he'd want to hear. Tell him there's a message from Robert Price.'

The shutter opened again, a furious eye appearing, then the door opened just enough to show the crowbar in the doorman's hand.

'Who are you?' he said.

Craik Tasered him in the face. The barb went through his cheek and the man fell to the floor, thrashing as the electricity pulsed through his muscles. Craik stepped over his body, into the dingy corridor. A second door slammed in her face.

'It's police,' a woman shouted. Craik tried the handle. Someone was leaning their weight against it. Craik took the crowbar from the man on the floor, got it into the crack of the door, then began slicing around, jabbing hard until she caught the person on the other side in the head. They cried out. She kicked the door open. A toilet was being flushed repeatedly. Someone else was trying to burn all their crack in the oven, filling the house with acrid smoke. The man she'd got with the crowbar had crumpled to the cigarette-burned carpet, clutching his skull. A woman convulsed on a mattress to the side. Eric was on his feet in the living room between two other men, one built like a weightlifter, one missing all his teeth and wielding a Samurai sword.

'Kirsty?' Eric said. 'What are you doing?'

'I wanted to talk to you about Robert Price.'

A range of expressions crossed Eric's face, none comfortable. 'What are you talking about, Kirsty?'

'People know what he's been up to. He's about to be taken down. You need a new friend.'

'You're chatting shit.'

'Price won't be able to protect you any more. They'll try to get you to turn on him for a reduced sentence. Still, even on reduced, a copper's buddy inside ... If you get inside, that is. I'm worried about what happens if all the people you've been grassing hear about it.'

Eric's companions turned towards him.

'Let's get you out of here,' Craik said.

'Eric?' one of the men said.

'This is bullshit,' Eric said.

Craik lifted her Taser again, this time for Eric's protection.

As she backed away towards the front door, he followed. They stepped over the doorman, moving rapidly along the walkway to the stairwell.

'Why did you do that?' he said.

'Because it's true. What's going on? Where's Nick?'

'Robert Price has been done?'

'Will be soon. I'm giving you a heads-up, a chance to get your shit in order.' They began down the stairs. She could see Eric thinking fast.

'I want protection.'

'Of course.'

'Nick's alive,' he said.

'I know. He came to you. What's the plan?'

'He said he had a deal.'

'Who's he selling to?'

'Steve Locke. If Locke can get the money by tomorrow.'

'Have you told Robert Price?'

'Of course. I had to.'

'What do you get for that? Cash? Protection?'

'He doesn't arrest my kids.'

'You've got kids?'

'I've got three, Kirsty. Price says the word and they're banged up. He's your people. Your house you need to sort out.'

'Did he tell you to say Belsey arranged Josie Summer's murder?'

'What do you think?'

'Tell me where the deal's going down.'

They left the stairs, into the car park, into the arms of an arrest team.

Craik was thrown to the ground. Her arms were wrenched behind her back, then cuffs closed around her wrists. She heard Eric swear as something similar happened to him.

Craik managed to turn her head on the tarmac to see at least ten officers in action. She looked for Robert Price, and when she couldn't see him, she felt relieved. She was lifted to her feet in time to see Eric being thrown into a van.

'Kirsty Craik, you're under arrest on suspicion of assisting the commission of homicide,' a man said behind her. 'You do not have to say anything, but it may harm your defence if you do not mention when questioned something which you later rely on in court.'

'I'll be saying plenty,' Craik said. 'Don't worry about that.'

FORTY

They took her to Holborn police station. Craik was marched to the custody suite where the DI on duty cautioned her again, and said Homicide were on their way. Her possessions were logged and removed. The custody officer, a man with bushy grey eyebrows, explained her rights.

'I'd like to request the presence of Imogen Lowell from Mattis Cartwright solicitors,' Craik said. 'But I need to start the interview immediately.'

'Okay. Personal phone call?'

She imagined calling Lawrence. It was almost worth it to hear his reaction. 'Not for now.'

'Medical help?'

'I'm fine. I really need to get on with it. I have time-sensitive information.'

The officer looked at her quizzically. Two constables led Craik through to a custody cell, where she sat for ten minutes before being unlocked and taken to an interview room where Chief Inspector Pawlowski and Detective Inspector Greg Hannaway were waiting for her.

Hannaway looked unslept and unshaven. He leaned back in his chair. Pawlowski was as fresh as anything, like she'd just woken up, hungry for blood. She started the tape and said her bit. Before they could ask the first question, Craik intervened:

'Can I ask if either of you know Detective Chief Inspector Robert Price in a personal capacity?'

Pawlowski glared at her. Hannaway gave an awkward smile. 'With due respect, Kirsty, we're not the ones here to answer questions.'

'I want to talk about internal corruption. I need to know this is secure.'

'You're here on suspicion of arranging the murder of Josie Summer,' Pawlowski said. 'And involvement in the shooting of an individual in Charlton this morning. Let's take things one at a time.'

'There's going to be a handover of up to one hundred kilos of cocaine tomorrow,' Craik said. 'Nick Belsey is going to sell it to a man called Steve Locke, but I believe that rival groups will attempt to steal the drugs when he does so. The FBI already have intelligence suggesting a large acquisition of arms in preparation for that. The man you arrested with me, Eric Jackson, has more details of where it's going to happen. We have the opportunity to stop a bloodbath, but this needs to be watertight.'

The two officers stared at her.

'Nick Belsey's dead,' Hannaway said.

'Well, he was on the Isle of Sheppey at eight a.m. this morning, so he may be not quite as dead as you think. Speak to Alicia Perez, a Mexican investigator currently based at the US Embassy.'

'Price has told us a few troubling things about you,' Pawlowski said. 'Including your ability to deceive.'

'I'm sure. Josie Summer had established that Robert Price was involved in trafficking significant amounts of cocaine into the UK. You might want to look a bit deeper into the identities of the men who tried to kill me this morning.'

Hannaway stopped the tape, spoke with his colleague. While they were deciding what to do, Craik's lawyer, Imogen Lowell, arrived. She was a tall, fiery woman. Craik knew her professionally, had always thought she must be a comforting presence to turn up in an interview room, never expected to have to find out. Lowell wore an appalled expression, which Craik felt was for her benefit.

'Kirsty. What's going here?' Lowell turned to the police. 'I need to speak to my client alone.'

'Quickly then,' Pawlowski said.

The police left the room. Craik explained the situation and the plan she was trying to get the police to take seriously.

'Kirsty, you're facing serious charges.'

'For a reason. I'm being set up. But I've got people out there, onside. I just need to make my case.'

The lawyer studied her eyes. 'Are you on drugs?'

'Pep pills.'

'What does that mean?'

Hannaway and Pawlowski returned, studying freshly printed sheets. Craik saw the FBI masthead.

'These arms you mentioned. Do you know any specifics?'

'No.'

'In the last few hours, several groups have been attempting to purchase guns, bulletproof vests and ammunition. They may have already acquired four assault rifles, two submachine-guns and several grenades, including flashbangs.'

Flashbangs, stun grenades: blind you for several minutes, deafen you for longer. Created for the SAS's counterterrorist wing.

'The flashbangs suggest a raid,' Craik said. 'A heist.'

'A phone attributed to the gun dealer, Sam Britton, was plotted moving to a property owned by a man called Alan Carney.'

'Carnage.'

'Carney.'

'Carnage is his nickname. He was involved with Danny Spiers in two Securitas robberies back in 2012. These are skilled, experienced players. You've got grounds for arrest.'

'If we knew where they currently were. It seems they've gone to ground.'

'You've lost them?'

'We never had them.'

'Can I see what you do have?'

'Not just yet. Keep talking.'

'Why aren't you recording this?'

'You want us to record?'

'That's procedure, isn't it?'

Hannaway hit the button.

'Wherever the handover is taking place, my hunch is Spiers and his men will be there to rob the drugs. Price has fed them the information he received from Eric Jackson. Someone like Spiers can recruit men for a job like this, no problem. This is an opportunity to catch them at it, but we have to keep the operation localised. Price will leak it, and then the whole thing's off.'

'But you don't have details.'

'I was about to get them when you arrested me. Eric Jackson has that information. Has he talked about Robert Price yet?'

'We'll worry about that. Any idea where the drugs are now?'

'No.'

'Where Belsey is?'

'No.'

'Do you think he's armed?'

'I very much doubt it.'

'But his emotional state is likely to be volatile.'

'I don't think he's the one who poses a threat.'

293

Someone knocked on the door. A female officer came in, carrying a laptop, spoke to the detectives aside. She showed them the laptop screen. Craik saw them study it with increasing concern. Hannaway scratched his stubbled cheek, then turned to Craik. 'Mr Jackson has decided to cooperate.'

'What a surprise.'

'He's given us some details of tomorrow's handover.'

'Where is it?'

Hannaway turned the laptop. There was a map up. Craik saw why they were all looking anxious. 'Tanner Street?'

Five minutes from City Hall, from the river, from a lot of business and tourism.

'And you think the weapons are part of a plan to ambush this handover?' Hannaway asked.

'Yes.'

Craik knew what everyone was thinking: tomorrow was the last Friday before Christmas. The area would be filled with several thousand people, a significant proportion of them drunk. Hannaway leaned forward, fixed bloodshot eyes on Craik. 'Start again,' he said. 'Tell us what you think we need to know.'

FORTY-ONE

Seeing the eagle tattoo was a wake-up call. Belsey had thought he was on top of things and forgotten quite how much heat he was generating. Had they really followed him over here? That suggested a worrying level of resources and commitment. But then he had to get into the mentality of people chasing five million quid's worth of drugs.

He moved fast now, checking for tails, using light evasion techniques to try to see what he was up against. It seemed he'd lost them. His phone rang.

'We can get three hundred together,' Steve Locke said. 'Best we can do for tomorrow.'

Belsey had been expecting this. In fact, he'd thought Steve would go lower. 'You're killing me. Three hundred? What time?'

'Eight p.m. Where we said.'

'Okay,' Belsey said. 'You've screwed me, but I'm out of time, I've got no choice. You know, if you try to fuck me about any more, I still have connections. You'd be looking over your shoulder for a long time.'

'No one's going to fuck you about. Just be there with what you've got.'

That meant Belsey had under twenty-four hours to prepare.

He walked towards Tanner Street, to recce the handover point. The riverside was already heaving, the business district alongside it also busy. This was how it would be tomorrow, only more so. London was getting ready for a break, demob happy, filling the pubs. Streets were choked by what described itself as a Christmas Tudor market, all the way up to the Thames, locals and tourists browsing stalls dotted around Hays Galleria and the mayor's headquarters, buying gourmet hotdogs and handmade scarves. Traders in temporary log cabins offered overpriced cider and mulled wine. A lot of them wore historical costume.

But the storage unit he was heading to belonged to the back world, behind the defensive line of the railway viaduct. The nineteenth-century brickwork shaped the territory beneath it, arch after arch lifting commuters away from the streets, stepping over alleyways, over the flow of time itself, leaving an endless stretch of shadowed portals.

Here was the hinterland of the once-working river: the old warehouses and older slums. Crucifix Lane, Druid Street, Magdalen. There was a magic here, Belsey had always thought. It felt like a lucky place.

There it was. Tanner Street. A battered iron door set into the bricks of the bridge: C&M Storage. Belsey walked past. The bridge would give them seclusion. It made entrances and exits tight.

If his plan worked, and Eric blabbed, whoever came after the drugs would use overpowering force. If Craik was on them, he'd have a multitude of police to deal with as well. They also liked to go in heavy, dominate the field of play. Belsey prepped his getaway, ready for all eventualities. If the police did their bit, then all main exits would be blocked. But there was a possibility he could get out. His closest opportunity for a sideways move was over a temporary fence and across a building site towards Tower Bridge. He took blocks of insulation from a skip and stacked them so he could climb the fence quickly. He didn't have to get arrested if he was clever. He just prayed that wherever Craik was she understood what he was doing and had been able to persuade the police to play along.

Let the countdown begin.

Shops were starting to close. No more sightings of the Jeep. Belsey walked into a bank and took a paying-in envelope and the chained pen and addressed the envelope to Kirsty Craik, then wondered what to do with it.

He walked along the river to Vauxhall, then crossed north. It was a strange sensation, being neither quite alive nor dead. A strange freedom, light and insubstantial, reminiscent of exile itself. He was a ghost, wandering through the locations of his life and not possessing them any more. King's Cross up to Camden, to idyllic Hampstead. So many memories he couldn't decide which to attach to each place, so they cancelled each other out and fell away, and the places emerged untainted as if he'd never existed. He was hungry, penniless, waiting on £300K. At the back of his mind, a small question kept voicing itself: could he get away with the money? Could he lead a group of organised criminals into the hands of the police and run with their cash? It was unlikely – unlikely he could get away at all – but you had to be prepared for the best-case scenario as well as the worst.

That meant being sharp tomorrow, which meant sleep. One thing he did have in his mind, among the remnants of his life, was an atlas of nocturnal sanctuary: sleeping options for those without roof or resources. He hadn't realised until now that it was one of the most precious things he possessed, but he must have maintained it for a reason.

It included all-night bars and cafés, various abandoned buildings, warm vents, forgotten corners. Hotels were open all night and had a lot of quiet, unpatrolled spaces. There was one on Tavistock Square, six mansion blocks knocked together. He'd attended the scene of a fatal overdose there once. The staff had led him through the labyrinth of corridors to an old linen room at the top where it seemed someone had set up home for a few months, entirely unnoticed, before making their last injection. Belsey had always remembered it. He'd think about that life up at the top of the hotel, and how they must have felt staking their claim to this corner of the world. It was one of those scenes that pops into your mind from time to time for no apparent reason. No reason, it seemed, apart from serving as a prophecy.

Belsey walked into the hotel, through its bright lobby, nodding to the night reception as he approached the stairs. He remembered the way. The room was still there. He went in and lay down.

FORTY-TWO

The senior team rolled in around 9 p.m. Craik's interview room got crowded. The assistant commissioner herself, Paula Walsh, arrived accompanied by her second-in-command, Bill Mannan. With them was the head of Met Intelligence, Clive Dent, a tall, tough-looking officer with silver hair and a boxer's crooked nose. Hannaway fetched extra chairs. Craik tried to recall their connections to Price. But there were too many individuals alerted now for her to keep track. Containment was in their hands.

Walsh said: 'Run us through it again.'

Craik spoke for over twenty minutes, telling them about their investigation into the missing load, the cartel and its chief importer, then about Josie's final hours. She wove in Price and Montgomery: Montgomery's tragedy, followed by her unit's focus on every other gang apart from those buying drugs from *el jefe*. She'd seen enough prosecution barristers in action to know how it worked. You didn't make big claims explicitly: you let details accumulate until they became too much for coincidence. Only when she'd fixed questions about Price in their mind, did she move on to the opportunity before them.

'How much is Belsey attempting to sell?' Mannan asked, when she'd finished.

'Possibly all one hundred kilograms. Could stretch to a street value of three or four million.'

'And how exactly did he bring it over?'

'A boat to Sheppey.'

'Where did you get this information?'

'From the FBI agents I'm encouraging you to contact.'

'And what do you expect to happen?'

'Belsey has ensured that Chief Inspector Price knows about it. So I expect Price to notify contacts of his who are in a position to reclaim this delivery. Several men in the network of dealers have backgrounds in armed robbery. This is what they do.'

'It all seems to hang on a lot of speculation,' Walsh said.

'There's only one way to find out.'

'And you really believe this is Nick Belsey setting it up for us, so to speak? Creating an opportunity to arrest these men?'

'I believe so.'

'Which could suggest it's entrapment,' Mannan said.

'He's not a serving police officer. There's no entrapment.'

'Which means this constitutes no defence on his part.'

'I doubt he's expecting any.'

'So why is he doing this?'

'Because it needs to be done,' Craik said.

There were a lot of raised eyebrows.

'You're still taking his side,' Walsh said.

'I'm saying this is where he's going to be. I'm leading you to him. That's hardly protective.'

'And will he come peacefully, if he is there?'

'If I'm there he will.'

Craik said it instinctively. She didn't know if it was true. She saw their wariness. It hadn't occurred to her that they might try to block her from her own op. But, then, she'd never sat this side of the interview desk before. It wasn't her op, she realised. It was her trial.

'He's going down. You understand that,' Walsh said.

'He would deserve some leniency.'

'Possibly. Possibly not.'

The officers discussed the warrants needed, including those for simultaneous raids on associated addresses, which would necessitate further teams, further risk of leaks.

'If we do this via conventional channels,' Craik said, 'Robert Price will hear and the whole thing will be off.'

'What do you suggest?'

'Creating a cover story.'

'Like what?'

'Classify this as an anti-terrorism op. High sensitivity, high urgency. Get officers from an external unit, not one that's worked with Organised Crime Command. I think it's very possible someone could give Price a nod. We need to be able to use the police system without it broadcasting what we're doing.'

'This could blow up in our faces in a horrible way,' the assistant commissioner said.

'It's going to kick off whatever we do. The real danger is not being prepared.'

'We can detain people before they get there.'

'We don't have track on them. And you won't have evidence. CPS will say we don't meet the threshold for a prosecution. I think we have what we need to get warrants to move quickly. There's a significant time pressure element.'

'It will never clear risk assessment.'

'What's the risk assessment of letting it play without us being there?'

Another knock on the door. The younger female officer stuck her head in. 'Phone call for the assistant commissioner.'

Hannaway suggested a break. The assistant commissioner went to take the call. When she came back fifteen minutes later she seemed sobered.

301

'What do you know about Dragutin Savic and Carlos Mendoza?' she asked Craik.

'ATO connections. They're also looking for the drugs.'

'Apparently they've gathered significant numbers of men and are trying to track Nick Belsey. The American ambassador has spoken to the Home Office. There's now governmental interest in this situation, and I've been asked to report directly to the Home Secretary.'

'Let's do it, then.'

'If these people are working with Daniel Spiers we're in trouble,' Walsh said.

'If they're not working with Spiers we're in real trouble,' Craik said. She watched the truth of this sink in.

Walsh turned to her second-in-command. 'Get preliminary observations on the gangs involved. See if you can confirm current locations. Get a full intelligence briefing on them from the relevant units: likely personnel, vehicles, access to weapons. But don't publicise what we're doing. I think we'd meet the criteria for deployment of AFOs, but we'd need to get that signed off now. Tonight.'

Authorised firearms officers. Craik grasped how real this was becoming.

Walsh turned back to her. 'Just to clarify: you remain under arrest.'

'That's not what I'm worried about right now.'

Walsh told Mannan to notify the commissioner, instructed someone else to get food and coffee. Then they began to break down the logistics: last Friday before Christmas; shoppers, drinkers, tourists. Instinct was to arrange a surreptitious evacuation in advance but there were too many people to achieve that without sending up a massive red flag. At the very least, they could fake a fault so no trains stopped immediately prior to deployment; organise a low-key road accident to close the adjacent roads. But that would involve the mayor's office and was unlikely to get approval anyway.

More officers arrived, two from the Flying Squad, one from the Tactical Unit: men and women with experience in major incidents and pre-planned operations. Confirmation came in: permission had been given for surveillance and communications interception of fifteen individuals connected to the guns and explosives that had recently changed hands. Almost all had previous for robbery or armed violence. But none were at their usual addresses or on their usual comms.

From what Craik could tell, a discreet surveillance unit had been placed on DCI Robert Price, although she wasn't privy to the intel coming in.

An operation like this would usually have a minimum two weeks' planning. They had less than twenty-four hours. Everyone looked at the map again. Craik floated the idea of using the Territorial Support Group. TSG was the muscle of the police, equipped and trained to deal with large-scale incidents such as riots. TSG also had its own firearms capability: Glock 17s and Heckler & Koch MP5s. Usually they were deployed in squads of twenty-seven officers: three carriers each with advanced driver, seven constables and a sergeant. Among those were trained medics.

Walsh agreed that contact should be made with TSG command. As they began to draw up geographical positioning, including vantage points for snipers, Craik saw that some of the intel going to the firearms officers concerned Belsey.

'Wherever the threat comes from, it won't be Belsey,' Craik argued. 'I don't want this to turn into a shoot-out. People have got an idea into their head about Nick Belsey. He's not dangerous.'

'We'll see about that.'

Craik was taken back to her cell, given a tray of microwaved food and a plastic cup of lukewarm tea. She worried that momentum would collapse without her there, that they'd chicken out. An hour passed. Her lawyer visited.

'This is a crazy state of affairs.'

'What are they saying?'

'Very split, from what I'm hearing. I don't know exactly what you've set in motion but the impression I get is that there are obstacles, a lot of challenges and quite a lot of doubt. I don't want this blowing up in your face.'

'Let's see how it goes.'

'I've just been told that the original suspect for the murder, Joshua Parish, has had all charges dropped. He's now being interviewed as a witness.'

'Good.'

'Are you sure?'

'Yes.'

'I hope so.' The lawyer studied her with concern. 'Try to get some sleep.'

Craik didn't sleep until morning. The ledge that was meant to serve as a bed was hard as a pavement. Every hour or so someone would turn up asking for more information. At 11 a.m. she finally drifted off and a couple of hours later the sound of unlocking woke her. DI Hannaway appeared. She was hauled back to the interview room. The crowd had departed. Craik was sweated one more time about the day of Josie Summer's death and her recent contact with Belsey, then told they were moving her.

Hannaway took her down to an unmarked Ford Fiesta. They tore through the streets of London, arriving finally at a broad, red-brick building in Clapham.

South London TSG base.

She was led inside and the sight took her breath.

Over fifty officers sat on rows of plastic chairs facing two large screens, one showing a map of the handover location, one with images of the men who might turn up. An operations briefing room. Body armour and tactical gear waited at the back. A senior officer wheeled in a whiteboard and began dividing people into tactical units for deployment.

Craik took a seat and gazed across what she'd unleashed. Pictures of Belsey circulated in hastily assembled briefing packs: Belsey in Sheppey; Belsey in London with Eric Jackson. How much liaison with the FBI was going on? Craik wondered. They had a map of the area in the handouts as well as up on the screen, every officer conscious that a map was a peaceful and unpopulated fantasy.

The tactical commander, Jim Straiton, took the front of the room with a chief superintendent from the TSG, Alison Mead.

'I know you're here at short notice, and we've all got presents to wrap. Basic outline: there's a very significant exchange of drugs and money scheduled for nine p.m. tonight, with credible intelligence that it's going to be jumped by men with a lot of firepower. Tanner Street, SE1, right in the middle of the city. That gives us less than four hours to get in position. So, as you can see, we're working under time constraints, and with a geographical challenge on our hands.'

Straiton outlined the gangs concerned, the individuals expected. There was no mention of Price, or the element of police corruption, but he emphasised the need for complete secrecy. No one was even allowed to message home.

'We know it's going to be crowded out there,' the commander said. 'What we don't know is exact numbers, methods of transportation and the details of weaponry.

305

Hopefully we'll be getting more intelligence soon, but this is the plan so far.'

The plan was to contain whatever unfolded beneath the bridge, creating a naturally sealed-off hot zone. Natural containment was a plus. The disadvantages were low visibility and the possibility that innocent passers-by got trapped. There was a two-hundred-metre stretch beneath the bridge. The key was timing it so that all civilians were clear, all targets beneath it, then moving in swiftly enough to split the gangs in two, isolating both groups.

'If it goes well, we take out a lot of narcotics and organised criminals. If we lose control of the situation we've started a war in a congested urban area.'

The TSG superintendent ran through local hazards, from an electricity substation to the railway, then the operational set-up: thirty officers in plain clothes posing as members of the public, another forty stationed nearby, including AFOs. They had secured access to two offices overlooking the approach and exit from the site.

Straiton turned to the map and indicated where unmarked vans had already been parked, and the adjacent buildings where firearms and surveillance were to be positioned. If it became a gunfight, the designated senior firearms officer would take over gold command. Floodlights and Tannoys would be used, and priority would switch to clearing the area. A helicopter was on standby for situational intelligence, but obviously it couldn't be flown over the site until the last minute.

'It will be radio silence, torches and laser sights off.'

Euston, Stratford and Hammersmith police stations were on stand-by to receive arrested suspects. Guy's Hospital had six ambulances ready to go.

The officers split into operational units. Hannaway took Craik aside.

'You've been given clearance to be there with me. We focus on Belsey.'

'Okay.'

'If this doesn't work, it's out of my hands. There'll be a lot of questions, obviously. For both of us.'

'I'll have a few questions of my own,' Craik said, but the anxiety was starting to get to her, the effort of convincing others she knew what was going on.

The first units began to deploy around 6 p.m. As new intelligence came in it was added to the boards. The remaining officers made final preparations. Then, just as people were starting to wonder if it was going to happen at all, a ripple of anticipation went around the room. Someone spoke to the commander, who returned to the front.

'Our Target One, Nick Belsey, is on the move. That's now confirmed. Let's go.'

FORTY-THREE

The day was crisp and bright, and Belsey felt good as soon as he awoke. He washed in the hotel's ground-floor toilet and readied himself for his big day. All he needed was something loosely resembling fifty kilograms of cocaine.

Tesco store security were not focused on the baking sections. There was a lot of chaotic last-minute Christmas shopping to hide in. He started with the Waterloo branch, picked up three kilos of flour, clingfilm, tape, bin liners and WD-40, walking straight out.

He visited six different supermarkets in total. When his load was becoming too much to carry, he took it to North Lambeth, to a secluded community garden near where the removals van was parked. He wrapped the flour in clingfilmed blocks, smeared them with grease, as if they'd had to bypass a lot of sniffer dogs, then wrapped them again in black plastic and taped it all down. Weight was more important than appearance. If it got to them sampling the stuff it was far too late. He had to pray police intervened first.

He wrapped a few more, then hid them in the back of the van beneath the old blankets and off-cuts of carpet. Then he went to steal some more, trying to imagine what the stash would look like.

By 7 p.m. he had fifty blocks. The outer wrapping was flimsier than he'd expected and he made a mental note not to drop any by accident. He'd only seen this kind of load on the news. Maybe the cartels used thicker plastic. Still, it was strangely exciting seeing them piled up.

The sky had darkened. A text came in from Steve Locke: *We're on. 8 pm.*

Eric had gone radio silent. Belsey would have liked to know if there was any whisper of Craik. He needed a lot of faith that her end of things was holding up. He went to the WHSmith's in Waterloo station, found an A–Z and made a final study of the approach to the drop-off, the streets nearby and potential escape routes, until he had it all memorised. At twenty to eight he returned to the van. No one was following him. He checked the load one last time, then got in.

This is it, he thought, starting the engine. He was up for it. He just didn't want to die, and found himself surprised by the strength of that feeling. Not so much a resistance to death as to the clumsiness of it: dying in a situation with a lot of stupid men waving guns around. It was a weak punchline.

He pulled the van onto Borough Road and began towards Bermondsey, conscious that he could be ambushed any time by any number of players. But nothing happened. Not yet. As he got closer to the riverfront he could see the coloured lights and excited families, people taking photos, spilling from the pubs. He left the main thoroughfare, heading into the back streets and circled round.

Were the police in place? Belsey glanced at a few of the parked vans as he drove by, low on their suspension. He felt sure that was them. All was ready. The time was now.

As Belsey approached the storage place, he slowed, tried to see what was going on. A Transit van already occupied the spot outside. He had nowhere to park. He stopped in the middle of the road.

Steve Locke came out, three men with him: Paul, Gary and a red-faced guy with sideburns. All looked charged.

'What are you doing there?' Locke said. Belsey rolled his window down.

'Where am I meant to be?'

Steve looked around. The driver behind Belsey blasted his horn. A queue of traffic was forming. The man from the Transit van began taking boxes into the storage unit. Locke spoke to him, came back to Belsey.

'Says he's unloading.'

The car behind Belsey honked again. Gary swore at them and began heading over.

'What the fuck's he doing?' Belsey said.

'Gary,' Steve said. 'Leave it.'

'You didn't tell me the space was shared,' Belsey said. He could see Locke's men eyeing up his van, their breath steaming in its headlights.

Locke spoke to them, then returned to Belsey. 'Let me in.' He climbed up, got into the cab next to Belsey. 'Keep driving. Straight on.'

'What's happening?'

'Change of plan. There's somewhere else.'

'Where's the money?'

'They've got it.'

Belsey checked his mirrors and saw Locke's three men following on foot. Two of them had rucksacks. 'They're coming with?'

'It's not far. They'll walk it.'

Would the police be able to respond? Belsey tried not to drive too fast, to let the operations teams know he was still cooperating, not about to run.

'What are you up to?' Locke said.

'Trying not to draw attention.'

'You're driving like you're pissed.'

'Where am I going?'

'Up the road. There's a parking place behind the Christmas market. I know the security there. They'll let us through.'

Belsey got to the first set of barriers. A cold-looking guard in a hi-vis bib shook his head. Locke got out. There was discussion with the security. Locke made a call, passed his phone to the security guard. Belsey watched, heart thumping now. Eventually Locke leaned in. 'They'll help us carry it inside.'

'Help?'

'Many hands, light work.'

'Fuck me, Steve. This is abysmal.'

'Let's get it done quickly. He says you can leave the van there for ten minutes. The place is around the corner.'

'Ten minutes won't do it.'

'Twenty, whatever.'

'How far is it?'

'Literally around the next corner.'

Belsey couldn't see it. He saw trees with fairy lights in the branches, City Hall glowing, and Tower Bridge as magical as the rest. And the market heaving with five hundred happy people.

FORTY-FOUR

The last of the police teams were in place with ten minutes to go. Craik had been instructed to join Hannaway in the back of what looked like a Royal Mail van, parked on a street parallel with Tanner, thirty seconds from the storage unit. Squeezed in with her were six officers and a live feed from multiple cameras. The office-block vantage points got good shots of the surrounding streets. Several of the undercover officers on foot wore hidden body cameras. Only one operational radio was allowed in the van, turned low. Ten similar vans waited within a five-hundred-metre radius of the RV point.

'Unit One in place.'

'Unit Two in place.'

Hannaway gave Craik an earpiece and a bullet-proof vest, which she strapped on. The radio crackled.

'We have a sighting of three males in a white Peugeot 508, approaching north along Tower Bridge Road. Registration comes up as stolen last night.'

That sent electricity through the van.

'They're slowing. FP Five, they're near you on Druid Street. They've stopped.'

'A second car has stopped behind them, a Vauxhall Corsa.' The plain-clothes officer read out the licence plate. 'Five IC One males inside.'

Eight in total, Craik thought. Spiers had brought his team.

'FP Five, can you see if they're armed?'

'Unclear. I can see the driver is holding a radio handset.'

Then the image changed again: another car on a different road.

'Can we get a reading on this vehicle? North side of Tower Bridge Road, corner with Long Lane, a Škoda Octavia, one occupant, also on radio.'

'Registration comes up as Metropolitan Police.'

'Local?'

'Not as far as we can tell.'

Craik saw the man in the driver's seat. 'That's Robert Price,' she said. She felt some vindication with her adrenalin. One of the foot patrol walked by.

'He's monitoring local police channels,' she said.

'Okay,' the commander said. 'Unit Seven, stay with the Škoda. Check there's no legitimate reason for him to be there.'

'What's Price going to do, do you think?' Hannaway asked.

'Keep an ear out. Make sure no one's on them.'

'Well, we've got him.'

'Not yet.'

'Confirmation,' someone said on the radio. 'Picking up comms between Target Two and the Met vehicle.'

Price securing things, Craik thought. Spiers ready to move in with seven other men. The radio set in the car started to broadcast.

'Stand by, stand by. Target One is approaching, driving a white Vauxhall Movano van with the markings Baros Removals. Vehicle is off Tower Bridge Road, on Tanner Street now.'

'There's Belsey.'

They kept the aerial shot tight on the dirty roof of the van as it progressed.

'Eight-Two to base, I have eyeball. Vehicle is towards the RV at speed three zero miles per hour.'

'Can confirm: Target Two's team, the Peugeot and Vauxhall, on the move as well.'

'Spiers has been alerted,' Craik said.

'They're tailing Target One.'

'Mobile units, begin approach,' the commander said.

They switched to the feed from the camera beneath the bridge and saw Belsey stop, his roof almost scraping the brickwork.

'Something's going on,' one of the officers said.

The traffic around them was growing bad-tempered.

'What is it?'

'Aggro.'

'I can see Danny Spiers and four men now out of the front vehicle, two visibly carrying firearms. Recommend we begin the cordon.'

Craik watched Spiers's fleshy, freckled bald head on the monitor, emerging from the car, scanning the surroundings as he tucked a handgun into his jacket then retrieved what looked like a pump-action shotgun from the seat.

'Target One's van is blocking the road.'

'Wait, he's leaving the location.'

'The men tailing him seem to be waiting.'

'They're returning to their vehicle now. There seems to be some confusion.'

Hannaway turned to Craik. 'What the hell is this?'

FORTY-FIVE

Belsey unlocked the back of the van and rolled the shutters up. Locke's men climbed in and he followed. There was a moment when Belsey pulled away the blankets to reveal the load sheltering in the darkness and everyone caught their breath.

'We've just to go fast,' Locke said.

'This is insane.'

'Take it to the staff area behind the big Christmas tree,' Locke said. 'We'll do the handover there. Get some fucking carrier bags or wrapping paper or something. Try to cover it,' he instructed his men, then turned to Belsey. 'I thought you said it would be in bags.'

'I thought you said we'd be doing this somewhere secure.'

'Let's go.'

They got a box of gift bags and started stuffing the bricks into these before hauling them out. A couple of the security guards helped, everyone taking several bags each, apart from Locke, who watched over them. Then they began to move through the crowd.

All stayed tight, hyper alert. Several hundred people surrounded them: carol singers, little kids, inebriated office workers. They were heading towards a giant Christmas tree covered with white lights. The market was too packed to get through easily and Belsey had to turn sideways to elbow his

315

way through the scrum. Each time he turned, he checked the crowd behind for anyone coming up on them. Then he saw the men in balaclavas.

'Steve, I think we've got a problem.'

Locke checked, then turned to Belsey, eyes fierce with terror.

'You've set something up.'

'Not me.'

'It's a fucking crew.'

They were almost at their destination. Behind the giant Christmas tree another row of safety barriers protected a patch of tarmac with generators and a Portakabin. But they weren't going to get there.

It was impossible to see how many masked men were steaming through the crowd, but those visible wore jackets big enough to conceal weapons. Now all the security guards had seen them and frozen. As the front balaclava got to Locke, he opened his jacket and pulled out a shotgun. A shopper screamed. The floodlights came on.

'Police,' a Tannoy said. 'You are surrounded. Place your weapons down.'

Craik ran towards the impending crisis, officers around her giving up on discretion, the worst-case scenario unfolding fast. The radio continued to give updates.

'We've got a confrontation.'

'This is it. Go, go.'

Craik's colleagues pulled on their identifying caps as they sprinted.

'Targets are armed, repeat armed. Do not approach. Unit Nine are taking up position. This is now a Unit Nine operation.'

Craik kept going, through shoppers fleeing in the opposite direction. When the floodlights came on, she was close enough to see men from every faction turning, stunned and half blinded. Then she saw Belsey.

He was watching all this unfold, standing near the Christmas tree, holding what looked like a block of cocaine. Craik moved towards him slowly. She could see officers pointing guns in his direction and held up a hand to stop them.

'Nick,' she said.

He turned, squinting against the light. Then he saw her and smiled. 'Kirsty.'

'Just walk towards me. Put the block down. Keep your hands visible.' He nodded.

Then she saw Robert Price.

He stood a few metres away, caught in the sudden deluge of halogen. Frozen in it, as if it was guilt itself. Suddenly he came to life. He produced his police badge and held it high. 'We've got him,' he said. 'I've got him, Kirsty.'

'I don't think so, Rob. Step back. Keep your hands in the air.'

Price looked around. 'What do you mean?'

'You're under arrest.'

She moved towards the chief inspector. Price reached to the back of his waistband and pulled a gun. Belsey turned towards him. Craik raised her hand again to stop him doing anything. 'I've got this. Rob, don't be stupid.' Craik took another step. Price eased the safety catch off.

Then a voice squawked in Craik's earpiece: 'Black Jeep approaching the barriers fast. Anyone know what this is about?'

Belsey saw Craik's expression change. A second later there was a crash from the front of the market, followed by a rattle of automatic fire. Everyone ducked or ran. Belsey dived towards Price, grabbing his wrist, angling the pistol down before driving a fist into his face. The chief inspector fell. Craik leaped on him,

317

swiping the gun away. Another blast of semi-automatic fire, closer this time. Belsey saw a spray of blood, then Eagle Tattoo marching towards him. He didn't want to leave Craik in the line of fire but he had a sense that the fire was drawn to him in the first place. He grabbed the kilo block as the tattoo got within reach. The man was armed to the teeth, an AR-15 in his hands, revolver at his side, hunting knife on his belt.

'Nick Belsey,' he said.

Belsey ripped the block apart in his face.

Flour exploded. The man spun away, gagging, as the white cloud engulfed him. He clawed at his eyes with the hand that wasn't holding the gun. Belsey turned and ran. He heard another shot, and when he glanced over his shoulder it was chaos. Some of the money had spilled from one of the rucksacks. A man in a balaclava was dragging himself through the artificial snow. Eagle Tattoo had been tackled to the ground. Belsey had no idea who was doing what. He headed for the riverside.

Someone shouted for him to stop. He kept going. He could hear people chasing but had no idea who they were. When he got to the river's edge, he saw that police had blocked the bridge. A shot whistled past his shoulder. He climbed the railings onto a narrow ledge. The Thames was black below him. It wasn't the impact that killed you, it was the shock of the cold. That was what he was thinking as he jumped.

FORTY-SIX

Twelve arrests, eighteen injuries, two dead: both members of Spiers's entourage. Robert Price sat against a market stall, hands cuffed in his lap, dusted with what turned out to be a lot of self-raising flour. Spiers was already in an ambulance under police escort.

Paramedics filled the place now. The two bodies had been covered, walking wounded triaged. The sirens of belated support teams were approaching, TV crews setting up. Craik looked for Belsey and couldn't see him.

She checked the police vans, then the ambulances. Consensus was that he was last seen heading in the direction of Tower Bridge.

'Was he hit?'

No one seemed sure.

There was a lot of blood among the flour on the ground. She followed it as far as she could. A group of officers huddled on the embankment, pointing torches at the water.

'This is where we last had visuals on him, ma'am.'

'Might he have crossed?'

'It was blocked. He didn't cross.'

They shone their torches under the ironwork, lighting ancient bolts the size of human heads, and rust-reddened stalactites.

Then down at the water again. It looked like oil. It looked like nothing that went in would ever come out.

'We'll search,' one of the local officers said. 'Maritime are on it. But the current's faster than it looks. Chances are he'll turn up next week by Deptford.'

'He was definitely here?'

'Definitely. Someone saw him go over the side.'

The commander was directing the aftermath when Craik got back to the market.

'This is quite a result, Detective Inspector. This is a lot of Christmases at once.'

'What about Nick Belsey?'

'He's not in the water?'

'Not visibly so.'

'That may be for the best.'

'What do you mean?'

'We may want to keep his contribution low-key.'

It took Craik a moment to understand what they were saying. Bury him. An inconvenience best not named. A medal of silence. She nodded numbly.

'Leave it to me,' the commander said.

'If something's happened . . .'

'Let's talk in the morning.'

'Do I remain under arrest?'

The commander laughed. 'I hope not. I'm sure there'll be paperwork to do, but as far as I'm concerned, you have the keys to the city. And the assistant commissioner agrees. Get some rest for now and we can do the official discharge in due course.'

Organised Crime Command was busy by the time Craik got there. Anti-corruption officers had begun taking apart

Price's office and placing it in evidence bags. The investigators nodded at her, turned back to their duties. Craik realised she was shaking.

She made herself some tea and sat down at her desk as if to begin a day's work. She didn't know what else to do.

'You should go home,' Weller said. 'It's going to be a long day tomorrow. The chief constable wants to line up a press conference. This is turning out to be even bigger than we realised.'

The idea of being at home felt bizarre. She wondered what Lawrence was doing now. Decorating the tree. Finding new sources for the brandy butter. Craik was considering her options when she saw the envelope at the top of her in-tray.

It was a cheque paying-in envelope, with her name on the front. The writing looked like Belsey's. Craik opened it carefully. Inside was a necklace.

She held it in her palm beneath the desk lamp. It had a thin gold chain and an oval-shaped pendant with a picture of the Virgin Mary. The Virgin's head was bowed, hands joined in prayer, feet floating above the ground. She was framed by pink roses.

Mexico, Craik thought. He brought me a souvenir.

Craik looked inside the envelope for a note. There was nothing. He could have written a note, she thought: a hello, a signature. She couldn't understand what was achieved by this mystery. The fool.

She checked the latest police reports for his name, then hospitals. Nothing came up. Maritime Police were continuing to look for bodies. They'd sent a diver down, but you couldn't thoroughly search the Thames. Eventually Craik put the necklace in her pocket and left HQ. She kept a hand on it as she walked. She thought it might tell her where to go.

FORTY-SEVEN

He hit the water hard. The shock sucked all the air from his lungs. Stay conscious, Belsey thought, as his body went numb. His mind shrunk to this one bright thought: keep terrified, keep conscious. He tried to thrash his limbs but they were jelly. His head slipped under and panic kicked in. Belsey was aware of a boat nearby, of its potential danger and how ridiculous he must seem as he drowned.

Something hit his arm. It had a flashing light attached: a life-saver ring. Belsey grabbed onto it. Now he could concentrate on his legs, kick his feet, get oxygen into his lungs. He was moving. He thought at first he was propelling himself, then realised someone was pulling a rope attached to the ring.

'Can you climb?' they said, as he got to the side of the boat.

Belsey reached for the ladder but his hands were useless. Someone gripped his arm. Then his feet were on a rung and that helped. He wrapped his arms around the sides of the ladder and in this way, with several hands pulling at him, he made it up to the deck where he collapsed. A lot of people stared down at him, some in party hats.

'Thank you,' he managed to say. His voice was slurred, teeth chattering. He was hustled indoors, into a boiler room, blissfully, soporifically warm. Someone gave him towels, someone gave him a blanket.

'Please,' he said. 'Don't stop your party.'

'We'll find you clothes.'

Belsey dried himself. He was okay. Shivering but alive. Bar staff gave him a T-shirt with the name of the boat on it, a jumper, some chef's checkered trousers and a pair of socks.

'What's your name?' a tall man who seemed to be in charge said.

'John.'

'We need to get you to a hospital, John.'

'Not right now. Just a drink. A whisky or something.'

They got him a large whisky. He could hear the dancefloor beyond the door, music and laughter.

'Fuck me, that's better.'

'What happened?'

'I don't know. One moment I was walking along . . . I think I slipped. Is that possible? I feel okay now.'

'Who should we call?'

'No one. I need to gather my thoughts. I'd really like to just catch my breath, and for you all to go back to having fun.'

After another ten minutes Belsey felt much better. He went out. Someone cheered as he emerged.

'You're alive.'

'Alive and well.'

He was momentarily the centre of attention, recipient of a lot of tipsy concern. It was the Christmas party for a PR company, everyone deep in the rations. The boat had two floors, a DJ, an extensive bar. Once it had been established that Belsey wasn't about to die, and nor had he sought to, people relaxed. Someone gave him another drink. Someone offered to pull a cracker with him.

'You're okay?'

'I'm okay. I was at the side of the river and just got swept up or something. Messing about. My fault.'

He went up on deck. Tower blocks and riverside pubs slid by. He saw the Blacksmith's Arms, which meant they were by Rotherhithe. A lot of small windows glowed up and down the sides of buildings, making the blocks look like Advent calendars. Belsey walked to the front of the boat where the tall man from the boiler room was in a cockpit working the ship's controls.

'Feeling better?' he asked.

'Much better. Where are we going?'

'Up to Canary Wharf, then back to Westminster.'

'What would happen if you just kept going? Out to sea?'

The man laughed. 'There's some pretty strong tidal streams, and a fair bit of commercial traffic. But it can be done. Not tonight, though. Not sure these people want to end up in France.'

'Have you asked them?'

'You ask them.' The man winked.

Belsey walked to the rear of the boat. It was empty and he could listen to the night alone. He could hear María Luisa singing 'La Golondrina'. That beach was special. Why had he only ever felt at home in places where he couldn't stay? He saw Kirsty Craik's face just before the chaos began and hoped she'd come through it unscathed. Glad he got that, at least. A minute. Less than a minute. But something.

The bar was free. He ordered another drink, a beer this time, then asked if they did margaritas and they fixed him one. Later he joked with some people about how he'd just joined the company and worked in the accounts department.

'Seriously?'

'Of course not. I was the guy in the water. You hauled me out.'

'You're that guy. You look different.'

'Because I'm dry now.'

It was easy to forget you were on a boat. When Belsey remembered, he felt safer. He had no idea what was going to happen when they eventually docked, but until that time he was okay. Maybe it could go on for ever. Dry land was the problem, he decided, on his second margarita: all the people standing there, thinking themselves secure.

Prosecco was going around. Someone added it straight into his cocktail. The dancefloor had taken off in a messy way. Belsey met Matt, an Australian guy, and Reese, who did computer stuff, and shot sambuca with them. Then he made everyone have a round of margaritas. The night was roaring in his bloodstream now.

'This must be an amazing PR company. You guys are golden.'

He showed them how to light shots and drink them burning. Then they went outside for cigarettes and he was telling his story again, about slipping and how it felt when he went under. Jane, who was in the design team, was particularly sympathetic. She'd woven mistletoe into her hairclip. She had a bottle of red wine but had misplaced her glass, which wasn't a problem for either of them, they established, passing the bottle back and forth.

'Jane,' Belsey said. 'You saved my life. Next year is going to be lucky for you. Do you feel that?'

'I was just saying that to someone.'

She gave him the bottle and he drank, watching Wapping slip away and the towers of Limehouse appear. The new riverside apartment blocks looked like they had a lot to learn. He searched the crevices between them for the old city but couldn't see it. It would be there, though. Everything was there. And that wasn't a problem right now because he was moving. He was sailing down the Thames, and the water was a firebreak, and all the flames of London had to watch him pass. Had to respect the fact that he was still here, unburned, untouchable, on a boat. Jane was saying something, lost against the churn of the engines, and when Belsey leaned closer he could see the lights of the bottomless city in her eyes.

'I'm asking if you like dancing,' she said, and she laughed. 'That's all. I'm asking if you want to dance.'

ACKNOWLEDGEMENTS

Many thanks to: Mike Grist, Tia Danckaert, Clare Smith, Zoe Hood, Zoe Gullen, Hazel Orme and Veronique Baxter. Biggest and most special thanks, as ever, to Jihyon and Taehee.

Oliver Harris was born in London and now lives in Manchester where he teaches at Manchester Metropolitan University. He writes the Nick Belsey series of detective novels and the Elliot Kane series of espionage novels.